G[illegible] is a New Zealander who came to Britain to complete a PhD study in the politics of education, and to work in that field. Since then, he has watched education become an annexe of national politics; and six years ago he took refuge in writing fiction. In that time, he has written several books and three television series – the latest of which is the BBC drama series, *Campaign*. He is currently working on a film screenplay and a novel.

Gerard Macdonald is forty-seven, married, with a son and a daughter, both of whom think there must be easier ways of earning a living.

Campaign

Gerard Macdonald

HEADLINE

First published in Great Britain in 1987
by HEADLINE BOOK PUBLISHING PLC

All characters in this publication are fictitious and any resemblance to real persons, living or dead, is purely coincidental.

British Library Cataloguing in Publication Data

Macdonald, Gerard
Campaign.
I. Title
823 [F] PR9639.3.M17/

ISBN 0-7472-0072-6 Hbk.
ISBN 0-7472-3099-4 Pbk.

Printed and bound in Great Britain by
Collins, Glasgow

HEADLINE BOOK PUBLISHING PLC
Headline House
79 Great Titchfield Street
London W1P 7FN

ONE

Early on Thursday morning, in a large house just off Barnsbury Square, North London, Sarah Copeland was talking on the phone in her front hall.

Sarah was an attractive woman with warm brown eyes and fair, shoulder-length hair, Sarah's face was only just beginning to show signs of the strain that came of being an intensely ambitious woman in an intensely competitive trade.

Sarah worked at Hamilton Forbes and Kent, one of the larger, and hotter, London advertising agencies. For the last three months, since her predecessor had been headhunted by Saatchi's, Sarah had been acting Creative Director. Much of her present attention was focussed on making the position permanent. To be Creative Director at Hamilton Forbes meant having a seat on the board.

There was a great deal of stress in Sarah's job. On the other hand, there were rewards; as one of London's creative top ten, she was very well paid indeed. Most of her salary, of course, she spent immediately. She played a notable part in the conspicuous consumption it was her business to promote. She was dressed by Giovanni Vanucci, one of her clients; she drove either a BMW or a Saab, either of which she would have liked to advertise. She had just passed one of advertising's most ominous landmarks, her thirtieth birthday. She would be thirty-one in April.

Sarah was holding the phone between chin and shoulder, and making notes on a yellow legal pad.

'Helen,' she said, 'it's not a good time to do this. It can't be seven o'clock yet – I'm not even dressed.' She was wearing a Vanucci slip, in a colour known as coffee cream. 'And I'm expecting a new au pair. Could you try to summarise it?'

She listened, made a note, then said: 'The Prime Minister?

Needs to be more radical?' She listened again. 'They want all private medicine? Cut funding for comprehensive schools?' She made more notes. 'That's what they're saying in the south-*west*? What do they want in the south-east? Public executions?'

The doorbell rang. A remote-controlled toy car moved slowly across the hall floor, stopped, then reversed.

'Helen,' said Sarah, 'it is absolutely no good your trying to give me all the data on the phone at this hour in the morning. I am standing in my hall. I don't have your charts. Daniel's waiting for his clothes – and now there's someone at the door. Hang on a minute –'

Sarah put down the phone and opened the front door. There was a taxi in the street. Rose Thompson, her new mother's help, was standing on the step with a suitcase and some sheets of copper. Rose was a pencil-slim girl who still looked like the art student she had recently been. Her eyes were a deeper brown than Sarah's, her hair was several shades darker, loose, and elaborately tied with dozens of tiny, yellow ribbons. She stepped carefully into the hall, avoiding the small cars and battleships that covered the carpet.

'I've got one more bag,' Rose said. She had a slight west country accent. 'And then the rest of my art stuff.'

'I'll be with you,' said Sarah. 'I'm just talking to someone –' She picked up the phone again and spoke to Helen, while Rose went out to the taxi.

'Helen,' said Sarah. 'Sorry. Back again. It was Rose. The au pair. The one who's also an artist. She's just arrived.'

'At this hour?' said Helen.

'It's a long and convoluted story,' said Sarah, 'which I won't tell you now. Listen. This place shows every sign of sliding into complete chaos. Daniel's upstairs. His little cars keep twitching. No one's done any ironing . . . What I really meant to say was, why don't you get a cab, bring all the charts and the data, come over here now, and explain the poll on the way in to work?'

The taxi drove away, going right around Barnsbury Square. Rose came into the hall, shut the door behind her, and put down her second case.

'I love you,' Sarah said into the phone, and put down the receiver.

'I am sorry,' she said to Rose. 'Someone I work with – trying to give me the results of an opinion poll in nine different counties. What do they want? More hospitals, or bring back hanging? Quite hopeless, over the phone, at breakfast time –'

Rose watched Daniel's car as it did a slow circuit of hall.

'Look,' said Sarah, 'I'm sorry to leave you like this, but I'll have to go in half an hour. Helen's coming over. We've got a big presentation today. To the Prime Minister, yet. Can I just show you how things work in the kitchen?'

She led the way toward the kitchen, then stopped and pointed at the sheets of copper which Rose had stacked against the architrave of the drawing room door.

'What's all that metal?'

'Those are my etching plates, Mrs Copeland.'

'Call me Sarah,' said Sarah. 'I'm not sure I *am* Mrs Copeland any more. My husband's not –' She stopped in mid-sentence and called up the stairs. 'Daniel!'

'What?' said Daniel. He was out of sight, on an upper landing.

'Rose has come to look after you,' called Sarah. 'You met Rose the other day. Will you come down and say hello?'

'I'm not dressed,' said Daniel. 'I haven't got a shirt.'

The phone in the hall began to ring.

'Daniel,' said Sarah, 'I've got a very busy morning. I've got to see the Prime Minister.'

'Who's he?' said Daniel.

'Can't you wear yesterday's shirt?' called Sarah.

'Shall I answer the phone, Mrs Copeland?' asked Rose.

'It's got blood on it,' said Daniel. 'Joshua bit me.'

'Joshua's a cat,' said Sarah to Rose. 'Evil animal.' She indicated the phone. 'Would you?'

Rose went to answer the phone. Sarah searched through a pile of unironed washing at the bottom of the stairs. She called to Daniel.

'Put the rest of your clothes on, love – and your vest, if that hasn't got blood on it. I'll iron you a shirt.'

Rose put her hand over the telephone receiver.

'They want Mr Copeland.'

There was a pause.

'Tell them I don't know where he is,' said Sarah finally. 'He hasn't been home all week –'

Rose uncovered the phone. Sarah lowered her voice.

'No. Don't say that. Say . . . say he's away. Till the end of the month.'

'I'm afraid Mr Copeland's away till the end of the month,' Rose said into the phone.

'It's so *stupid*, all this,' said Sarah, speaking to herself. She brushed her blonde hair back from her face, and went into the kitchen with the folded washing.

In the street outside Sarah Copeland's house, Stephen Hallam was parking his Porsche Carrera.

'Not quite her sparkling self these days, our Sarah,' he said.

Helen was collecting computer printout from the back seat of the car.

'Nothing wrong with Sarah,' she said. 'Just lost her au pair.'

'And a husband. Both in the same week. Now that, my love, is careless.'

Helen packed the printout into a leather satchel.

'If I do start this agency of mine,' said Stephen, 'do you think Sarah would come in?'

Helen opened the passenger door.

'You're not going to ask her today?'

'Running out of time,' said Stephen. 'David's only got another couple of days in New York.'

'Don't you think Sarah has enough on her plate?' asked Helen, 'I mean: just at this moment?'

Sarah stood in the middle of her kitchen, pointing items out to Rose.

'Washing machine stays on the cool cycle,' she said, 'or it turns everything into dolls' clothes. Dryer over there. Dishwasher needs that rinse aid stuff, but Janine forgot to get any. Janine was your predecessor. Bread's in there. Daniel has sandwiches at the moment – he's stopped eating school dinners. He has two Marmite, two paté, two cheese and jam.'

'Together?' asked Rose. 'Cheese and jam together?'

'Weird,' said Sarah. 'He likes it.'

The doorbell rang. Sarah moved toward the hall.

'Damn,' she said. 'Helen already. Look – could you do Daniel a shirt? Board – iron – spray starch if you need it – all in that cupboard. Unless Janine found a new hiding place for them. She did for everything else.'

'Shirt for today?' said Rose.

'Poor love's half naked,' said Sarah. She opened the door, and Helen came into the hall. Helen was Sarah's oldest friend, a blue-eyed woman in her early thirties, with brown hair layered softly around her face. She and Sarah had started work in the same week at Doyle Dane Bernbach, when Helen was twenty-four. Apart from one separation, they had worked together through the intervening years.

'Helen,' said Sarah, 'hold on a minute – Rose: I must go. Crisis day. But there's one thing – if my husband should ring –'

'You still haven't heard from him?' asked Helen.

'Not a word. But, Rose, listen. My husband – he's called Paul, and he has just the trace of a Yorkshire accent – and if he does ring, will you please try and find out where he is? I just don't know where he went. It's so –'

There was a pause.

'Strange,' said Helen.

'And today,' said Sarah to Rose, 'just today – don't let Paul talk to Daniel. Daniel's upset. You know: father's gone, au pair gone. The last au pair, that is.'

'They didn't . . .?' asked Rose.

Sarah was collecting a leather clipboard and a sheaf of notes from the hall table.

'Didn't what?' she asked. 'Swan off together? My husband and the au pair?'

Rose nodded.

'My husband knows a lot of very attractive, sane women,' said Sarah. 'Why should he go off with Janine?'

TWO

Sarah drove a BMW 328 CSi. It was a very fast car, which averaged just under fifteen miles an hour on the way in to Jermyn Street. While Sarah drove, Helen demonstrated electoral maps and charts.

'This is what I was trying to tell you on the phone,' she said. 'The strategy says we sell the idea of Britain being one nation. Then you look at these opinion poll figures – you look at the north-east, you look at Scotland, you look at Wales – I mean, politically, it's like dealing with a whole set of different countries.'

'What's that mean for us?' asked Sarah. 'In terms of getting the government back?'

'We have to adjust the advertising for each of the areas,' said Helen. She held up a computer-generated map, printed in several colours. 'Look at this. Attitudes to the National Health Service. Down here, in the south, what do they want? Private hospitals and medical insurance.' She pointed to north Wales, coloured green on the map. 'Up here, that's about as popular as bringing back the poorhouse.'

Sarah halted for a Vauxhall that was blocking the road, and swore under her breath.

'Has Stephen seen that chart?'

'Well, he went through all the data –' said Helen.

Sarah turned and looked at her.

'When? Last night?'

'Yesterday evening.'

'After I left you?' asked Sarah. 'How did you get to my place so quickly this morning? Cab?'

'Actually,' Helen muttered, 'Stephen went in early –'

'Thought I heard the Porsche,' said Sarah. 'You never learn, do you, love? I suppose he stayed the night – telling you his latest agency scheme?'

'By the time we finished, it was after midnight. Stephen really didn't –'

'– feel like driving back to Kent at that hour,' said Sarah. She went on to the right-hand side of the road and accelerated past the Vauxhall. 'Poor, dear Stephen. Don't you wonder if his wife's ever thought of moving a little bit closer to London?'

The Hamilton Forbes and Kent advertising agency was confortably positioned in the league table above the smaller firms which lived dangerously in Soho, and the two leviathans which dominated the business. It occupied an enviable site in the middle of St James's; for which the freehold was held separately to discourage asset-stripping takeover bids.

According to trade gossip, HFK was London's most consistently creative agency, but a little shaky on the management side. None of this was apparent to the passer-by. The façade was discreetly prosperous, with only the agency name visible, in Palatino caps, to indicate what went on inside.

Beside the agency's glass doors, Mike Sutherland was buying copies of all the papers which gave racing results. Sarah stopped her BMW in the road beside him, got out, and called.

'Room in the car park?'

'*Jawohl, mein Frau*,' said Mike. He gave the BMW a mock-fascist salute, and went on inside. Sarah drove into the agency's parking lot, where she was the only non-director to have a reserved space. Helen turned to watch Mike Sutherland as he carried his papers away.

'That creep's started getting here early,' she said. 'Could he be after your job?'

'Just dumb enough to think he could get it,' said Sarah, parking the car. 'The day they put me on the board is the day Sutherland starts looking for another agency.'

The reception area of Hamilton Forbes and Kent was a vast open space, all marble, travertine and glass, in shades of grey, strawberry fool and pistachio green. Behind a curved reception desk, one of the secretaries, Carol, was talking to Jane, who was the agency receptionist. Carol was telling Jane her plan for getting a room in Dee's house. They both paused and watched as Mike Sutherland came through the glass doors from Jermyn Street.

'Morning, girls,' said Mike. 'Nice to see you working hard. So early in the morning.'

'Morning, girls, he goes,' said Jane, as Mike entered one of the lifts. 'No wonder his wife left him. Alessandra must be out of her mind.'

'At least Mike's sort of young,' said Carol. 'I mean, I said to Sally: How old's David, then? What is he: is he thirty-nine? Is he forty?'

'Thirty-nine,' said Jane. 'Alessandra told me.'

'What I mean,' said Carol. 'I said, Sally, be serious. You do that, you'll find yourself popping down the Post Office, pick up his pension for him.'

'You'd better scoot,' said Jane. 'Here's Sarah.'

Sarah came through the swing doors, arguing with Helen.

'You've got it wrong,' said Helen. 'What I'm saying is – the peace talks might get somewhere. What happens then? We go into the election, advertising peace through nuclear weapons –'

'Peace is a bomb in the backyard,' said Sarah.

'Absolutely. But what happens if they agree to a nuclear-free Europe next month? We'll look bloody stupid if we've just put out a series of election ads saying we need more missiles.'

'Don't hold your breath,' said Sarah. 'Peace talks are about shuffling missiles around, not getting rid of them. They take a few away, then they put in others. It's called strategic balance. Keeps the military employed.' She called to Jane: 'Messages? No?'

Carol was pretending to help Jane sort through the morning's mail.

'Never stops working, does she? Think she has any sex life?'

Jane looked after Sarah and Helen as they went through to the lifts.

'I know she fancies Nick.'

Carol stopped pretending to work.

'Sarah? Fancies *copywriter* Nick?'

'You watch how she changes,' said Jane. 'Soon as he comes back.'

'Wish he was back,' said Carol. 'She's not the only one that fancies him.'

'Sarah's got an advantage,' said Jane.

'She's not that sexy,' said Carol.

'Not sexy,' said Jane. 'She's his boss.'

Sarah got out of the lift on the first floor, the home of agency's creative department. At the moment, it was also Sarah's empire; as acting Creative Director, she was in charge of twenty-four very highly paid copywriters and art directors. Sarah watched some of them at work as she paused to plan with Helen how to handle Gordon Lochhead. Gordon was the agency's deputy managing director, and the main opponent of Sarah's promotion to the board.

In the middle of the first floor was an open-plan area where Sarah's junior creative teams worked. Junior creative teams are partnerships of young art directors and copywriters. Often, they are recruited straight from college, and learn to work together on the first stages of imagining ads. In theory, the AD does the visual side of it, and the writer does the words. In practice, there's no firm boundary between the two. The ideas can come from either of them.

Talking to Helen, Sarah gave part of her attention to one of her recent recruits, a notably beautiful black girl called Dee Vincent, whose fall of her braided hair, glowing skin and sculptured cheekbones drew the eye like a magnet. Dee was the art director half of one junior creative team; she was West Indian and, Sarah knew, was active in both black and feminist causes.

The other half of the team was Nick Faulds. Nick lived with Sarah's secretary, Sally Byfleet. They had both gone on holiday at the same time but, rumour had it, not together. Nick was now on his way back from Barbados; or so Sarah hoped. She had sent him a telex saying she wanted him back at work today, but so far, there was no sign of him.

Dee's family also came from Barbados, but she herself had been born in Kennington. As a rule, she was a calm and elegant young woman. Just now, though, she showed every sign of being very angry. She was talking intensely to Warren, the agency's senior art director. She turned down volume on a cassette recorder so that Warren gave his full attention to her.

'It's supposed to be an ad with a *Russian* tank,' she said. 'They give me a pic, and the hell it's Russian.' She showed a photographic enlargement. 'This is an American tank.'

Warren peered at the enlargement.

'Who's going to know?'

'If Stan knows, a lot of other people are going to know.'

'Sod it,' said Warren. He moved away toward the office he shared with Sarah. 'Get another pic.'

'*Me* get another pic?' called Dee. 'I've got half the political campaign to do. I've got four finished roughs to go to Downing Street this afternoon. Andy's gone. Your daughter hasn't turned up. Nick's not here. How do you think I'm going to spend time getting more pix?'

Warren went into his office and shut the door. Sarah left Helen and walked over to Dee's desk.

'I'll get Jenny to find the photo,' she said. 'Try not to shout at Warren this early in the morning. It's not his best time.'

'Not my best time either,' said Dee. 'Get here at sunrise – if you ever saw the sun in this place – agency's empty, we've got a presentation this afternoon, they send me the wrong stuff, I've got no copy for the National Health –'

'I told you,' said Sarah. 'We're shooting the National Health on video. After lunch. In North London Women's Hospital.'

Dee stopped work.

'They let you shoot in a hospital?'

'It's closed,' said Sarah. 'That's one thing you can find these days: closed hospitals. You can have the print copy for three p.m.'

'Jesus,' said Dee. 'Thanks. And you want a finished rough by five?'

'Four-thirty,' said Sarah. 'We leave for Downing Street at five.'

'Magic,' said Dee. 'Did I tell you Linda's waiting for you?'

Gordon Lochhead came across the creative department, walking fast. Gordon was Scottish and, at forty-four, the oldest executive in the agency. He had narrowly missed becoming Managing Director when the board chose a younger man, David Postgate. David had been Deputy MD at Y and R; he was good looking, charming and apparently casual in his management style. Gordon made no secret of detesting the man; and made no secret of his view that David did none of the real work of running the agency. The fact that David was now in New York had fired Gordon's resentment almost to melting point.

He switched off the cassette recorder on Dee's desk, and spoke to Sarah.

'I thought we had a meeting in my office.'

'Neither of us is there,' said Sarah.

'I'm on my way. Make it in half an hour,' said Gordon. 'I hope you are.'

Sarah took Gordon's arm and led him out of Dee's hearing.

'Coming back to that other discussion,' she said, 'I've done what you asked. I've thought about it. And I've decided that I am not having you shift my staff around. More particularly, I am not, repeat not, having Mike Sutherland selling nuclear weapons to the British voting public.'

Gordon looked around the creative department. Dee, Warren and Helen had stopped work to watch him and Sarah.

'I simply asked Sutherland,' he began.

'I understand,' said Sarah. 'You asked a writer, who has all the sensitivity you normally associate with water buffalo, to advertise medium-range missiles. I have now moved him back to his proper metier, which is selling little tubes of Tropic Tan to yuppies on their way to Kenya. The missile ads I'll do myself.'

'You are not yet creative director, Sarah,' said Gordon. 'Remember that; you are merely acting in the post.'

'If I'm acting, I'll act,' said Sarah. She moved back to Dee's desk.

Gordon paused, then turned and went in the direction of the lifts.

'Who did you say was waiting?' Sarah asked Dee.

'Linda,' said Dee. 'She came in early.'

'Apart from you,' said Sarah, 'she's the only person who does. Maybe it's living with Alice.'

The main office was shared by Sarah and Warren as the agency's senior creative team. At thirty-six, Warren Greenbank was a solid man with hair brushed straight down over his forehead. He had worked with Sarah for the last nine years. It had been one of the industry's great partnerships. Together, they had won every award to be had; many of them several years in a row. In the past year, though, they had won nothing. Warren publicly blamed Sarah's promotion, and the amount of administrative work she now did. More privately, Sarah put the blame on Warren's drinking. Whatever the reason, they were no longer the close creative team they had once been. Increasingly, Sarah went to others to discuss her ideas. Increasingly, Warren worked alone in their office.

Warren was now at his desk, ignoring the phones that were ringing on Sarah's side of the office, considering that to be the task of Sally Byfleet, who was Sarah's secretary. Sarah's secretary was supposed to be in Rome, and was in fact in New York. Either way, she was not available to take phone calls.

Warren's half of the office was cluttered with objects: Rapidographs, felt pens, markers, layout pads, light boxes, decorative objects like Brasso tins and Daniel Webster cigar boxes, art deco figurines, malachite elephants, and a magnet board of roughs, photos, ad proofs and cartoons.

Sarah's half of the office was meticulously tidy by contrast. Its furniture was high-tec in black and primary colours: acid green, chrome yellow and solid red. On the desk were three phones, one in each of these colours. Linda was answering the yellow one as Sarah walked in.

'It's Gordon,' she said. 'Wants to know if we can make the meeting fifteen minutes earlier.'

'Tell him no,' said Sarah. 'We're going to have to talk him through this absent animatic,' she said to Warren.

Warren was watching Linda.

'You go a beaut shade of brown there,' he said. 'How was Oz?'

Linda put the phone down.

'Oz was OK,' she said. 'It's coming back that's hard. Sydney's eighty-five in the shade. Get off the plane at Heathrow, yesterday afternoon, and there's hail coming down. Cold as a welldigger's ass, to quote Tom Waits.'

'God knows what your biological clock's doing,' said Sarah. 'Come on. Tell us. In three sentences: how did the filming go?'

'I can tell you in three words,' said Linda. 'It was disaster. They say we have to go to Australia to shoot the perfect body, in the perfect pool, in perfect antipodean light. Great. Costs megabucks to fly a crew out there. Second day, gaffer hits the tequila, manages to empty our perfect pool.'

Warren started to laugh.

'Put it on record, Sarah. I'm not the only tequila freak in the trade.'

'Not hard to refill the pool, surely?' said Sarah.

'Refilling the pool wasn't the problem,' said Linda. 'Problem was, the overflow blocked. So when Gary empties the water out, he washes away a rather nice little Double Bay property. A colonial-style villa, which is – or was – one step down the hill.'

Warren and Sarah looked at Linda.

'Price of property over there,' said Warren, 'that must be the most expensive shoot since *Heaven's Gate*.'

'No question,' said Linda. 'We came away with six Tropic Tan shots, at a price of about two hundred thousand a picture. Insurance should help, unless someone tells them Gary was wrecked at the time of our mishap. Sarah: I dragged myself out of bed, still thinking it was the Australian evening, because there's a message on my machine saying you wanted to brief me.'

'I do,' said Sarah. 'Have you heard the political news?'

'Have you ever tried finding political news in a Sydney paper?' asked Linda.

'This particular item hasn't hit the press anywhere,' said Warren.

'Prime Minister's calling an election,' said Sarah. 'Middle of next month.'

'Christ,' said Linda. 'That soon?'

'And you, sweetheart, seem to be producing the party political broadcasts.'

'Starting after lunch,' said Sarah.

Warren's phone rang. He picked it up and listened.

'A Chocolate Elf?' he asked incredulously. 'Not mine. Sounds like a Mike Sutherland stroke of genius, that.' He put the phone down forcefully.

'After lunch we are doing a video shoot in a closed hospital,' said Sarah to Linda. 'It's an insert into a party political. Quote: the National Health Service is in good hands, unquote. The video has to be shot for zero editing, be ready to show at five this evening.'

'Shown to whom?' said Linda.

'The Prime Minister,' said Sarah. 'But right now, we have a meeting with Gordon Lochhead, God help us. I'll tell you more on the way down.'

THREE

Gordon Lochhead's office was furnished to look more like the domain of a banker than an advertising man. It was a long room, papered in a dark Zoffany design, and hung with prints of exotic flora, reproduced from Joseph Banks' botanical masterwork, *The Florilegium.*

At one end of the room was an oval mahogany table. At the other was a vast mahogany desk. Gordon was standing in front of the desk, holding on a white phone, and speaking at the same time to Stephen Hallam. Stephen was a young and personable account executive, who privately claimed to have slept with every nubile woman in the agency; most recently, Helen. The new designer diseases had curbed, but not radically changed, this aspect of his life.

Stephen Hallam was helped in his sexual pilgrimage by dark good looks; and even more by the sense he gave of explosive masculine energy, barely restrained. He wore his dark hair brushed back and, in Gordon's opinion, a little too long. He also wore the agency's most expensive Italian suits.

Now, Stephen was listening to Gordon with his characteristic smile, which Warren had once described as the contented expression of a wolverine devouring the remains of his mate.

'No use having a damn board meeting if David's back from New York,' said Gordon. 'Whole point is to get a vote of no-confidence while the man's out of the country.' He spoke into the phone. 'Lochhead speaking. Sarah Copeland is not here. I know she should be. I'm saying she's not.'

Just then Carol, Gordon's secretary, showed Sarah and Linda into the office.

'Correction,' said Gordon. 'She just walked in.'

'Someone wants you, my love,' said Stephen, with his grin.

'Stan, said Gordon, indicating the phone. 'Wants to know what videorecorders we are taking to Downing Street.'

'U-matics,' said Sarah. 'Three of them, and a spare. Checked, ready to go, four-thirty.'

'Four U-matics,' said Gordon and put down the phone. Helen and Warren came into the office and took seats at the oval table.

'Now,' said Gordon. 'For a moment, I am the Prime Minister. The door of the White Room in Downing Street is over there. I shall come in across the room like this, accompanied by the Minister of State and the chairman of the party.'

'Chairperson,' said Sarah. 'Mrs Clarkson is a woman.'

'The term chairman has nothing to do with the sex of the holder,' said Gordon. 'You, as a copywriter, should know that, Sarah. Now. I want you, Helen, sitting there. You will be in a similar position at Downing Street this afternoon. Stephen, beside Helen. Sarah, beside Stephen. What's Liz doing?'

'You mean Linda,' said Sarah. 'She's getting the TV brief.'

'Perhaps you've forgotten,' said Linda to Gordon. 'I've been shooting swimsuits in Australia.'

'Linda's going to do the party politicals,' said Warren.

'Understood,' said Gordon. 'Liz, you sit over there, on Warren's left.'

Linda moved around the table and took her seat.

'I'm Linda,' she said. 'For heaven's sake, Gordon. I've only been away two weeks.'

'I want you to remember,' Gordon told her, 'that this is going to be a very short election campaign. Everything said here is completely confidential. No gossip. It is absolutely vital to keep the opposition parties in ignorance as long as we can.'

Sarah said: 'I'm sure Linda's aware of all this.'

Gordon displayed a copy of the *Express*. Its headline read: *Election. It's Autumn – Official.*

'The Prime Minister,' said Gordon, 'is giving the public impression that the election will be later in the year. Meanwhile we, and the Party, are preparing a creative strategy, buying space and services, fine-tuning the electoral machine.'

'I do know how these things work,' said Linda.

'One person talking out of turn,' said Gordon, '– even one person – that could mean losing our client. And our client losing the election.' He turned to Linda. 'Just keep it in mind. I tell everyone the same thing.'

'Indeed he does,' said Sarah quietly to Warren.

'Now,' said Gordon, 'since our Managing Director has chosen this moment to be in New York, I shall introduce our team when we arrive at Downing Street. I shall give our advertising strategy for the Party, answer questions, show a selection of print advertising for the national newspapers.'

Stephen was checking through a pile of finished roughs that Warren had brought in.

'All the prints ads are here,' he said.

'Understood,' said Gordon. 'What about the television?'

There was a pause.

'Not ready,' said Sarah finally.

There was another pause.

'You told me,' said Gordon, 'that you would have an animatic, ready to show the Prime Minister, by this morning.'

Warren produced a set of photographic enlargements and pushed them across the table toward Sarah.

'The idea,' said Sarah, 'was to do ninety seconds of a party political broadcast on why we need to keep the bomb.'

'Theme was: missiles protect your family,' said Stephen. 'We wanted a set of shots – cosy home, good parents, rosy-cheeked children.'

Sarah held up one of the photographs. It showed two bad-tempered and ill-favoured infants.

'And look what research came up with,' she said. 'Pix weren't worth putting on the rostrum.' She held up another photograph. 'Look at these kids. I really can't see anyone blowing up Russia to save this lot.'

Gordon stood. He leaned over the table. His Edinburgh accent became more marked when he was angry.

'This,' he said with emphasis, 'will be a television election. It will be won or lost on the bloody box. And you tell me that we are going to put an election package to the Prime Minister this afternoon – with no television. Is that what you're saying?

'No, it is not,' said Sarah. 'I said the animatic wasn't worth finishing. I'm going to do something simpler. We're shooting a video insert this afternoon, to put across the message that the government is looking after the Health Service. We shoot for minimal editing, have it checked and ready to go to Downing Street by four-thirty. Unless you have a better plan?'

The phone on the table began to ring.

'I can tell you what I think of *your* planning,' said Gordon. 'I think it's amateur. I think it's a disgrace to a professional advertising agency.' He picked up the phone and spoke into it. 'Carol? I thought I said no calls?' He listened. His tone changed. 'Ah. Well. Put him through.' He covered the receiver and spoke to Stephen. 'The Chairman. That little matter we were speaking about.'

Stephen looked across the table at Sarah. She was watching him with close attention. Stephen gave her a particularly wide smile, as Gordon began a low-toned conversation with the company Chairman.

Outside Gordon's office was a smaller office, belonging to his secretary. Carol had made a distinctive space for herself, filling it with a miniature jungle of plants, among the foliage of which stood small replicas of Snoopy and Woodstock, and framed photos of Carol's parents, taken at the seaside.

Carol was watering one of the larger plants, a maidenhair fern, when Alessandra stopped in the doorway of her office. An exceptionally beautiful blonde, Alessandra's manner was described by her friends as cool, and by her enemies as deep-frozen. She was personal assistant to David Postgate, the agency's managing director and, as such she knew a great deal about David's affairs; including the affair he was now conducting in New York.

'Call from Downing Street,' said Alessandra. 'They want to bring the presentation half an hour forward. Prime Minister's got some foreign affairs crisis.'

'Oh, *sugar*,' said Carol. 'Why don't you tell Gordon?'

'Because I'm not his secretary,' said Alessandra. She went on down the passage toward the photocopier. Carol sighed, and knocked on the door of Gordon's office. It opened immediately as Gordon pushed past her.

'I shall be with the Chairman,' he said as he followed Alessandra down the passage.

'Downing Street's put the presentation half an hour forward,' said Carol to Sarah.

'Dear God,' said Sarah. 'That's all I need. Let me have the phone.'

'Coffee?' Stephen asked Linda, as he preceded her out of the office. 'I haven't really welcomed you back from Down Under, have I? Nor congratulated you on drawing the short straw for the party political broadcasts.'

Linda walked with Stephen down the carpeted corridor towards the agency restaurant.

'What does that mean, exactly?' she asked.

'You've seen party politicals,' said Stephen, 'all the charm and fascination of a feminist documentary.'

'Bang,' said Warren to Helen. 'Right through the foot.'

'I might be fascinated,' said Linda. 'Being a feminist.'

Stephen smacked his left wrist with his right hand.

'Stephen Hallam,' he said. 'How could you forget?'

Warren, Helen and Linda entered the restaurant. Stephen paused beside Alessandra, who was photocopying the last pages of a political contact report. He put his hand on her waist and slid it gently downward.

'If I had your body,' he said, 'I wouldn't wear loose clothes.'

Without shifting attention from her copying, Alessandra removed his hand.

'You don't have my body,' she said.

'Not as often as I'd like,' agreed Stephen. 'But I could meet you in the wine bar about seven. What would you say to that?'

Linda, Helen and Warren joined a noisy media-buying group who were young enough and slim enough to be eating sticky cakes on the far side of the restaurant. The restaurant itself was a new innovation at Hamilton Forbes. It was David Postgate's idea. He thought an in-house restaurant and wine bar might cut down the time his staff spent lunching in the Firenze, and other Mayfair watering holes. The restaurant had not been open long enough to show whether he was right or wrong; but it was usually full until quite late in the evening.

'Thought Gordon might have mellowed while I was away,' said Linda.

'Uh huh,' said Helen. 'Still doing the deputy managing director bit.'

Sarah came into the restaurant and collected her coffee.

'I hear he may not stay deputy,' said Warren. 'Plans to be manager.'

Stephen walked across the restaurant with Sarah.

'How are things at home?' he asked. 'Still no husband?'

Sarah's expression changed.

'For a few hours, Stephen, I was trying to forget that.'

'I'm sorry,' said Stephen. 'Clumsy.' He moved closer. 'But, if I may whisper a sybilline word, life here might be easier if you didn't handle Gordon quite like that.'

'I shouldn't have to handle Gordon. He shows all the outward signs of being a grown man.'

'Do you happen to know what David is doing in New York?' asked Stephen.

'Staying at the Plaza, having his way with my secretary,' said Sarah. 'Damn him. Just when I need her. Just when we need David, come to that.' She looked closely at Stephen. 'Why? What's that got to do with Gordon?'

'Apart from what he does in bed with your secretary,' said Stephen, 'our Managing Director has just bought an American agency. Pater Paolozzi and Klein.'

'Dear God,' said Sarah. 'Pater Paolozzi's huge. They've got United Foods.' She paused and thought. 'What's David going to pay for it?'

'More than we can afford, according to Gordon,' said Stephen. 'He's upstairs now, persuading the Chairman of that fact.'

'Ah,' said Sarah. 'You mean, the board won't back David?'

Stephen smiled widely, and shook his head.

A wall phone rang. Warren went to answer it.

'And if the board don't back David – ?' said Sarah.

'Sarah,' called Warren. 'Phone for you.'

'We shall have ourselves a new Managing Director,' said Stephen. 'Guess who.'

Sarah began to move towards the phone that Warren was holding.

'Oh, shit,' she said. 'Not Gordon?'

Stephen nodded.

'So, my love, you have a choice. Stay here – working for Gordon – or come in with me. New agency: Hallam and Copeland.'

'You never stop, do you, Stephen?' said Sarah as she took the phone. 'Sarah Copeland,' she said. Then she heard her au pair's voice, and she was engulfed by sudden, irrational panic.

'Rose?' she said. '*Rose*? Tell me – is there something wrong with Daniel?'

Rose was standing in the hall of Sarah's house, speaking on the phone, and trying to hear a series of faint sounds from upstairs.

'Really, Mrs Copeland,' she said, 'Daniel's all right. I mean, it's nothing physical. They just – well they rang, they said they couldn't find him at the school. It was one of the teachers. She said she couldn't find him at playtime.'

Rose listened, then spoke again.

'No. He came straight home – that wasn't a problem, Mrs Copeland. But he won't talk to me, and I can't get through to your mother – and what happened was, he'd been crying, and he was sort of curled up, rocking himself backwards and forwards, and I didn't know if he'd ever done that before: Mrs Copeland?'

Sarah, standing in the restaurant at Hamilton Forbes, and still holding the phone, paused for some moments. She was fighting against a persistent guilt; against the recurrent sense that she should be at home with her son, not in these pistachio-painted offices which claimed most of her waking life. Finally, she spoke to Rose.

'No,' she said, 'something must have happened to Daniel. I'll come back and see him.' She checked the time. 'Listen, Rose: we're going out on a shoot – if I leave now, I could just dash home on the way. Stay with him, will you? I'll be there in half an hour.'

Sarah hung up the phone, stood for a moment undecided, then walked quickly out of the restaurant.

In the reception area, Jane was talking on two telephones at once. On the first phone, she said: 'Putting you through now, sir.' On the second phone, she said: 'Dee, you don't do that these days. Tell her you get nasty diseases. Tell her, if he won't take a test, don't go away with him.'

Sarah paused by the marble reception desk.

'Jane,' she said, 'I'm sure this life-giving advice, but I need your attention for a couple of minutes.'

'Talk to you soon,' said Jane, and put down the phone. 'Sorry, Sarah.'

'Do me a favour,' said Sarah. 'With Sally away. Call Jeremy, tell him I've got to call in at home – on the way to the shoot – won't see him till after the presentation. Call Simon, tell him come in, if I'm out he should talk to Dee. OK? Anything desperate, get me on the car phone. And there's a note for Stan. I want him to have it in the next five minutes. It's about Downing Street. For the next couple of hours, I'm going to be at the North London Hospital for Women.'

'I am sorry,' said Jane. 'Is it serious?'

'It's not personal,' said Sarah. 'The hospital's closed. It's where we're shooting the ads for the Health Service.'

Twenty-three minutes later, Sarah parked outside her house, so fast that the BMW hit the kerb. She left the car unlocked, and was trying her key, clumsy in haste, when Rose opened the door from inside.

'Oh, thanks,' said Sarah. 'Where is he? Where's Daniel?'

'He's in the kitchen,' said Rose. 'I was just trying to –'

'I'll do it,' said Sarah. 'Whatever it is.'

She went into the kitchen. There was no sign of her son. There was a slight, sharp sound. Sarah looked around the end of the dresser. Daniel was curled up there. He still wore his school uniform and he held a thin, dry stick. He was snapping small pieces off it. They were neatly broken and of uniform length. Sarah knelt down beside him.

'Daniel, love – what's wrong?'

'Nothing,' said Daniel.

'Something must be wrong, my love,' said Sarah. 'Did something happen at school?'

Silence.

'Daniel?'

Sarah gently turned his face towards her.

'Was it – ?'

'This boy Gavin,' said Daniel suddenly. 'He said Daddy went off with Janine.' He broke another inch from the stick. 'Did he?'

'Daniel,' said Sarah, 'I don't know where Daddy is. I'm sure he's going to telephone, and tell us –' She glanced surreptitiously at her watch. 'Why did this boy think Daddy went away – with Janine – ?'

'Grandma told somebody in the delicatessen. And Gavin's Mummy was in there too.'

'Oh, darling,' said Sarah. 'I am sorry.'

She took Daniel in her arms. His small, stiff body began to relax.

'When *is* Daddy coming back?'

Sarah hesitated.

'Daniel – I'm not sure when he's coming back.' She waited. Daniel said nothing. 'Would you mind very much, if Daddy didn't come back?'

Sarah stroked Daniel's face. He closed his teeth on one of her fingers.

'Daniel – *don't*!' said Sarah. She tried to prise his mouth open. 'You're hurting me. You're *hurting* me!'

As suddenly as he bit, Daniel let go his mother's finger. He broke free of her and ran out of the kitchen. Sarah's eyes were full of tears. She stood up and looked around the kitchen.

'Oh, screw it,' she said.

Then she swept two dozen dinner plates off the dresser and followed Daniel out of the kitchen.

In the agency, Mike Sutherland was running up the stairs to the first floor. Mike was a squash player. He preferred stairs to lifts. He caught up with Warren just before he turned in to the creative department.

'How would you like to work on a beer account?' he asked.

Warren stopped.

'Sutherland,' he said, 'we have a presentation to the bloody Prime Minister this afternoon. Everyone else is buzzing round like a blue-arsed fly – and you're on about beer.' He opened the door of the department, paused a moment, then closed it again. 'What sort of beer?'

'New brew,' said Mike. 'Scunthorpe Six X.'

'Kidding,' said Warren. 'They don't make beer in Scunthorpe.'

Mike kept pace as Warren walked back to his office.

'Of course they don't make beer in Scunthorpe,' he said. 'I invented the name. Client wanted something that sounds pretty damn strong.'

'Is it?' said Warren.

'Joking,' said Mike, 'you try it some time. Three pints, guaranteed. Turns your brains to spinach.'

In Helen's office, Linda was helping organise data for the afternoon's presentation. Computer printouts were stacked in folders of a dozen different colours.

'It was while you were away,' said Helen. 'Sarah's husband disappeared.'

For once, Linda seemed genuinely shaken.

'Paul? Disappeared? With someone else?'

'No one knows,' said Helen. 'Least of all Sarah. She said he just packed a bag and went. No note: nothing. Pass me that yellow folder, will you?'

'I always thought,' said Linda, 'it was the one straight marriage that worked –'

'Me too,' said Helen. 'Devoted father. Except, something odd. Paul came in for a drink one evening – just before we were approached over this account – and more or less said he felt he didn't figure in Sarah's life.'

'I have to go out to shoot,' said Linda, picking up her bag. 'What did he mean: didn't figure?'

'Said it was work first with Sarah; Daniel second; and him somewhere third. That's how he saw the marriage.'

Linda paused in the doorway.

'Then what happened?'

'Nothing *happened*,' said Helen, putting the word in verbal quotes. 'It wasn't like that. He was in tears. I just sort of held him. It was like holding a child.' She started another set of folders. 'I said: Paul, love, it comes with the territory. That's why my husband left. Couldn't cope with my career.'

The phone began to ring.

'Did you tell Sarah?' asked Linda.

'Would you tell Sarah?' said Helen. 'If her husband was crying on your shoulder?' She turned away and picked up the phone.

Sarah was still in her own house. She was sitting on the stairs, and listening to Rose. Rose stood on the landing above her.

'Daniel's OK now, Mrs Copeland,' she said.

'I can't do this,' said Sarah.

'I'll read to him,' said Rose. 'He's better now.'

'I can't do it. I can't do this job on my own. And look after him. They say, well, you get the same money as a man. Why shouldn't you do what a man does? But when did you last see the chairman of your bank picking little Julian up from school?'

There was a pause and, from somewhere above them, the mewing of Daniel's computer.

'I'm not saying he wasn't supportive,' said Sarah.

'Who's that, Mrs Copeland?' asked Rose.

'Paul. My husband. To be honest, he was very good with

Daniel. I suppose, if you think about it, Paul played with him more than I did. But playing's the easy part. Whenever there's a crisis, you find Paul's got a class to teach, and it's me that gets in the car and comes home. And when you get there, the au pair's waiting for you. Heart sinks. You find she's mentally packed her bags. Or physically. It's a nightmare: present company excepted; I hope. And it never was my husband handling that.' She paused. 'Now he's not here to handle anything.'

'Mrs Copeland,' said Rose, 'I'm sure Daniel's all right. I'll read to him.'

'He likes *Fantastic Mister Fox*,' said Sarah. 'It sends him to sleep.'

'I'll read to him,' said Rose again. 'You go out and shoot your film.'

FOUR

Sarah's political promo was directed by Clayton Yock. Clayton was a director of television commercials and pop videos. He was a young man with pale skin and dyed black hair, who carefully maintained his south London accent, and who despised any art which was less than completely commercial. Now he was standing at the top of a flight of stairs in the deserted North London Hospital for Women. He was shouting, so that echoes bounced off the green-tiled walls.

'Get the sodding gear up here, will you, Gary, if that's not too much trouble for you, son. And where the fuck is Sarah Copeland, anybody know? I want to talk to her.'

'Don't we all,' said Warren, going into a disused ward.

Inside the ward, there was more activity than there had been since the hospital closed. Beds were lined up in the north corner. In one of the beds was Vera Forrest, an aging actress. In the other was a more distinguished actor, of similar vintage, called Bassett Syme. Looking after them was a nurse called Judy Axford.

Judy Axford was a real nurse; an SRN. She had been chosen, from a computer-generated list of possible candidates, by Helen Marriott, the agency's chief planner. Helen chose Judy for several reasons. She was young, she was photogenic, she had a high credibility-factor when panel-tested – and her husband had left her for another nurse. This last was an important consideration. It meant that Mrs Axford was now the single mother of three young children; and it also meant she desperately needed money. For an appropiate fee, therefore, Judy was willing to say that all was well with the National Health Service. Not all of her colleagues would do the same.

Around Vera, Bassett and Judy was all the paraphernalia of

a video shoot: cameras, tracks, cables, boom microphones, lights, and monitors. Fran, a makeup girl, was colouring Vera Forrest's face in the pallor of ill health. Linda Prentice, standing in for the absent Sarah, was talking to the young nurse, who had never before been on film.

'Just be natural, Judy,' she reassured the girl. 'Play yourself. Don't worry if you feel a bit nervous – everyone's nervous the first time.'

'Where'd you turn up these troglodytes?' the director asked his first assistant.

'You listen to what she's saying, love,' said Vera Forrest to Judy. She propped herself up on her pillows, and the cameraman readjusted his focus. 'End of the war, I remember, I was playing that girl in whatsername. *Flare Path*. Terence Rattigan, it was. Talk about nervous. Needed three pair of knickers a night.'

Outside the building, Sarah drove her BMW into the hospital car park. She switched off the engine, put on the handbrake, and sat for a moment, looking up at the empty building. There had been a protest, she remembered, when it was closed last year. From the top storey windows a banner still hung saying: Keep North London's Only Hosital for Women Open.' Over the last nine months, the lettering had run in the rain.

Sarah got out of her car and began to climb the hospital stairs. She slipped on dampness and went slower. At the top she paused and caught her breath. She went into the nearest ward. Warren was standing at the door.

'Where the hell have you been?' he asked. 'Linda just decided to start the shoot without you.'

'Domestic crisis,' said Sarah. 'Daniel's – Daniel's upset.'

They walked into the ward. It was a chaos of activity.

'You went home to see your kid – three hours before we go to Downing Street?'

'Warren,' said Sarah, 'you don't have to run home and see Kim, because you've got a wife to do all that. I don't have a wife.'

'Nor do I,' said Warren. 'Not at the moment.'

'I'm sorry, love,' said Sarah. 'Stupid of me.' She went up to Linda, who was assessing a three-shot of the nurse and two patients.

'I'm told you're ready to go.'

'We ran out of time,' said Linda. 'But now you're here, you do the questions to the nurse. Read them. You'll be out of shot.'

'I know,' said Sarah. 'I planned this shoot. Remember? You were in Sydney, destroying villas in Double Bay.'

Clayton, the director, was shouting at the makeup girl.

'Slap some more paint on her face, will you, love? Supposed to be at death's door, isn't she?'

'The name's Vera,' said Vera with dignity. 'What have I got, nurse?' she asked Judy Axford.

Sarah spoke to Linda, indicating Judy Axford. 'Does the nurse know her lines?'

'I said, what have I got?' asked Vera. She turned to Bassett Syme in the next bed. 'What have you got, Bass?'

'He can't speak,' said Warren. 'He's had a stroke.'

'Judy's reading her lines from cue cards,' said Linda. 'Try a card,' she called.

The assistant floor manager began to whistle a song called *From a Jack to a King*. The song dated from about the same period as he did. He held up a cue card. Vera Forrest sat up in bed and inspected Bassett Syme.

'If you know what's wrong with him,' she said, 'why don't you know what's wrong with me?' She spoke confidentially to the nurse. 'I played Camille once. In rep, just after the war. She was dying of TB, that girl. I'd have played her very different, darling, if she'd had rabies.'

'Judy,' called Sarah, 'could you look as if you're caring for the man in that bed –'

'Bassett,' said Vera.

'– and then just look up and say to camera what's on that cue card.'

'Just who do you think's directing this, darling?' Clayton asked Sarah.

'Rabies,' said Bassett to Vera, 'you need flecks of foam.'

Judy tucked in Bassett's sheets, looked up, and read from the card.

'*Yes, I've always wanted to be a nurse. I can't think of any work that's more satisfying.*'

'That's it,' shouted the director. 'Get out of shot, makeup girl, whoever you are – bloody makeup, always in shot – and someone elbow that bloody bedpan, will you? – OK, all right, let's get something moving here, shall we? Someone prop up Bassett Syme, will you?'

'If Bassett's had a stroke,' said Vera, 'you leave him laying down.'

'Dear God, he can be a tonsillectomy,' said Sarah. 'Just do it.'

'Quiet,' screamed the director. 'And for God's sake, run that machine up to speed, will you?'

At the agency, Stephen Hallam had paused on his way in to Gordon's office, in order to have a quiet word with Alessandra, the managing director's personal assistant. He ran a finger lightly through Alessandra's hair.

'Such a blonde *mane*,' he said. 'God clearly designed you for riding. Any word of your lord and master?'

'Inside the agency,' said Alessandra, 'I really prefer that you don't touch me.'

'Not at all your attitude outside the agency,' said Stephen. 'What I was specifically wondering was whether David had changed his return flight.'

'If he does, I'm sure he'll let Gordon know. And I'm sure Gordon will tell you.'

'Aren't you the soul of discretion?' said Stephen. 'See you at seven.' He blew Alessandra a sketch of a kiss, and went in to the deputy managing director's office.

Gordon was behind his vast mahogany desk, speaking on the phone. 'I thought perhaps five for five-thirty,' he was saying. 'Don't imagine it should take too long. It's mainly the New York business I think you should know about.' He made his farewells and put down the phone.

'Board meeting all arranged?' asked Stephen.

'Everyone confirmed, except Simon Forbes.'

'Rather significant exception,' said Stephen.

'No one knows where Forbes is,' said Gordon. 'However, Carol's tracking him down. I have a tie for you.'

'A tie?' said Stephen. He looked down with surprise at the silk Paul Smith creation he was wearing.

Gordon opened a mahogany clothes press at the far end of his office. Inside were a number of dark suits, each with an appropiate shirt and tie. Gordon selected one of sober shade.

'Don't want you meeting the Prime Minister wearing a pink tie,' he said. He passed the tie to Stephen, who began to loosen his own.

'Another little naughtiness,' said Stephen. 'I learn that David put down Sally's trip to New York as a company expense.'

'She is his secretary,' said Gordon.

'She is *a* secretary,' said Stephen, with emphasis. 'Not his. Unless you give the possessive pronoun it most fundamental meaning.' He turned to look at Gordon. 'But you do realise that if our Manging Director does survive this board meeting – and if he does get the government back in – he'll be in a very strong position? That it might be us on the outside?'

'– it might be *we*,' said Gordon, pedantically.

Stephen waited.

Gordon took up a characteristic stance. He stood with his hands behind his back, leaning forward slightly from the waist.

'David will not survive,' he said. 'The man's a figure from a Greek tragedy. There is a central flaw in his character. On the verge of victory, he betrays himself. He's done it before. He will do it again. In fact, he is doing it now.'

Stephen finshed knotting his tie.

'In what way?'

'Why, in his right mind.' asked Gordon, 'should David take on the project of advertising the government, and then fly to New York, and buy an agency he can't afford to pay for? The man is destroying himself.'

'With a little help,' said Stephen.

'Oh, I may have to finish the process,' agreed Gordon. 'But believe me, I couldn't do it without David's own gift for self-destruction.'

The phone rang. Gordon picked it up, listened, and put it down again.

'They've started the shoot at the hospital.'

'Should bloody well hope so,' said Stephen. 'Since we're hoping to show the finished video to the Prime Minister in about three hours.'

At the North London Hospital for Women the same thought was going through Sarah's mind. Out of shot, she was questioning the young nurse, Judy Axford.

'Nurse Axford,' she said, '– if you don't mind my interrupting your work – can you tell me whether you enjoy working as a nurse in the National Health Service?'

Judy looked up from ministering to Vera Forrest. She glanced at her cue card.

'*Yes. Very much,*' she said. '*I've always wanted to be a nurse. I can't think of any work that's more satisfying.*'

The sound recordist swung his boom microphone back over Sarah's head.

'But Nurse,' she said, 'what about this talk of cuts in the Health Service?'

The camera followed Judy as she rearranged the flowers between Vera's and Bassett's beds. The boom swung back to her.

'*Well,*' she said, '*we don't really think of it as cutting. It's more like pruning – taking out some of the dead wood.*'

'So what you call pruning,' said Sarah, 'has actually been good for the Health Service?'

Judy looked back to camera.

'*Yes, I think it has. Most of the dead wood's gone now. You know, the administrators doing nothing much, the bureaucrats, the overpaid managers. That's what I call pruning –*'

The assistant floor manager nodded to Vera.

'That's right, my dear,' said Vera. 'I prune me roses –'

'Hold it,' shouted the director. 'Hold it! Cut! Sorry, loves. Let's take it again. Pick it up at "overpaid managers". I'll do a single of Vera.' To Vera he said: 'It's not The Archers, darling. You just happen to have some roses. All right?'

'Can I be Yorkshire?' asked Vera.

'No you can not,' said Clayton. 'Nothing ethnic.' To the cameraman he said: 'All right? Can we go again? Turn over. Run it up to speed.'

'I prune me roses,' said Vera. 'Makes them come out wonderful in spring.'

'Wait till I shout "action", will you love?' asked Clayton. 'Action!'

Sarah said to Judy: 'So what you call pruning has actually been good for the Health Service?'

'*Yes, I think it has*,' said Judy Axford, speaking straight to camera.

'I prune me roses,' said Vera for the third time. 'Makes them come out wonderful in spring.'

The director signalled to Sarah.

'So you're saying, Nurse Axford, that the people who really do the work – the nurses and doctors – they've been protected?'

Judy glanced at her cue card.

'*Yes*,' she said. '*I think the government's been very fair to the doctors. And to us – to the nurses*.'

Vera was looking at Bassett Syme in the next bed.

'Excuse me, Nurse,' she said. 'I don't like the sound of Bassett's breathing.'

'Cut!' shouted Clayton. 'Cut! Cut! Bloody cut!'

Linda peered at the old actor.

'He's asleep, that's all. Wake him up, will you, Fran?'

'And put a bit of powder on his forehead, while you're at it,' said Clayton. 'Stop him glinting.'

'You are a real nurse, aren't you?' said Vera to Judy.

Judy hesitated.

'Why don't you direct it, darling?' said Clayton to Vera.

'Yes, I am,' said Judy. 'Or I was.'

'Dear God. Look at the *time*,' said Sarah to Linda, in agonised tones. 'We ought to be back in the agency by now.'

'Well, Nurse,' said Vera, 'you come and have a good look at poor old Bassett. I think all this medical business might have been too much for him.'

FIVE

Gordon Lochhead was waiting for Sarah when she came back into the agency. He called down to her from the mezzanine floor as she ran through reception.

'Do you realise,' he shouted, 'that this whole presentation is waiting on you –'

Sarah came up the staircase.

'We're advertising the NHS,' she said.

'I know what you're advertising,' said Gordon. 'It's the only part of this damn package that isn't ready to show the PM.'

Trying to run up stairs in a pencil skirt put Sarah at considerable disadvantage. She paused before going along the passage to her own department.

'Listen, Gordon,' she said, trying to breathe evenly, 'one of our actors nearly died on us. Imagine it. In the *Mail*, or the *Mirror*. Great publicity for the Health Service.'

'Don't go into some long explanation,' said Gordon, keeping pace with Sarah as she went into the creative department. 'We should have left. Downing Street made a change.'

'I need another ten minutes,' said Sarah. 'What do you mean: a change?'

Warren emerged from the production department.

'Message for you, Sarah,' he said.

'The change,' said Gordon, 'is that we are now meeting the Prime Minister at Party headquarters. Priory Square. Which is why we should be leaving early.'

'Dear God,' said Sarah. 'Has Stan moved the equipment?'

'That,' said Warren, 'is what he sent the message is about. Megapanic.'

'I'll call him,' said Sarah. 'Gordon – I am not showing an unchecked video to the leaders of a political party on the verge of a snap election. So I shall be another ten minutes, checking it. OK?' She went into her office.

'We leave in five minutes,' called Gordon. 'Precisely.'

Sarah was keying Stan's number into her phone.

'The man still thinks that precise equals efficient,' she said over her shoulder to Warren. Into the phone she said: 'Stan, we're leaving in ten minutes for Priory Square. Come up here with a checklist of equipment, will you?' She listened, then said: 'Dear God, yes I mean *now*.'

Forty minutes later the representatives of Hamilton Forbes and Kent were sitting in the book-lined Agincourt Room at the Party's headquarters. There was a silence, until Sarah extracted one of the leather-bound volumes behind her, and found its pages uncut.

'Our masters don't seem to do much reading,' she said in a whisper to Helen.

'Put that book back,' said Gordon, quietly, but with emphasis.

Sarah was doing so when the door of Agincourt opened and Francis Salk came in. In his late thirties, Francis Salk was a rising star of the Prime Minister's entourage. Political gossip had it that he was willing to do a number of things that Neville Henderson himself could not even contemplate. Certainly, Henderson found him indispensable. For this election, Salk had been given the title of Prime Minister's media adviser, though his duties were considerably wider than that.

Sarah surveyed the media adviser with almost equal interest and distaste. Before he had been headhunted by Downing Street, Salk had worked for a large confectionery firm, Fowler Rutherford Foods. It was there Sarah first met him. Their dislike was mutual and immediate. Sarah objected to Salk's tiny, figure-conscious meals, his blow-waved hair, his androgynous perfumes, and his infinite capacity for bitchiness. Salk's objection to her, she suspected, was more general – and centred on the fact that she was female.

Francis was now leaning intimately over Gordon.

'Mr Lochhead,' he said, in his characteristic half-whisper,

'we are just a mite late. But you will be pleased to know that we are ready for you now.'

Salk led the way through an interconnecting door into the much more imposing Marlborough Room. There he joined two other people who were sitting on the far side of the Marlborough's oval table. One was a heavily-built woman with the face of a pale but intelligent bull terrier. This was Mrs Merle Clarkson, a barrister who became chairperson of the Party when two male predecessors had failed to reform its sclerotic bureaucracy.

Beside Mrs Clarkson sat Geoffrey Talbot, the Minister of State for Army Affairs, and Minister in charge of campaign planning. Sarah found herself looking at him with considerable interest. Geoffrey Talbot was an imposing man, just beginning to get heavy, but still notably good looking. His darkly curling hair was almost untouched by grey. Sarah briefly and vividly imagined him in bed, then brought herself sharply back to the business at hand.

'Mrs Clarkson, our Party chairman, you will know,' Francis Salk was saying. 'And Geoffrey Talbot – Minister of State for Army Affairs – who is coordinating our campaign this year –'

'Do sit down,' said Mrs Clarkson to the group from Hamilton Forbes. Mrs Clarkson had assumed a benign appearance, which was entirely misleading. She bent her apparently amiable gaze on Gordon.

'Mr Lochhead and I have met more than once. I should say, straight away, Mr Lochhead, that I am deputising for Mr Henderson.'

'For – the Prime Minister?' said Gordon.

'Who sends his apologies,' added Francis Salk.

'Caught up in this Middle Eastern business,' said the Minister.

'So, Mr Lochhead,' said Mrs Clarkson, 'the floor is yours.'

Gordon rearranged the papers in front of him.

'Madam Chairman,' he said, 'Minister; Mr Salk. I am afraid I have to begin with an apology. Our managing director has unfortunately been detained in New York –'

'Then we are both deputising,' said Mrs Clarkson crisply. 'I for the Prime Minister: you for your managing director. Now. You know who we are – I am not sure that I know everyone on your side.'

'Ah,' said Gordon. 'My apologies, Madam Chairman.' He indicated Stephen. 'Stephen Hallam, account director, will – if you accept the package we are putting forward – Stephen will be handling the day-to-day progress of your election advertising. Under my supervision. Mrs Sarah Copeland is our creative director and will oversee the actual creative strategy. Liaising of course with you, Minister.'

'Closest of liaison,' said Geoffrey Talbot.

Gordon pointed to Helen.

'Mrs Marriott,' he continued, 'is what we call, in our jargon, a planner – which means that she is in charge of research on your account. Our agency rates research very highly –'

'So we understand, Mr Lochhead,' said Mrs Clarkson, 'from your quite lengthy written submission. Francis? Geoffrey? Questions? No?'

'Now, Madam Chairman,' said Gordon, 'this is our creative strategy for the product we hope to be marketing.' He paused for a moment. 'You notice that we talk of your Party as a product. We use that term for three reasons –'

'If you don't mind my interrupting, Mr Lochhead,' said Francis Salk, 'we had our other advertising agency in here earlier today. They also hope to handle this election for us, and they explained – at rather wearisome length, I thought – why Her Majesty's Government should be treated as a saleable product. So perhaps we might skip that bit? Time being short. We have, in fact, quite a number of questions – to do with the coming election – that we should like to put to you and your team. If your group will bear with us?'

Gordon, his prepared speech in ruins, stared at Francis Salk.

'Ah. Of course,' he said. 'Only too happy.'

On the first floor of Hamilton Forbes and Kent, Warren was on his way back from the bar, and was looking for Dee. Dee was still at work, finishing a storyboard for a television commercial. Warren sat heavily down on the edge of her desk and peered at what she was doing. Dee spoke without stopping work.

'Are they still at Downing Street?' she asked.

'Priory Square,' said Warren. 'And the answer is, in all probability, yes. Imagine: Sarah and Francis Salk. Are these the people you want deciding on your government for the next five years?' He was examining a giant cereal packet that stood on Dee's desk. 'Chocolate Flakes now, young lady? Change from the bomb.'

Dee glanced at a sketch that was fixed to her magnet board: a poster rough she had done that morning. It showed a missile with a Union Jack on its nuclear warhead. The headline was: *We won't use it. But aren't you glad we could*?

'I work on other things beside the political account,' said Dee. 'You think people stop buying Chocolate Flakes just because there's an election? Anyway, we don't know if we've got the account yet.'

'People,' he said, 'don't yet know that there is an election.' He opened a small, rustic door in the cereal packet. 'What is this cute little contrivance for, do you suppose?'

'Careful,' said Dee. 'We're using that in the shoot. Have you been down in the bar?'

'Couple of quick tonics,' said Warren. He discovered a hairy dwarf inside the packet and extracted him. 'Does this little fellow come out the door, or what?'

'That's the Chocolate Elf,' said Dee. In bible-belt accent, she sang:

'One, two, three, it's the Chocolate Elf,
Hopping along the grocery shelf.
Four, five, six, before anyone wakes,
He puts choc-olate on your Chocolate Flakes.'

'Come back, Squirrel Nutkin. All is forgiven.' said Warren. 'Must be a relief having Nick away, if he writes stuff like that.'

'It's not a relief,' said Dee. 'I'm up to my bloody eyes in

work, and Nick's swanning around the West Indies. Means I got to use Mike Sutherland's copy.'

'That I would not wish on my worst enemy,' said Warren. 'You know Sutherland's found himself a beer account? Scunthorpe Six X. Seriously strong beer.'

Warren tried to jam the Chocolate Elf through the door in the fake cereal packet. Doing so, he knocked over the genuine packet. Chocolate-coated corn flakes cascaded over Dee's storyboard.

Dee wearily poured the cereal back into its packet.

'Warren,' she said, 'don't even think about working on a strong beer account. There's a lot too much alcohol in your life already.'

In the Marlborough Room, on the south side of Priory Square, the Minister of State for Army Affairs was coming to the end of his list of questions. All dealt with the techniques of selling his Party to the electorate: most were uncomfortably detailed. The group from Hamilton Forbes and Kent were looking older and more worn than when they came in, a little over an hour earlier.

'My last question,' said the Minister, 'is how long you would need – from the point of view of advertising – to make sure that you had a head start over the opposition parties? How long would you say, Mr Lochhead?'

It was not a question to which Gordon had an immediate answer.

'Head start,' he said. 'Over the opposition parties.'

'By head start,' said Mrs Clarkson, 'I think the Minister actually means an unshakeable lead.'

'If I may come in here,' said Stephen, 'I would suggest we need something in the order of ten days before the opposition realises that an election date has been set. Let us suggest that – later this evening – you and the Prime Minister decide to accept the election package we are offering. Ideally, then, we should like lead time to the end of next week. We could do a great deal that would make it hard for anyone else to catch up with us.'

Francis Salk looked at Stephen with the thoughtful scrutiny of a snake watching a young rabbit.

'And exactly how would you use those ten days, Mr Hallam?'

Stephen indicated Sarah.

'The first stage, I think, is Mrs Copeland's department.'

Sarah glanced at her notes.

'Our initial priority,' she said, 'is to refine the creative strategy. We need full agreement between ourselves and the Party as to how we re-sell you – the present government – to the electorate. We then translate that into further campaigns which the present company, together with the inner Cabinet and the Prime Minister, would approve.

'Or not,' said Francis Salk blandly. 'And the next stage?'

'Is to book whatever can be booked,' said Stephen, 'both for your own use and to pre-empt other parties. An obvious example is poster sites.'

Stephen picked up a miniposter from the table in front of him, and displayed it. On a vast area of white space was a simple typographical message, which read: *If you want law and order, you know who to vote for.*

'This particular poster is for polling day,' said Sarah. 'By then, research suggests, we should be able to do without a Party logo.'

'We gather that, as a Party, you are not short of funds,' said Stephen. 'Therefore, we should be able to book so many prime poster sites that any other party will have great difficulty running a poster campaign at all.'

'Not a tactic we can use with other media, I imagine,' said Mrs Clarkson.

'Television, of course, Madam Chairman, we can't book,' said Gordon. 'Not for a political campaign. European radio, yes. Cinemas for a particular youth segment, of which our Mrs Marriott will give the parameters. Press, unfortunately, expands to meet advertising demand; not a great deal we can do about that. But we would mount a very extensive PR operation: something the others will find it hard to match.'

'In the time that we leave them,' added Stephen.

'But it is the area of creative strategy,' said Gordon, 'which offers –'

'– probably the greatest time advantage,' said Sarah. 'We shall continue to develop the campaign which you will see later this evening in the Wellington Room next door. The opposition, meanwhile, will still be fighting in their committees, trying to agree on policies acceptable to all sections of their political machine. As Stephen says, while they are doing that, we shall be booking film production time and video crews, to shoot and edit your Party election broadcasts. That's very hard for anyone else to do at the last minute, with the sort of production values we are getting now.'

'May we ask exactly how long you can delay the election announcement?' said Stephen. 'That is, how long the Prime Minister can delay it?'

'Not too long, is the answer to that,' said the Minister of State. 'One or two papers are getting uncomfortably warm.'

'Surely,' said Helen, 'most of the press is picking an October polling date?'

Talbot flicked through the papers on the table in front of him.

'*The Sun* says: End this Indecision! Second lead, I notice to an article on the shame of a teenage mother. Plus topless picture of the lady in question. *The Mirror* has: PM Goes for Autumn Election? – with a question mark. The *Express* says: It Looks Like October. As does the *Mail*.'

'Very reliable papers, the *Express* and the *Mail*,' said Francis. 'As we all know.'

Rose, the new mother's help, could hear the phone ringing in the kitchen of Sarah's house. She put down the book she was reading to Daniel.

'What happens to Golog?' asked Daniel. 'Does he kill all the Trilobites?'

'You could read the next page yourself,' said Rose, as she went into the kitchen. 'Then you'd know what happens to the poor little Trilobites.'

'I hope they do all get killed,' said Daniel. 'Every one. When are we having something to eat?'

Rose didn't answer. Daniel heard her pick up the phone and say: 'Mrs Copeland's house.' She listened. 'I'm afraid Mrs Copeland is at – well, she's still at work. Can I help?' She listened again. 'Oh, I'm Rose,' she said. 'The new au pair. Mother's help. And you'll phone later? Shall I say who it was?' A pause. 'It's who? *Paul*?' Then she said: 'Oh. I am sorry. You're Sarah's *husband*?'

At Party headquarters in Priory Square, Sarah was discreetly watching Gordon. His face was lightly flushed. A faint dew of moisture stood on his skin. Mrs Clarkson was speaking directly to him.

'To summarise,' she said, 'you are saying that the Prime Minister should wait two weeks – or at least ten days – before asking the Queen to dissolve Parliament?'

'That is my feeling, Madam Chairman,' said Gordon.

'Can you be sure of doing all we have discussed in ten days?' said Francis Salk. 'Can you be sufficiently far ahead of our opposition?'

'You realise,' said Geoffrey Talbot, 'that we shall be crucified by our own Party if we go early to the country – and then lose the majority we now hold?'

Gordon seemed to be formulating some reply; but did not speak.

'We have looked at the timings quite carefully,' said Sarah. 'Barring any unforseen disruption, we can keep to that schedule.'

'We think we can get you another five years,' said Stephen.

Geoffrey Talbot spoke to his colleagues.

'Probably keep the papers at bay,' he said. 'Not a vintage year for quality of journalism.'

'Fortunately for us,' said Francis Salk.

'Before we move on,' said Mrs Clarkson, 'might I ask our advertising friends about a couple of specific issues? First of all, unemployment. How would you propose to deal with that?'

Gordon looked to his right, then to his left.

'You mean, how would we deal with the problem in terms of advertising?' asked Stephen.

'No other obvious way of dealing with it,' said the Minister. 'Massage the figures once more, and they'll die of exhaustion.'

'Helen?' said Gordon.

Helen looked up from her notes.

'Our research,' she said, 'indicates that the unemployed are now less likely to blame their state on world recession, or even on the trade unions. Rightly or wrongly, they do think that unemployment has something to do with government policies. Many of the employed, in fact, share that view. In our sample, a very high proportion did.' She checked her data. 'Sixty-three per cent.'

'Which seems to suggest,' said Stephen, 'that our advertising might show a slightly higher level of compassion for the unemployed.'

'While still throwing the main responsibility, of course, on the trade unions,' added Gordon.

'Intrigued to know,' asked Geoffrey Talbot, 'how you propose doing both of those things.'

'At the same time,' said Francis Salk.

'We have five full-page press ads, Minister, directly addressing that issue,' said Sarah.

'And those are next door?' asked Mrs Clarkson. 'Where you have assembled all your videotape machines?' She stood, leaning heavily on the table. 'In that case, this seems as good a time as any for our adjournment to the Wellington Room.' To Geoffrey Talbot, she said: 'I shall be interested to see how our friends propose selling our employment policies to the nation.'

'Never the easiest of tasks,' Stephen said quietly to Sarah.

Mrs Clarkson paused at the door and turned.

'And then, perhaps, a cup of tea,' she offered.

'I'm going to need more than tea,' said Sarah to Stephen.

* * *

At Hamilton Forbes and Kent, the bar was now crowded with agency staff. Gordon's secretary Carol Braithwaite came and sat down at a table where Dee and Warren were in conversation. Carol often said she wondered how she got into Hamilton Forbes. Out of her hearing, others asked the same question, for Carol was the agency's oddity. For a start, she had a distinctly downmarket accent, originating somewhere in south-east London. Then there was her appearance. Where the rest of the agency secretaries tended to slim elegance, Carol had an exuberant body, constantly in conflict with the tight shirts and skirts she always wore.

In Gordon's eyes, though, Carol had one quality which outweighed all the others. This was loyalty. She had worked for him at his previous agency and, in three years, had never been involved in its internal politics. There were those who suggested that Carol took no part in power struggles only because they were over by the time she heard about them. But, whatever the reasons for her loyalty, Gordon appreciated it. He had resisted to several attempts to replace his secretary with a more presentable personal assistant.

'Are they back yet?' Carol asked. 'I mean – Gordon and Sarah and Helen and Stephen? Did they see the Prime Minister? Warren, are you listening? Did they get all the political stuff through? Are we going to be the agency for the election?'

'No, they're not. I know who you mean. No, they didn't. Yes, but I wish I wasn't. How would I know? Ask Sarah when she comes back,' said Warren, answering Carol's questions in their original order.

Dee, who was fond of Carol, tried to soothe her.

'No sign of them yet,' she said. 'They must have been there' – she checked the time – 'like three hours.'

Mike Sutherland came across to the table and sat down heavily. He carried a bottle, wrapped in a linen napkin, which he had brought with him from the restaurant.

'Mike,' said Carol, 'what have you got in there? Come on. What *is* it, then?'

'Blind product test,' said Mike. 'As seen on television. Special challenge for the professional boozer here.'

Dee put her hand on Warren's arm.

'Don't encourage him, Mike.'

Mike poured a glass from his wrapped bottle, and passed it to Warren.

'What'd you say it was, old son?'

Warren drained the glass. He gasped for air.

'Liquid smack, that's what I'd say it was, Sutherland.' He breathed deeply. 'Ahhh. Why bother injecting if you can drink the stuff?'

'Stop you getting AIDS off the needles,' said Dee. 'So what is it?'

Mike unwrapped the bottle to show the label: Scunthorpe Six X.

'Killer,' said Warren. 'Who put that in our bloody bar?'

'Client tells me,' said Mike, 'he goes: "Listen, we're looking for test markets." I said, "Right, mate; you're on." More formal language, but that was the gist of it. Put us down for twenty dozen in the house bar, I said.'

'Twenty dozen,' said Warren, cautiously sipping what was left in his glass. 'Twenty dozen of them, you'd get half London legless.'

'Seriously, Mike,' said Dee, 'if it's too strong for Warren, should you be unleashing this stuff on the rest of the British population?'

In Priory Square, it was getting dark. Sarah, Gordon, Helen and Stephen filed out of Party headquarters. They spoke in subdued tones.

'My God, that was hard,' said Helen. 'Do you think they'll buy it?'

Stephen was unlocking his Porsche.

'Depends on the Prime Minister,' he said. 'Depends on the election date they've got in mind.' He put a hand on Helen's shoulder. 'Listen, my love. I need a few words with Sarah. One or two things to settle. But why don't you meet me back in the bar? Could buy you a largish bottle of bubbles.'

'After that session, Stephen,' said Helen, 'I warn you I may need more than one.' She got into a taxi that had been ordered for her.

Sarah left Gordon. She unlocked her BMW, collapsed into the

driver's seat and phoned her own house. Stephen opened the passenger door and waited till Sarah had finished talking to Rose.

'All well?' he asked.

'Rose says Daniel's all right. Seems to have got over –'

She paused.

'Over what?'

'Oh – an upset. Earlier in the day. Missing his father,' said Sarah. 'It happened before the National Health shoot.'

'Which, incidentally, went down very well the Minister,' said Stephen. 'Very taken with that nice little nurse.'

'Just as well,' said Sarah. 'Seeing we've got nothing else on video.'

'Indeed it is,' agreed Stephen. 'Now, my lady. Your friend and colleague Warren is apparently organising what he does so well – a select little piss-up in the agency bar. Which I think we all richly deserve.'

Sarah started her car.

'Oh, I've no doubt I deserve it,' she said. 'I've also no doubt what Daniel will do if I don't get home in time to finish *Fantastic Mister Fox*. Shut the door, will you, Stephen; and I'll see you tomorrow.'

Stephen got out of the car and shut the passenger door. He stood for a moment, watching the BMW as it went fast around Priory Square. Then he got into his Porsche and made a phone call of his own.

In the agency bar Linda, the film producer, was talking to Alessandra Castorina.

'I couldn't believe it,' she said. 'There they were, going off this afternoon for a presentation to the Prime Minister – and the managing director's still in New York.'

Alessandra was personal assistant to David Postgate, the managing director in question.

'Well, it's no secret,' she said. 'David's desperate to get hold of an American agency. He heard Pater Paolozzi were coming up for grabs in New York, and there was no holding him. As far as I know he just jumped on a plane – didn't even tell the board he was bidding.'

At the next table, Mike Sutherland was shouting at Warren, trying to make himself heard above a dozen conversations around him.

'All these booze accounts just pussyfoot around it,' he announced. 'The parts other beers can't reach. All that coy stuff. I say, come out with it. Tell the punters: you want to get wasted, this is the way. Scunthorpe Six X.'

'I heard there was – well, some other reason,' said Linda to Alessandra. 'For David going to New York.'

'Doesn't gossip get round?' said Alessandra acidly. 'How long have you been back from Sydney? Eighteen hours?'

Mike Sutherland was attempting to pour Warren another glass of the Seriously Strong Beer. Warren covered his glass with one shaking hand.

'Get away, Sutherland,' he said. 'I was hoping for a few more years of life.'

'David told me to book a couple of seats for New York,' said Alessandra to Linda. 'So I went through the whole bit: what does your wife like, window or aisle, non-smoking, any special food – ? Then Sarah comes in and says Sally suddenly decided to take her holiday that week.'

'Holiday in Rome.' said Linda.

'Rome pronounced Manhattan,' said Alessandra. 'By the time Sarah told me, it was all around the agency. David was taking Sally to New York – three days, four nights, at the Plaza, no less.'

'I got this idea for a TV commercial,' shouted Mike loudly at the other table. 'You have this big Scottish lad. He's laid out on the ground, and his mate says, "Hey, Jimmy, who hit yeh?" And the guy on the ground – blissful – he says: "It was the Scunthorpe Six X, Jimmy."'

Helen walked into the bar. Linda saw her first, and called:

'Helen! How did it go? How was the Prime Minister?'

'And where's Stephen?' added Alessandra.

'Awful, to the first question,' Helen said. 'Prime Minister wasn't there – got tied up with some foreign policy crisis. And Stephen's coming later, he's parking the car.'

Helen turned to Mike and Warren, who were still in noisy disagreement.

'How about one of you nice men getting me a drink?'

Mike got to his feet as rapidly as his condition allowed.

'Oh no you don't,' Warren warned him. 'Not that strong.' He turned to Helen. 'Stay where you are, love. Don't drink anything I haven't bought. In particular, do not accept anything from Sutherland here.'

Sarah unlocked the door of her house and called to Rose, who appeared from the kitchen with flour on her hands.

'I was wondering when you'd get back, Mrs Copeland,' she said. 'I mean, Sarah. How was the – do you call it a presentation?'

'You do,' said Sarah. 'And it was a nightmare. Minister asks you what to do about unemployment. What do you say?'

There was a pause. Sarah started up the stairs.

'Well,' said Rose finally, 'perhaps they could put up some more factories?'

'Not this lot,' said Sarah. 'Is Daniel in bed?'

'Mmn,' said Rose. 'He went straight to sleep.'

Sarah stopped, halfway up the stairs.

'You mean – I rushed home to see him – and he's *asleep*?'

'He was still up when you called from the car,' said Rose. 'But then he just sort of wilted. Couldn't keep his eyes open. I think it was the day. Coming home from school at lunch time and –'

'– getting upset with his mother,' finished Sarah. She came down stairs again. 'Dear God. Asleep. I could have stayed for the party at the agency.'

'Well, I'll be here,' said Rose. 'You could go back.'

Sarah looked at her, then shook her head.

'Too late,' she decided. 'Time I got there – no. I shall open one of Paul's oldest clarets, which would annoy the hell out of him if he were here.' She went into the drawing room. 'I'll wait and see if the agency phones. Which reminds me – my absent husband didn't by any chance call, did he?'

'I forgot to say,' said Rose, 'but yes, he did.'

* * *

At nine forty-five in the evening there was a call from Downing Street to say that the Prime Minister had accepted the Hamilton Forbes package of election advertising. Five minutes later, the agency bar had turned into the scene of a full-scale celebration. Champagne bottles were set on every table. Stephen was moving from table to table, kissing the younger and more available women. This culminated in an especially long and sensuous encounter with Alessandra.

'It could be the break, my love,' he said, finally separating his mouth from hers. 'Got the government – just look at the publicity we're going to get. Across the country: three weeks, total saturation. Look what it did for Saatchis in '79. Number fifty-three in the league, or whatever, right up to number one.'

'You've got lip-gloss on your mouth,' said Alessandra, offering a napkin.

'It's an achievement, sweetheart,' said Stephen. 'All right you sitting there, looking blonde and bloody beautiful. You didn't have to face up to Ministers and Party chairmen and convince them you could re-elect a goddamn government with five million unemployed.' He pointed at full bottle of Dom Perignon. 'Give us some of those bubbles, and then I'll take you out for supper somewhere.'

Alessandra poured a glass of champagne and said: 'You do mean supper?'

At the next table, Helen was shouting to make herself heard above the noise.

'Someone should tell Sarah we got the account.'

'Phone's in the usual place,' Mike Sutherland shouted back.

'If I trusted myself to stand –'

Stephen abandoned Alessandra. He moved to Helen's table and cautiously picked up an empty bottle of Scunthorpe Six X.

'It's this lethal stuff Sutherland's selling,' he said. 'Destroys your central nervous system.'

Warren came back into the bar and sat down, almost missing his chair.

'You see what I mean?' said Stephen to Helen.

Warren was staring fixedly at the six bottles of Dom Perignon in front of him.

'What's all this, then?' he asked. 'Did they? Did they phone?'

'They did indeed,' said Stephen. 'While you were in the powder room –'

'Can't afford that stuff,' said Warren. 'Just bathing my brow, all I was doing.'

'During the half hour you spent in the men's lavatory,' said Stephen, 'we had a surprisingly friendly call from Downing Street.'

'Prime Minister's approved it,' said Linda. 'For the last – nine minutes – it's been all on. Election. Our ad package. No major changes.'

'No shit,' said Warren. He opened two bottles of champagne and began to pour. Most of the champagne went into the glasses.

'Here's to the coming erection,' he said.

'I'll call Sarah,' said Linda. 'Tell her the news. While I still can.'

Stephen tried his champagne, managing to keep an eye on Alessandra while watching Linda make her way across the crowded bar.

'A toast to Mrs Sarah Copeland,' he said. 'At home alone with the infant. An example to us all.'

Sarah was sitting in the darkness of her drawing room. A bottle of her husband's claret, half empty, stood on the table beside her. She was listening to Ravel's Piano Concerto in G Major on compact disc. Suddenly the door opened and the room was full of light.

'Sarah?' said Rose. 'Phone for you –'

Sarah didn't move.

'The agency?' she asked.

'No –' said Rose. She hesitated. 'He sounds very – disturbed –' She paused again. 'I think it's your husband.'

SIX

Suite 301 has one of the most favoured rooms in New York's Plaza Hotel. It is very large. It is away from the lift shafts. It is away from the traffic, and looks over the greenest part of Central Park. For all these reasons, 301 is favoured by illicit lovers – the ones who are affluent enough to afford its very high tariff.

David Postgate was one of those who could, and occasionally did, afford suite 301. David was managing director of Hamilton Forbes and Kent, a position he had held for only eighteen months. Before that, he was deputy in one of the larger American agencies – an experience that left him determined to run his own transatlantic operation. His appointment to HFK had bitterly divided its board members, a small minority of whom favoured Gordon Lochhead. But David was now confident that he could either charm or persuade the board into accepting him as manager of the global network he so clearly foresaw.

In advertising circles, it was generally agreed that David Postgate looked well suited to the part of international executive. At the age of thirty-nine, he had kept the lean fair-haired looks of a younger man; though years of corporate infighting were just beginning to leave their mark. As time went on, David dressed more expensively, favouring those shades of blue which brought out the still startling blue of his eyes, against perpetually suntanned skin.

David's friends were inclined to emphasise his charm and political skill. His enemies noted his willingness to lend a hand only to those on the rung above him. Lovers, if asked, referred to his surprising gentleness in bed. This gentleness was one of the reasons why Sally, Sarah Copeland's secretary, had agreed, after some thought, to spend a weekend with him in New York, instead of the West Indies with her live-in lover, Nick.

At three o'clock in the morning, Sally was sleeping on the left-hand side of the emperor-sized bed in the Plaza's suite 301. David Postgate was lying tense against her body. He was awake, and considering their ages. Sally was then twenty-four; just over fifteen years younger than he. David was wondering whether she was too young to be a wife.

When the phone beside the bed began mewing softly, David brushed Sally's cloud of dark hair away from his face. He lay for a moment, looking out the window at the city-glow in New York's night sky. Then he lowered his face back into Sally's hair.

'Phone,' he whispered.

Either Sally was awake, or she came back to consciousness quickly.

'Do you think –' she asked '– do you think I'm in New York to be your secretary?'

David leaned over her naked back and grabbed the telephone cord.

'Of course not,' he said. With one hand he pulled the phone closer along the bedside table; he cupped the other around Sally's breast. 'You came as my plaything.'

As he spoke, the phone fell off the marble table, and stopped ringing.

In London, it was eight in the morning. Sarah was alone in her lime-green office at the agency. She sat on the edge of her desk, going through her in-tray, and holding on the phone. The receiver was cradled between chin and shoulder. A paintbox of lip colour was open beside her.

'Yes. I am still waiting,' she said into the phone. 'Mmn. For David Postgate.' She listened. 'Well, if he didn't answer the first time, try again.' Sarah picked up a typed agenda for a board meeting. To no one in particular she said, 'Come on, damn you.' Then her tone changed as the phone was answered in New York.

'David,' she said. 'It's Sarah. Yes: in London. So what time *is* it over there?'

* * *

In the Plaza Hotel, David climbed over Sally and got out of bed. Naked, and carrying the phone, he went across to where his gown was hanging.

'God knows what time it is,' he said. 'Awesomely early.'

He pulled on his gown, sat down on an immense couch, switched on a wall lamp, and inspected his watch. 'Sarah, it is three o'clock. Do you mind my asking – what on earth possessed you to ring at this hour of the night?'

'It's not a social call,' said Sarah. 'Something I thought you should know. In your absence, they approved our election package. The Prime Minister's giving us ten days' clear run, then he's getting the Queen to dissolve to Parliament.'

'I'm delighted,' said David. 'With any luck, it's going to give us the same sort of boost it gave bloody Saatchi's. But couldn't you wait till I was out of bed?'

'Does that sentence have a singular subject?' asked Sarah. 'And in any case, that wasn't the urgent bit of news. The urgent item is today's board meeting.'

'What board meeting?' said David.

'You might well ask,' said Sarah. 'It's been so arranged that one copy of the board's agenda is now in the post to you – and the other one's lying on your desk in London.' Sarah glanced down at the typed sheet she was holding. 'Or was, until Alessandra gave it to me.'

There was a silence. Then David asked: 'When is this board?'

'End of the afternoon,' said Sarah. 'Five o'clock, London time. And the first item on the agenda is a motion to annul your takeover of the American agency.'

'If they throw that out,' said David, 'they're throwing me out.'

'Absolutely,' said Sarah. 'That is why I think you should get yourself on Concorde – or anything else that will get you over here before five. Otherwise, you may well be unemployed by the time you return me my secretary.'

Warren was coming across the creative department toward the office he shared with Sarah. He looked surprisingly bright, given the amount of alcohol he had taken on the night before. He was telling Mike Sutherland a convoluted American joke.

'There's this bunch of Polacks, middle of winter, and they're pushing this house down the freeway. Guy comes past in a Chevy –'

'You told me,' said Mike. 'I heard it.' He strode off to look for Dee. Warren went into his office where Sarah was still on the phone to New York. He picked up the roughs he needed for his meeting with Helen, waved to Sarah, and left. Outside the door, he almost ran into Stephen, who was leaning quietly against the wall. Warren went past, then stopped and looked back. Stephen had not moved; he seemed slightly embarrassed by Warren's scrutiny.

Inside the office, Sarah was saying: 'If you do get a plane, David – then call me. Or call Alessandra. I'll meet you at the airport. Tell you what's happened while you were in flight.'

Warren was still watching Stephen, who indicated the office.

'That's – Sarah?' he asked.

Warren inclined his head and listened.

'No,' he said. 'Arnold Schwarzenegger. Why don't you go in, Stephen, if you're so interested?'

Stephen went into the office and Warren went on toward the lifts.

Sarah, who was putting down the phone, looked up to see Stephen watching her.

'You really have no sense of privacy, do you?' she said. 'I suppose you heard that conversation?'

'I did,' said Stephen. 'Soup to nuts, as they say in our American agency.'

In New York, David Postgate said, to himself as much as anyone else, 'That goddamn Gordon Lochhead.'

Sally was still in bed. She had her eyes shut, but she was awake.

'What's Gordon done?' she said.

'Nothing much,' said David. 'Yet.' He picked up the phone again. 'But this afternoon, he's arranged a board meeting to have me thrown out of the agency. Me. The fucking managing director.' Into the phone, he said: 'Sorry. Talking to someone else. Is that reception? OK. Well, I want two flights to London. Any airline. Just as long as we get there by mid-afternoon.'

In London, Sarah was walking fast across the agency's creative department, on her way to the meeting in Helen's office. Stephen Hallam kept pace with her.

'I'm simply suggesting,' he said, 'that for an intelligent woman, you do some remarkably silly things. Like that call you made to New York. My love: you are backing the wrong man.'

'I am?' said Sarah.

'Gordon's going to be running this place. Not David.'

Sarah paused by Dee's desk, but out of her hearing.

'Why do you get so bitter about David?' she asked. 'I know he hasn't put you on the board. But I'm not a board director either.'

'For you, love, the way is still open,' said Stephen. 'Apple of the man's eye, aren't you? For me, it's clearly not. If he was going to put me on the board, Sarah, he would have done it by now.'

Stephen turned and began descending the stairs to reception. Sarah called after him.

'I thought you were meeting with me Warren and Helen? Advertising to the unemployed?'

'My dear,' said Stephen, 'I have been in this place since seven o'clock. Working for our political masters. Without food or drink. Now, I am going to have breakfast, in that very expensive little caff down the road, pretentiously known as the Firenze.'

The Firenze Restaurant is well known in St James's for its business breakfasts. Some of the customers have, for one reason or another, not been home the previous night. Others are hoping that they, and their breakfast companions, will not be recognised.

Gordon Lochhead, who was eating at a corner table, came into the latter category. As Stephen sat down, Gordon was closely examining a jar of marmalade.

'Says it's made in Somerset,' he said. 'Somerset Marmalade. More like Saudi Arabia, if you ask me. Tastes like camel dung. Glad it's not one of our accounts.'

A waitress brought Stephen coffee. Gordon pushed across to Stephen the agenda for the afternoon's board meeting.

'Confirmed. Five, for five-thirty. Directors all coming. Except for David, I trust.'

'Coffee tastes foreign, too,' said Stephen.

The waitress brought Stephen his usual breakfast of kippers.

'Perhaps we ought to get Alessandra to call New York,' said Gordon. 'Let her talk to David. Read him that agenda, some time this afternoon. What do you think?'

'Really I don't think it's necessary,' said Stephen, starting on his kipper.

'It's a demonstration, surely?' said Gordon. 'Means we have made every effort to keep our managing director informed.'

Stephen extracted a minute bone.

'It's not necessary, Gordon,' he said, 'because Alessandra has already given Sarah a copy of this agenda. Sarah, not being mentally retarded, can see exactly what we are doing with this board meeting. And, for reasons of her own, she does not want the meeting to succeed. I am afraid she does not want you running the agency.'

Gordon paused, toast in hand.

'Sarah's got the agenda?' he said finally. Then he said: 'But I really fail to see what the woman can do about it. Apart from Simon Forbes, all the directors have confirmed –'

Stephen continued with his breakfast.

'It's not what Sarah can do about it,' he said. 'It's what she has already done. About ten minutes ago, she phoned David in New York. Told him you had fixed a board meeting this afternoon – which was set up to sack him.'

There was a pause. Then Gordon said: 'Must be the middle of the night over there.'

'But New York,' said Stephen, 'is not London. You may have

noticed, it does not close down at night. At this moment, I imagine, David's desperately trying for a seat on whatever will get across the Atlantic before five this evening.'

Gordon sat still for a moment. Then he brought his hand violently down on the table. China jumped, and fell.

'Damn the bitch!' said Gordon. He stood up violently, almost knocking over a waitress who had come to remove a broken cream jug.

Stephen watched Gordon push his way out of the restaurant.

'Well, sweetheart,' he said to the waitress. 'What's the damage?'

In New York, Sally was lying upside down on the floor of her bedroom. She was wearing a green leotard, which fitted her very beautiful legs like a second skin. At the moment, those legs were touching the carpet behind her head in a difficult, but reputedly health-giving, yoga position. She was also trying to reach the phone, which David had left on the floor, and which was now gurgling quietly.

David was shaving in the bathroom with a razor which he advertised, and which was supposed to adjust itself automatically to American voltages. When Sally called, he came out of the bathroom and leant down so that he could see her face, which was still hidden by her legs.

'Room service say, do you want croissants with your hash brown?' she asked. 'Apparently they have eighteen kinds.'

'Of croissant?' said David. 'Truly, an ad man's paradise. I'll take the French variety.' He picked up the phone and asked reception whether they had found him a flight.

'Absolutely anything that flies,' he said. 'As long as I have seats by five-thirty this morning. I'll take Air Alaska, if there is one.' He listened. 'Your computer's down? Well, in this technological dystopia, could you just try a telephone? As in, the instrument we are both using now?' David listened again, then put the receiver down and spoke to Sally.

'Seems they can only find one seat to London.'

Sally brought her feet gently down to the floor. She lay on her back, looking up at her lover.

'Looks like someone stays another day, doesn't it?'

David took out his wallet.

'You came over to see New York,' he said. 'Stay the rest of the week.' He held out a handful of credit cards. 'Take the company plastic.'

'Another week?' said Sally. She tried another yoga position. 'Sarah would be climbing the walls.'

'You may be Sarah's secretary,' said David, 'but I am Sarah's Managing Director.' The phone rang again. 'At least – I am until this afternoon.'

Moaning, Sally curled suddenly into the shape of a foetus. David dropped the phone and knelt down beside her.

'My love? What is it?'

'All this yoga,' said Sally, on a painfully indrawn breath, 'and I bloody well get *cramp*.'

In London, it was nine in the morning. Carol, came into the agency reception area carrying a maidenhair fern so large that she was almost hidden by it. Jane, at reception desk, could hear her voice from behind the foliage.

'They're really touchy plants, these are, Jane, so I'll *kill* anyone that lets it get dry. Doesn't like draughts. Wants its leaves spraying. Keep it warm. Talk to it. Jane? Are you *listening* to me?'

Carol tried to clear space for the fern at one end of the reception desk. Jane was on the phone. She covered the receiver.

'Gordon's chasing you,' she said.

'Aaagh,' said Carol.

'He just came through here like an Ethiopian chicken,' said Jane. Then, into the phone: 'Sorry, sir. Your extension is still holding.'

'Thought the old bat was out for breakfast,' said Carol, referring to Gordon. She peered round the fern at something she could see through the glass doors which led out on to the street. Then she tugged at Jane's cream silk sleeve.

'Hey! Jane! *Nick's* back!'

In Jermyn Street, Nick was paying the driver of a black cab.

Even at a distance, he looked wonderful. He was wearing white linen and his skin was deeply tanned. Appropriately enough, he looked like a piece of advertising art.

'That tan,' said Carol. 'Oh, to die for.'

Nick came into the agency. Only one thing spoiled the visual effect. He was limping.

'Jane,' he said. 'Missed you madly.' He looked at the fern. 'Who's behind the bush? Is that the lovely Carol?'

Nick kissed Carol, who went an attractive shade of pink. Jane put two calls through, then said, 'The lovely Carol shouldn't be necking with you, Nick. There's a very unhappy Gordon waiting for her upstairs.'

Gordon Lochhead was in his office, talking to Mike Sutherland. Jane was right. He was far from happy.

'The marketing message,' he was saying, 'is that tax cuts help the poor. People have the idea that tax cuts are for the rich. In your copy, I want you tell them: that's wrong. Everybody benefits.'

Mike Sutherland was on his way out. He paused.

'How do you get a tax cut if you don't pay tax?'

Gordon registered despair.

'Try to get across the notion of tax thresholds, Sutherland. The rich get reductions: the rest get higher thresholds. When we're selling the government's tax policy, that's the idea we have to sell.' He pushed into Mike's hands a bulky, photocopied document. 'Treasury statement. It's all in there. Written for three-year-olds.'

Gordon followed Mike out of the office. Carol was now at her desk in the outer office. She was looking busy.

'Ah, Carol,' said Gordon acidly. 'Deigned to turn up, have we?'

Mike Sutherland made his escape. Gordon leaned over Carol's desk to show her a report she had typed the previous afternoon.

'Just have a look at your typing,' he said. '*That*, Carol, in the interests of grammar – that needs to be a noun.'

Carol looked first at the sentence, then at Gordon.

'I was away the day they did nouns,' she said.

'Type it again,' said Gordon, pronouncing the three words slowly and with maximum control. 'But first, I want you to phone all of this agency's directors. The message is this: could they come half an hour early for the board meeting this afternoon –'

'Early for the board meeting,' said Carol, writing herself a note.

Stephen entered the office, carrying a number of videocassettes and an index card.

'– and,' said Gordon, 'say I should like to have an urgent word with them, before the meeting proper.'

Stephen put the card down in front of Carol.

'First call to Simon Forbes,' he said. 'Reputed to be at that address.'

'If Forbes is not there,' added Gordon, 'get his present location. Keep trying until you do find him.' He led Stephen into his own office and said, more quietly, 'Meeting could be troublesome. If David does get back.'

'More than troublesome,' said Stephen. 'You may well lose the vote.'

'I presume David will phone his P.A. from New York.'

'Alessandra,' said Stephen, who had a personal interest in her.

'Alessandra,' said Gordon, who didn't. 'Would she tell you if he did phone? If he had a flight?'

Stephen shrugged elegantly. Gordon stared at him.

'I thought you could charm the knickers off anything female.'

'Who am I to say?' replied Stephen modestly. 'But in this case, it's not her knickers we need.'

In the agency's conference room, Sarah, Warren, Helen and Linda were sitting at one end of a long walnut table. There was no ambient light. At the far end of the room was a huge video screen, which showed a mob of yelling kids pouring through the gate of a comprehensive school.

'It's library film,' said Linda. 'I thought of using it for the education-isn't-what-it-used-to-be bit of the first party political.' She held up a rough of a press ad Warren had produced. It showed a picture of two youths in leather jackets. The headline read: *Teachers call them kids with special needs*. Under the picture was a second display: *We call them thugs*.

Sarah was still watching the screen. She shook her head.

'Whatever film you use has to show teachers. Teachers not controlling their kids.'

'Peddling all this progressive nonsense,' said Helen.

'Have to pin the responsibility on the teaching force,' said Sarah. 'And the local authorities.'

Linda switched off the video image.

'Ah, well,' she said. 'Back to the archive.'

Sarah and Helen moved to the door.

'How's your son liking school?'

'Daniel?' Sarah asked. 'Daniel's not liking it at all at the moment. But that's temporary. I hope.'

They walked down the passage together.

'Which reminds me,' said Sarah. 'Can we have a word?'

Following Helen into her office, Sarah was surprised to find herself trembling. Helen noticed her tension.

'Is something the matter?'

'Maybe you can tell me that,' said Sarah. She was trying to keep her voice under control. 'Last night, I finally heard from my husband.'

Helen looked at her and waited.

'After all this time,' said Sarah, 'I still haven't seen Paul. Now, ten days after he leaves, I have this one phone call. Wouldn't tell me where he was. Wouldn't say where he was living. But he told me something else. He said he'd seen you.'

There was a pause, and the soft hum of a computer running. The two women watched each other. Then Helen reached out and put her hand on Sarah's. Sarah shook it off.

'Helen – I don't want sympathy,' she said. 'I want to know what the hell is happening with you and my husband.'

'Paul's been round to the flat twice,' said Helen finally. 'He said he couldn't talk to you any more.'

'Ah,' said Sarah. 'So that's the problem. Can't talk to me. Can talk to my friends.'

'Sarah –'

'Listen,' said Sarah. 'You talk to whomever you want. Help them with their difficulties. But for Christ's sake, Helen – you knew I was banging into the bloody furniture. Paul walks out without a word. I don't know where the hell he is. Don't know if he's OK. Can't even tell if I've still got a husband. Don't know if Daniel has a father. And now I find that you've been seeing him.' She took a breath. 'Do you know how I feel? Let me tell you. I feel betrayed.'

'Betrayed?' said Helen. 'Oh, great. For nine years, I've listened to you – I've covered for you – I've watched you climbing up the ladder – treading on everyone's fingers – and now, because *your* husband comes to *my* flat – his idea, let me say, not mine – *you* feel betrayed.'

Sarah came around the table and stood close to Helen.

'What am I supposed to think?' she asked. 'It's not a man that Paul goes to when he leaves my house. It's not anyone we know that's plain and safe and motherly. Oh, no. It's the one of my friends, who everyone fancies, and who happens to be living on her own.' She paused. 'If this was just a bit of sisterly help, why didn't you say you knew where he was?'

'Why do you think?' asked Helen. 'Because Paul made me promise not to tell you. That's why. He's not happy, Sarah.'

'*He's* not happy.'

'Listen,' said Helen, 'before you go on with these accusations, let me tell you I didn't like it, either – being caught between a friend and her husband. It's not what I want. I told him that. Who do you think made Paul phone you last night?'

'You?' said Sarah.

'Me,' said Helen.

Returning to the creative department, Warren stopped beside Dee's desk and looked at the tank she was drawing.

'Sarah not back?' he asked.

Dee didn't look up.

'You work in the same office,' she said. 'Why do you always ask me? Last seen, Sarah was down in the conference room, watching video clips.'

'Anywhere but here,' said Warren. He put a business card down on Dee's desk. 'There you go. Steven Yeates. Does really nice retouching. Get him to put a hammer and sickle on that tank.'

Dee picked up the photo, inspected it, then passed it to Warren.

'Stan says it's not Russian. Says it's an American tank.'

Warren peered at the print.

'Who's going to know that?'

'If Stan can tell –'

'Ah,' said Warren, 'the way they bloody niggle. Russian tank – American tank – Get some more pix then.' He walked away toward his office. Dee shouted after him.

'Me get more pix? Listen, Warren. I've got half the political campaign to do. Your Kim hasn't come. Nick's in Barbados –'

Warren stopped and pointed toward the lifts.

'Nick's not in Barbados, maan. Beach boy's back.'

Nick was walking across the creative department with Mike Sutherland, and explaining his bandaged foot.

'Playing football, that's what did it. Down there, they can't afford a ball.'

'No shit,' said Mike.

'Play with a sort of big round rock.'

'No shit,' said Mike again.

Nick moved his hands well apart from one another.

'Rock about this size. Really heavy.' He was about to go on when Dee ran at him and wrapped him in her arms.

'Hey, Nick,' she said. 'Brill! You're back!'

As Dee was greeting Nick, Helen and Sarah came through the department. The way they walked, you would not have taken them for close friends. There was an almost tangible tension between them.

'What I'll do,' said Helen, attempting to pour oil on already troubled waters, '– I'll ask Paul if he'll go and see you.'

'You,' said Sarah through gritted teeth, 'will ask my husband if he will come and see me. Now, that is friendship.'

The two women went through the main door, into the passage, and out of sight. Warren, who urgently needed to consult Sarah, went after them at a run.

Nick, sitting on the edge of his desk, was telling Dee about Barbados.

'The water,' he said. 'You can see right down through it – right down to the sand. Just a pale wash of colour.'

'I remember,' said Dee. 'The blues and the greens –'

'Magic,' said Nick. There was a pause; then he said: 'But you know what I really liked?'

Dee waited.

'Nobody talked about the price of property. I mean, nobody said, Look, man, I'm telling you – this time last year, buy my hut for three stick of sugarcane – and *this* year – is ridiculous, man – she worth nine and a half stick –'

Nick's eye was caught by Dee's rough of a Russian tank. He picked it up.

'What the hell's this?'

'While you're away,' said Dee, 'Prime Minister decided we're going to have an election.'

'You're making this up as you go along,' said Nick. 'There's nothing in the papers.' He looked at the newspaper he was carrying. 'Admittedly, I only bought the *Mail*.'

'Hasn't been announced yet,' said Dee. 'Another ten days.'

Nick dropped into a chair and put his injured foot up on the desk.

'Well. As big Mike says: no shit.'

SEVEN

In New York it was now four o'clock in the morning. David was about to leave for JFK Airport. One of the Plaza bellboys was carrying his luggage to the lift. David was in his bedroom, saying goodbye to Sally. Sally was sitting on the edge of the emperor bed, still in her leotard, massaging the back of her leg.

'If they've taken the luggage,' she said, 'then you ought to go.'

'You still don't believe me, do you?' said David. Holding her, he could feel her ribs through the leotard. 'I promise: I will do it as soon as I get back. The moment I've settled this business at the agency, I'll make the house over to my wife.'

'David,' she said, 'I'm not interested in houses. I think you ought to go and get your taxi.'

She was thin. He could feel each of her vertebra.

'They call them cabs over here. Not taxis. I was thinking, Sally – we could live out of London. Even Oxford –'

'What would I do in Oxford?'

'You'd love it,' said David. 'I was brought up outside Oxford. In Woodstock; edge of Blenheim Park. If we lived there, I could work a shorter day. Spend more time with you.'

The phone began to ring. Sally pointed through the window at the Manhattan skyline.

'You've just bought – what is it, down there? – the fourth biggest agency in New York? I couldn't believe it when I saw it – and you think you're going to work shorter days?' She picked up the phone and listened, then put it down again. 'Your taxi – your cab – is getting impatient.'

David kissed her.

'Believe me –'

Sally pulled her mouth away.

'I do believe you – when you say it. But, actually, when

you're not here – when I'm missing you – when I just want to make love to you – I know it's not going to be like that. It's going to be like *this*. Whatever you feel about me – there's going to be some reason why you really have to catch the next plane.'

David lifted her from the bed.

'Sally: if I don't catch this particular plane, I may lose my agency. It happens. The board could end my contract. Literally. I could be out on the street this evening.'

Sally limped to the door and opened it.

'Well, go then. Bloody well go. But don't pretend it won't be like this the next time we're together. If there is a next time – There'll be some panic in that place down there – Pater Parazzi –'

'Pater Paolozzi,' said David.

'Whatever it is,' said Sally. 'And then you'll have to get the next flight to New York –' She was trying not to cry. 'Now, will you catch your damn plane? I'm sorry to go on like this. It sounds like we're married already, doesn't it? I just do hate the way you always have the world's best reason for leaving – But if you are going, will you please, *please*, go?'

In London, Sarah was working in her office with Warren. As a creative team of writer and art director, they had spent a lot of time working together in the past nine years. Now, they spent much less. Sarah was acting as head of the department; and Warren was finding it increasingly hard to concentrate. A partnership that was once one of the best in the advertising business was now visibly breaking up. It was like the end of a long marriage. And, as at the end of a marriage, there were moments of reconciliation. This was one of them: Sarah and Warren were producing a series of print ads on the state of the National Health Service.

'Next one's a magazine ad,' said Sarah. 'We want to get across the idea of *caring* for the Health Service.' She held up a colour photo of Nurse Judy Axford, which had been taken after the previous day's filming in the empty North London Hospital for Women. 'Maybe use this shot of the nurse. Build up the good associations – warm, caring woman –'

Warren was sketching a full-page advertisement. He spoke without looking up from his layout pad.

'Professional earth-mother.'

'This is serious, Warren,' said Sarah. 'We've got a lot more of this stuff to do.' She looked across at Warren's scribble. 'OK. Big photo of Judy Axford, in nurse's uniform – and copy has to get across the message, I'm a nurse . . . I look after the sick . . . and the government looks after me . . . between the lines, we're showing how the government looks after the Health Service –'

'Cue, thousand violins,' said Warren, still sketching.

'So: for a headline,' said Sarah, '*If you want to know about the Health Service, ask a nurse*.'

Warren rapidly lettered this on layout paper over the background area of the photograph.

'Bit long, isn't it?'

Sarah wasn't listening. She had just caught sight of Nick, limping in from the lifts. She was surprised by her own reaction. In the midst of her preoccupation with her missing husband, and with the problems of political advertising – there came a sudden, unwished-for eruption of pure desire. Sarah had a crazy impulse to walk across the creative department and, in front of all her staff, to touch Nick's suntanned body. She held herself still, trying to bring her mind back to the work at hand. Tense, motionless, she could hear her own breath.

Warren stopped work. Sarah became aware he was watching her.

'Nick's back!' she said; then called: 'Nick!'

Warren went back to drawing in tramlines of body copy.

'No concentration,' he said to himself.

Nick came into the office, watching Warren but talking to Sarah.

'Got the old man working,' he said. He dropped into one of Sarah's lime-green chairs, which made a nice contrast with his tan. 'I was just – this moment – coming in to report back.'

Sarah sat and looked at him.

'Such a wonderful colour. Like those sweet biscuits you get in Vienna.'

'Edible?' asked Nick.

'If you like sweets,' said Warren, finishing his magazine rough.

Sarah leaned forward and pushed a sleeve of Nick's cream shirt further up his arm.

'Same colour all over?'

Nick rolled his sleeve back down again.

'I get very nervous when people do that,' he said. He looked at Sarah, then looked away, through the glass dividing wall, into the next office, which belonged to Sarah's secretary. 'Where's my lovely Sally?'

'Didn't she tell you?' asked Sarah.

Warren looked up from his work. Out of Nick's sight, he put a marker-stained finger to his lips. Sarah smiled slightly.

'Sally's in New York,' she said. 'With David.'

For the first time since his return, Nick had nothing to say. His mind went back three years to the time Sally moved in with him: the whiteness of her body and the darkness of her hair and how immensely young she was. Then, like cloud-shadow, there was another memory: of her retreating into herself over the last year, departing alone, coming in late.

Nick found himself staring blankly at Sarah. She was waiting for him to speak.

'Sally went away with David Postgate?' he said finally. It was that he found hardest to accept.

Watching Nick, Sarah nodded.

'Well,' he said. 'Well. What a –' He paused. When your life changes, there are no words. 'What a – faithless girl.'

There was a silence. Warren had stopped work and was looking from Nick to Sarah.

'So,' said Nick. 'I might have to find a new flatmate.'

'Looks as if you might,' agreed Sarah.

Increasingly uneasy with this interchange, Warren was about to interrupt, when he caught sight of a gorilla shambling sadly across the creative department. He went rapidly out of the office and followed the moulting animal. Sarah looked after him, and then spoke to Nick.

'Even if Sally doesn't think so,' she said, 'it is nice to have you back.'

Warren caught up with the gorilla in a small staff kitchen, where it was looking for instant coffee. The gorilla was an actor called Ivor Barclay-Smith, who was booked for a sunscreen shot. Years before, Ivor had been at art school with Warren; then he became an actor. Since that moment of decision, his career had not gone well.

Ivor still had his optimistic days, when he imagined playing West End leads: but clearly this was not one of those days.

'Ivor,' said Warren, 'you're supposed to be across the street. You must know where the bloody studio is by now.'

Ivor bent a hairy face toward Warren.

'I wanted your advice,' he whispered. 'It's not business. This is personal, Warren.'

Warren took Ivor's paw, led him further into the kitchen, and closed the door.

'I haven't been sleeping –' he began.

'Ivor,' said Warren, 'I've heard it. Where does a six-foot gorilla sleep? Answer: anywhere he wants to. Could you at least take that damn face-mask off?'

Ivor pushed the mask up into his hair. Beneath it he looked pale and, Warren thought, unwell.

'It's serious, Warren. Susan says to me – well, she says – I mean, her words – she says I'm not sufficiently masculine.'

'I guess you weren't dressed as a gorilla at the time?' said Warren. He passed Ivor the coffee he'd been looking for.

'Ah, come on, Warren. You were my best man. You knew Susan before I did.'

Warren nodded reminiscently. Susan Barclay-Smith had been a unanimous choice as the art school's sexiest student.

'And she's gone off with the picture-framing kit.'

This brought Warren back into the present.

'With what?'

'The picture-framing kit. It's the only way I make money, apart from' – he indicated the gorilla suit – 'apart from this.'

'Listen, Ivor,' said Warren. 'Why don't you just finish your coffee, then go down to the studio as unobtrusively as you can. I know you can't be entirely unobtrusive, dressed like that.'

'Then what?' asked Ivor.

'Then we do the sun-tan shot,' said Warren, 'and we talk about your marriage afterwards in the bar. Couple of quiet beers.'

'You won't forget?' said Ivor. 'Who else knows me this well?'

'Probably Susan does,' said Warren. He closed the door on Ivor and walked thoughtfully back to his National Health advertisements.

Outside David Postgate's empty office, the beautiful blonde Alessandra Castorina was working at her word processor. Stephen Hallam paused in the doorway and held out an earring. It was a large piece of red amber in an intricate silver mount.

'My cleaning lady found it,' he said. 'When she was making the bed.' He did his Sarf London accent. 'She said: "I suppose this is yours, Mr Hallam?"'

Alessandra looked from the earring to Stephen.

'What did you tell her? Amber matches your eyes?'

Stephen removed from Alessandra's in-tray the agenda for the board meeting that afternoon. With his other hand he pressed the earring to his own ear. It was a surprisingly feminine gesture for an apparently masculine man.

'I said, "Just one little earring on a Saturday, Mrs Searle. With a suspicion of eye-shadow."' He indicated the agenda. 'Board meeting today? Will David get back from New York in time?

Alessandra's blue eyes watched him without expression.

'I really don't know, Stephen,' she said. 'Do you?'

Warren had left the office to art-direct his sun-tan shoot. Sarah was briefing Nick on the election campaign.

'For this election,' she said, 'we're not having a single creative platform.' She went to the wall map. 'Helen – my friend Helen – ran a computer analysis of the Party's opinion polls. She's done a report this thick.' She indicated coloured sections of the map. 'Briefly, in these yellow areas, we're taking a compassionate approach – keep the Health Service intact, index-link pensions, measures to bring down youth unemployment –'

'What's the grey part?'

'Hard-line territory,' said Sarah. 'Different set of ads. Mike's writing them. Hit the unions. No closed shop. Educational choice –'

'Meaning private schools?'

'And schools that have been pulled out of the State system. Plus private hospitals. And a good strong nuclear defence line – Most of it's in there.' She passed a typed brief to Nick. She was looking at him, not at the document. 'Have you noticed? The tan brings out the colour of your eyes. . . . Promise not to wash for a week.'

'For you,' said Nick, 'anything.'

Stephen Hallam knocked on the door of Gordon's office and went in. Gordon, the agency's most meticulous dresser, was standing in front of a full-length mirror, adjusting the line of his shirt cuffs. He spoke to Stephen without taking his eyes from the mirror.

'Has Alessandra heard from David? Is he coming back?'

'Wouldn't say. Lovely lips are sealed.'

'If David does get here –' said Gordon. He paused, and tightened his tie. 'The man has so much meretricious charm. He could swing the directors. Could change their decision, in fact.'

'Indeed he could,' said Stephen. 'If you recall, I pointed that out before you got into this particular game.' He checked the time and led the way out of the office. 'We should be downstairs.'

Gordon followed Stephen out the door.

'At the time, there was no alternative. Apart from letting David get an even tighter grip on this damned agency.'

Stephen called a lift.

'There has always been an alternative,' he said. 'I've outlined it more than once. You set up your own agency. We do have the ingredients. You as chairman. I do account direction; Helen does planning. And Sarah takes the creative side.'

The lift doors opened. Stephen and Gordon entered.

'Can you imagine,' said Gordon, 'can you imagine me going into partnership with that woman? I would not willingly ride in the same car as Sarah Copeland.'

'One gets used to anything,' said Stephen. 'And there's really not a lot of choice. We won't get a better creative director. Plus – there's at least three accounts – which we badly need – that she could take out of this agency.'

Stephen and Gordon left the lift. They walked along a passage toward the conference room.

'You are offering me one third of an infant agency. This afternoon, I may have control of a very large one.' Gordon indicated the space around him. 'Surely a better bet?'

'Oh, indeed,' said Stephen. 'If that's the way it works out. But you will have to line up all the directors, and present them with an extremely convincing case. And you'll have to do it before David does.' The two men paused at the door of the conference room. 'Which does mean finding Simon Forbes. Very soon.'

In the photo studio, Ivor Barclay-Smith was brushing what looked like dandruff from his gorilla suit. Warren took the brush from his paw and pushed him in the direction of the cyclorama.

'Just get up there and have your picture taken, will you, Ivor?' he asked.

Dee came into the studio, carrying a sheaf of notes.

'Sarah says, are you shooting the political stuff?'

'*Wild Thing*,' said Warren. He held up a tube of jungle-printed sunscreen. 'On that set.' He pointed at what looked like Douanier Rousseau's vision of a tropical island. 'Doesn't look like an unemployment ad, does it?'

Dee persisted. 'Sarah said, in studio B, she wants single shots for law-and-order.' She consulted a list on her layout pad. 'One: football hooligans, two: muggers, three: promiscuous sex and spreading AIDS.'

'An' the big baaad Rasta man,' said Warren. Then, noticing Dee's expression, he added: 'No offence, love. I sometimes forget what colour you are.'

'He surveyed the set, on which two female models in swimsuits were now crouching beside an electric radiator. 'And you tell Sarah that her stuff gets shot after I've done this lot.'

Dee was also surveying the set.

'Are you getting the gorilla back?'

Warren stopped on his way to the front of the studio.

'We're working,' he said, 'in a so-called creative hot shop. Now: today, I'm doing skin shots.' Again, he held up the tube of suntan lotion. It was labelled – in pink on green – *Wild Thing*. 'This is your yuppies-in-Kenya-seriously-expensive-sunscreen stuff. OK. I can do a standard boring sexist shot.' He indicated the two models, who were now being sprayed a tasteful shade of brown. 'Or we make it more fun. Sort of Where the Wild Things Are. Jungle Girls Meet Teenage Godzilla.' He pointed to the back of the set, a grove of artificial palm trees. 'Gorilla comes out of that lot, picks up one of the chicks. Ancestral memories of Fay Wray, or what?'

'Well,' said Dee, 'thanks for the philosophy. I'm just telling you, Sarah's dead against the gorilla.'

Helen Marriott, the agency's political planner, was working in her high-tec office. She was surrounded by computers, monitors, graphics printers and fax machines. Now she was dividing her attention between Linda, and a VDU, which showed the latest poll of voting intentions.

'The trouble is,' Linda was saying, 'Sarah still thinks of herself as married. That's half the problem. It's not a separation. It's not a divorce. It's just – Paul's disappeared.'

Helen, who knew where Sarah's husband was, hesitated before answering.

'Paul hasn't disappeared,' she said eventually. 'He's just not living with Sarah.'

The graphics printer on the desk finished charting the poll results. Helen tore off the chart and scanned it briefly.

'Government's down again today. Gone down every poll this week.'

'What do you mean, Paul hasn't disappeared?' asked Linda. 'Sarah doesn't know where he is. She apparently spent half last week calling round, asking people if they'd seen him.'

'I know,' said Helen. She began to work again on her computer keyboard. 'It was awful watching her. I couldn't believe the difference.'

'Difference?'

'Well – you know the way she always used to work,' said Helen. 'Right from day one, when we started at Doyle Dane. Fanatical. Everything done better than it had to be. Everything on time.'

'And home life in chaos,' said Linda.

'Oh, sure. Home life in absolute chaos. Paul running round picking up the pieces – buying the pesto when anyone came to dinner – but the last couple of weeks it wasn't even like that.'

'I was away,' said Linda. 'Sydney.'

'Well, Sarah was quite different. All systems down. Not just at home: here as well. Copy late. Missing meetings. I've never seen Sarah so – so untogether.' The phone rang. Helen picked it up. 'Mind you, she's better now. And Nick's back, which helps.' She listened to the phone, then put it down. 'Jane, in reception. Says Rachel Someone's down there waiting for you.'

'Aaaah, damn,' said Linda. 'Rachel Hall.'

She went out, passing Stephen in the doorway.

'I suspect that Rachel was Linda's lover-before-Alice,' said Stephen to Helen. 'However, enough gossip. Business call. Warren says you have some research on identification of political parties. Do we, for example, need logos on posters?'

Helen pointed at a bookshelf behind Stephen.

'There's the research. All five volumes of it. But if you go along to the right-hand end, you'll find a single slim-ish volume of summary. I think you want chapter eight. Maybe nine.'

Helen watched Stephen take down the summary and leaf through it.

'Leaving aside Linda's sex life, Stephen – do you ever wonder about your own?'

'Almost constantly,' said Stephen, reading rapidly through a list of summarised research findings.

'Sarah's says you've got your eye on Alessandra.'

'If Sarah said "eye", she has a most curious notion of anatomy.'

'Health aside,' said Helen, 'is that wise? Sleeping with David's secretary – while you and Gordon are trying to get him out of the agency?'

Stephen put down the volume of psephological research. He spoke with unusual force.

'Wisdom, my love, has nothing to do with it. You go to bed to get away from wisdom. Sex is the one thing left that doesn't depend on being wise. It's the one time that all the murderous virtues don't matter.'

'And I thought it was just a pastime,' said Helen.

'No pastime. Believe me, sex is the only liberation we have left. In between getting and spending, this is our last fine and private place, my love. It's the one time we can switch off the radiophone and just be human again. As in: "Lay your sleeping head, my love – Human on my faithless arm." Remember that couplet? You should: you gave me the book.'

Helen nodded. Stephen picked up the research report again: but he was not yet finished.

'Take sex away, they might as well open up the skull, put in the microprocessor – and programme it for meetings.'

'Talking of which,' said Helen, 'aren't we due at a progress meeting in the conference room?'

Gordon was already in the conference room when Helen and Stephen entered.

'Late,' he remarked. He pointed at a back-projected transparency on a screen at the end of the room.

'Location for the *Wild Thing* shoot.'

'Looks like Tahiti,' said Nick, who was sitting on the far side of the table.

'It is Tahiti.'

'Not possible,' said Helen, arranging her papers. 'It's the French nuclear weapons factory. Think of the associations.'

'That's why we changed the product name,' added Stephen. 'It used to be called *Tahiti Tan.*'

'In any case,' said Sarah, 'Warren's trying a set. Shooting it some time today, in fact. Sort of Rousseau-comes-to-Stills-Studio-B.' She glanced at Nick and dropped her voice. 'With that tan, we should have used you as a model.'

Gordon was moving down his status list.

'Now. Progress on the political campaign. Carol?'

Carol, who had been wondering whether Alessandra really liked her, came to mental attention and passed across a checklist.

'Several items slipping,' said Gordon. 'Nine days till the election's announced – and National Health Service still to be re-shot. Press ads not finished.' He looked around the table. 'Perhaps someone can tell me why?'

'I'm supposed to be writing the print and the posters,' said Nick. 'I only just got back from holiday.'

'So I heard,' said Gordon. 'Curious time to have a holiday, in the run-up to an election campaign.'

'I haven't even seen the first hospital shoot,' said Nick. 'Also it's sort of difficult getting a tight brief.'

'Come on,' said Stephen. 'An extremely full brief exists on how we handle the Health Service. Cabinet's very touchy about the whole business.'

Sarah turned on Stephen.

'Stop brushing it aside,' she said. 'There's a problem here. We've simply underestimated how strongly people feel about the Health Service. What we've produced so far simply doesn't address itself to that.'

Gordon leaned over the table toward Sarah.

'You're not suggesting, I hope, that we change a political platform – less than a month before polling day? Tell me. Is that what you're suggesting?'

'If the platform's not right,' replied Sarah, 'then, yes, I would suggest changing it. Let me give you just one example.

Of many.' She reached across to a video recorder in front of Nick. 'Is this on the right clip?' she asked Helen.

Helen nodded. Sarah switched the machine to play. On a video screen at the end of the room appeared the image of a woman, aged about thirty. The weariness of her expression made her seem older.

'This,' said Sarah, 'is a woman called Sue Holland. Mother of three young children. She was in the last voters' panel that Helen brought together.' She increased volume on sound.

Looking straight to camera, Sue Holland said: '– there's my youngest in hospital, with the nurses that tired from working all night, they can't keep awake – and there's my friend's Mum, she's been waiting a year and half to have her hip done, and she's nowhere near the head of the queue – and we've got our local hospital – which was great – it's been closed down, and the big hospital, it's had the kitchens shut because they're so full of cockroaches – *cockroaches*, in a hospital – Look. You ask the doctors. They know the Health Service shouldn't be like that.'

Sarah switched off the recorder. There was a moment's silence, then Stephen spoke.

'Reinforces my point,' he said. 'Public's only getting the negatives. We have to give them the good news about the Health Service.'

'What good news is this, Stephen?' asked Helen.

'For example,' said Stephen, 'higher government spending, new larger hospitals opened, reorganised administrative level –'

'Exactly,' said Gordon. 'We can't afford to be defensive. Not on this issue. We could run a whole series of ads, telling the good news.'

'If I were the opposition agency,' said Sarah, 'I'd run a comparable series: hospitals closed, services cut, vital equipment not ordered, waiting list figures massaged downward – the whole service being run down for the benefit of the private sector.'

'But,' said Stephen, 'we are not an opposition agency. We have to make the best of what the government gives us.'

'Oh, I realise that,' said Sarah. 'I'm simply suggesting we may convince more of the voters if we stay this side of fantasy.'

In Stills Studio B, the suntan shoot was nearing its end. Ivor Barclay-Smith in his gorilla suit held a model called Fabienne in his arms. He was wilting under the strain. Warren bent over the photographer, an elegant young man called Robin Gellhorn.

'Robin,' said Warren, 'just shoot the thing, will you. Before the gorilla's flat on his bloody back.'

A bank of flashes fired into silver umbrellas and the gorilla put the girl down on to an artificial beach of real sand.

'OK,' said Warren to the photographer. 'Now a three-shot. Gorilla sunbathing. Try sunbathing, love,' he shouted to Ivor.

The gorilla lay awkwardly down on the sand.

'I'm unbearably hot already,' he said. 'It's hard work, holding that girl.'

'Thanks a lot,' said Fabienne, who was arranging herself on the sand beside him. 'My love.'

A young man entered the studio. He was dressed in deliberately torn clothes and his hair, in spikes, was gelled to death. He looked from Warren to the gorilla.

'I'm Tony Tosser,' he said. 'Am in this lot?'

'Next studio,' said Warren. 'You're the political shot.'

'OK, governor,' said Tony Tosser amiably. 'Can I say something?'

The bank of flashes fired as Robin Gellhorn immortalised the island scene.

'It's just, I seen gorillas at the zoo,' said Tony. 'They don't lie like that, squire.'

'I'll sort out my problems,' snapped Warren. 'You sort out yours.'

'Me, I got no problems,' said Tony Tosser. He went into the next studio, where he was due to represent unemployed dole-fiddling youth.

'Nor me,' said Warren. 'When I was your age.'

Tosser was gone.

Sarah was still in the conference room some minutes after the progress meeting ended. Nick, too, stayed behind when the room emptied. He sat watching Sarah.

'Being away, you forget what it's like.'

'Gordon?' said Sarah.

'Gordon,' said Nick. 'The whole business of office politics. People edging along the wall. Protecting their backs.'

'It's the way you survive,' said Sarah. She resisted a sudden temptation to touch Nick's suntanned arm. Instead, she collected her papers, got up, and walked slowly out into the passage. Nick followed her. Alessandra, returning to her office, stopped to speak to Sarah.

'David phoned from New York,' she said quietly. 'Should be on a flight to London by now. He said to ask – can you meet him at Heathrow? About four fifteen?'

Sarah checked the time. It was after midday.

'You know how porcupines mate?'

'With difficulty,' said Alessandra, going into her office. 'If you can't get there, I can. But I think David wants to see you.'

'Believe me, it's nothing personal,' said Sarah. 'If anyone wants me in the next forty-five minutes, I'm going to grab a coffee, then over in the photo studios.'

Gordon and Stephen were waiting for Sarah as she came into the agency restaurant. They closed in, one on each side of her. Sarah looked from one man to the other.

'What is this? Abduction?'

'Stephen tells me that you phoned David in New York this morning,' said Gordon.

This was not something Sarah had expected. She paused.

'It seemed the right thing to do,' she said finally.

'Why, exactly?'

'Well,' said Sarah, 'I thought it was – unwise – to have a board meeting, which might decide the shape of the agency, without the managing director.'

'David happened to be in New York,' said Stephen. 'Of his own choice.'

'And he happens not to have the agenda,' said Sarah. 'That

was not his choice. Do you two mind if I get myself some coffee?'

Stephen and Gordon followed Sarah to her table. Gordon's manner had changed. He seemed to be making an unusual effort to ensure that Sarah understood what he was saying.

'Let me put it to you: our Managing Director has gone to New York and, with minimal consultation, has bid for an agency much larger than this one. Provisionally, the bid has been accepted – simply because Pater Paolozzi are in financial trouble.'

'Badly needing a white knight,' said Stephen. 'Though that may not be everyone's picture of David.'

Gordon spoke to a hovering waitress.

'Two more of us to come,' he said. 'In the meantime, dry sherry.'

'Usual,' said Stephen.

'Not staying,' said Sarah. To Gordon she said: 'I may not agree with the takeover –'

Gordon interrupted her.

'The takeover's the easy part,' he said. 'The hard part is actually running an American agency. Toughest advertising market in the world. And this place is scarcely a model of management. So what makes you think – or David think – we can run a larger agency?'

'On the other side of the Atlantic,' added Stephen.

On the far side of the restaurant, Nick, Dee and Linda were serving themselves salads. Nick paused in spooning out tabbouleh and stared at Tony Tosser who had crossed the road from the photo studio to take lunch in the agency. Tony was accompanied by a young woman called Slagheap. Both of them, though gentle-natured, were of terrifying appearance.

'Don't tell me,' said Nick to Dee. 'We got the AIDS account as well.'

Dee turned to look at Tosser and Slagheap.

'They're the sex-and-violence shots,' she said. 'Foretaste of what it's going to be like if the government doesn't get back.'

Linda indicated two middle-aged men who had just entered the restaurant.

'That's the other end of the account,' she said. 'On the left, the Minister of State for Army Affairs. The pretty one's Francis Salk.'

'Should I know Francis Salk?'

'By repute you should,' said Linda. 'He's supposed to have brought us our present political rulers.'

Sarah's intensity matched Gordon's. She was leaning across the table and pushing her hair back with both hands. It was a nervous habit.

'You say you don't know David's rationale for buying an American agency. I can tell you David's reasons. In his view, agencies will only survive the next decade if they can handle global accounts. What's happening now is a massive concentration of wealth in the largest corporations. That's what the Reagan-Thatcher time was all about. Letting the corporations loose. Now the world market's run by a few big transnationals.' She grouped condiments together to demonstrate. 'There's IBM, Bechtel, Exxon, DEC, General Foods, Mitsubishi, ICI, Lockheed, Sony, Frick, Shell, General Motors, Ford –' she indicated an expanse of tablecloth – 'and the rest of them are out there in the cold. Scratching for crumbs. We can't live on the little accounts –'

'The trouble with that analysis –' began Gordon, when Stephen touched his arm. He looked up, then stood up, to greet Geoffrey Talbot and Francis Salk.

'Minister,' he said. 'Francis. Stephen Hallam you know. You've met Sarah Copeland?'

'Mrs Copeland was at your most interesting presentation,' said Geoffrey Talbot, sitting down.

'The artistic dynamo behind the whole business,' said Francis Salk to Sarah, with a surprising degree of venom. 'I heard the other day that you were in London's creative top ten. Wonderful notion, I thought – a creative top ten. Would Blake or Botticelli have made it, I ask myself.'

'There are a lot of people who don't make it,' said Sarah.

'Some other time, we could try a historical list. At the moment, I have to go across to our photo studio.' To the Minister she said: 'We are shooting some of your advertisements this afternoon.'

The Minister was not listening. He was staring across the restaurant at Slagheap and Tony Tosser, who were eating a substantial free lunch.

'Good heavens,' he said. 'Do those two young people work for you?'

'For you, Minister,' said Stephen.

'For – ?' said Talbot.

'Those are the feckless unemployed,' said Sarah. 'On whom we all squander our hard-earned taxes.'

'National press campaign against unemployment benefit. Runs in the week of the ninth,' added Stephen.

'Ah. The scroungers,' said the Minister, suddenly enlightened. 'Costa del Dole. Excellent.' He turned to look again at Tosser and Slagheap. 'They're not models?'

'Do they look like models, Minister?' Stephen asked. 'Those two are straight off the Hammersmith dole queue. We do appreciate the Party's – sensitivity on that point.'

'You would if you'd been involved in the last election,' said the Minister. Indicating the punks, he turned to Salk. 'You've seen them, Francis? If those two don't bring in the lower-middle-class floating vote, I can't imagine what will.'

Sarah stood up to leave.

'Encouraging to know that not all advertisers take three-hour lunches,' said Salk waspishly. 'And I gather that we are seeing some of your creative efforts tomorrow?'

'Tomorrow afternoon,' said Stephen. More quietly, he said to Sarah: 'Do you happen to be free this evening?'

'I don't,' said Sarah. 'My au pair is.'

'Business discussion,' said Stephen.

'Later this afternoon, or tomorrow,' said Sarah. 'I like to have business discussions in public places.'

'Very cautious woman,' said Francis Salk, watching Sarah leave the restaurant.

'Only in some areas of her life,' said Stephen. 'In others, she can be quite reckless.'

EIGHT

Daniel turned into his front garden, and bent down to pick a shell out of the sea-gravel on the path. Rose stood and waited for him.

'Do you know who's the strongest boy in our school?'

Rose named the only boy she could remember. 'William?'

'William's not a bit strong,' said Daniel. 'Gavin punches William up almost every playtime. Gavin's much the strongest.' He pocketed his shell, ran to the front door, and waited while Rose found the keys.

'Do you like Gavin?'

'Well,' said Daniel, 'his Mummy and Daddy don't live in the same house. His Daddy doesn't even live in England.'

Rose unlocked the door. 'Didn't you know that before?'

'Of course I didn't,' said Daniel. 'At our school, you don't talk about things like that.' He ran ahead of Rose to the kitchen. 'What have you got me for lunch, Rose?'

'Cheese sandwiches,' said Rose. 'And biscuits and terrine.'

'Tired of terrine,' said Daniel, opening up the sandwiches. 'Yuck. This is cheddar. I hate cheddar.'

Rose said something under her breath.

'What?' said Daniel. Then: 'My Daddy's coming home this evening, Rose.'

Rose tried to read his expression.

'Do you really know that, Daniel? Or do you just think it would be nice if he did?'

'I'd like some tea,' said Daniel. 'Actually, Rose, I know my Daddy's coming home, because he came to my school, and he said he's bringing me a battleship. And a new cat.'

Rose switched on the electric kettle, and got Earl Grey teabags out of the cupboard.

'You've got a cat. 'You've got Joshua.'

'Joshua's dead.'

'I don't know why you keep thinking Joshua's dead,' said Rose. 'Joshua was up on the bench eating monkfish this morning. But if you do know Daddy's coming home, hadn't we better tell your mummy?'

'I don't want to tell Sarah anything,' said Daniel.

As her son was finishing his sandwiches, Sarah left the photo studios. She crossed the street at a run and came back into the agency with Helen, who was returning from lunch at the Firenze.

'There was something else I meant to say to you.'

Helen paused, just inside the agency's glass doors, and waited.

'About my husband,' said Sarah. 'If you do just happen to see him again, you might say that Daniel now doesn't like going to school. Insists on coming home for lunch. And he's generally being very difficult. See what Paul makes of that.'

Helen said nothing, but started to walk toward the lifts. Sarah kept pace with her.

'It's like those crazy families where the parents don't speak to each other. They communicate through one of the children.'

Helen called a lift.

'Thank you very much,' she said.

Stephen, Gordon, Francis Salk and Geoffrey Talbot were coming slowly down the stairs from the restaurant. It had been a long and heavy working lunch.

'Surely there's always some sort of scandal before an election. Some sort of moral panic?' said Stephen.

'This time,' said Francis Salk, 'the gods may be with us. The rent boys seem to fading into race memory. One or two nasty little things in the City, of course –'

'But nothing,' said the Minister, 'that we can't screw down tight for the next few weeks.'

The four men acknowledged Sarah and Helen, but did not break their progress toward the street and the waiting limousine. Alessandra, coming from the opposite direction, paused beside Sarah.

'I called Heathrow,' she said quietly. 'David's plane's on time. Might even be a few minutes early.'

She went on towards the reception desk. Helen looked from her to Sarah.

'Heathrow? David's flying back early?'

'I'm trying to get him here for a board meeting this afternoon,' said Sarah. She indicated Gordon, who was talking to Stephen as they came back into the agency.

'If David isn't back here by five, there's a good chance that Gordon will be running this place by tomorrow. God help us.'

'Amen to that,' said Helen. She looked at her watch. 'Hadn't you better leave, if you're going to meet a plane?'

'I've gone,' said Sarah. 'You might do me a favour and tell Jane I won't be back in the office until later this afternoon.'

The car park at Hamilton Forbes and Kent was an enclosed, and highly expensive, piece of St James's real estate. Parking space was limited to board directors; and Sarah was not one of them. It had taken some skilled political in-fighting to get herself a space for the BMW, which she was now manoeuvring past Gordon's dark-green Jaguar. Just as she was clear, Stephen opened the passenger door and got into her car. Sarah jammed on the handbrake.

'What the hell are you doing, Stephen?'

'You're going to Heathrow?'

Sarah paused. Then she said: 'I am. Now, would you please get out of my car?'

'Give me one minute,' said Stephen. 'The way you drive, you'll get there.'

Sarah switched off the car engine.

'I have a message from Gordon,' Stephen said. 'He's prepared to confirm you as creative director.'

Sarah had not expected this.

'And board director?'

Stephen nodded. 'Always assuming that David – for whatever reason – doesn't make this afternoon's board meeting.'

Sarah sat for a moment, tracing the circumference of the rev counter with one fingernail. She considered the offer.

'Always assuming,' she said finally, 'that Gordon could deliver on his promises.' She restarted the car. 'Are you getting out? Or do you want to come to the airport?'

While Sarah was driving to Heathrow, Nick was sitting in the agency's darkened conference room. He was watching the videotape that Sarah and Linda had shot for the National Health Service. Linda, sitting on the other side of the table, was running the recorder.

'It was a dreadful shoot,' she said. 'Complete panic, trying to get it ready for five p.m. But the nurse is good.'

'I know,' said Nick. 'I've been told to use her in all my print ads. That big blue-eyed stare to camera.' In the half-light he made a note to himself. 'I meant to tell you, when I came back yesterday, I saw someone at the airport – looked like your Alice.'

Linda lived with a young, blonde lawyer.

'In all likelihood,' she said, 'it *was* my Alice. I love that term: "my" Alice. They keep inviting her to legal conferences. Colorado. Siena. New Caledonia. Great legal centres of the world.' She switched off the videorecorder and rewound the tape. 'How many attractive young barristers are there?'

'Sisterhood, Linda.'

'I know,' said Linda. 'It's awful. Never thought I'd say the word – but I get jealous.' She paused, then said: 'I'm not the only one. Sally had a bad time with Sarah when you two were living together.'

Nick stood up and switched on the conference room lights.

'Well, Sally seems to have solved that one,' he said. 'Left me on my own.'

'Like Sarah,' said Linda.

Sarah was coming out of Heathrow's Terminal Four. Beside her, David was carrying a single leather travelling bag. For the first time in Sarah's experience, he seemed older than his thirty-nine years. She stopped and looked at him.

'You look exhausted,' she said. 'I hope you're up to this board meeting.'

David walked on toward the car park; Sarah kept pace with him.

'You woke me up,' he said, 'about three o'clock this morning. Since then, I've had to pack, book a flight, get to JFK, get across the Atlantic –'

'And make arrangements for my secretary,' said Sarah. She opened the boot of her car, and David dropped his bag into it.

'You knew I was with Sally?'

Sarah unlocked the car doors.

'I was one of the last to know. I heard about two days after you left. Until then, I thought Sally was in Rome.'

David dropped into the passenger seat of the BMW and closed his door.

'It's actually quite serious,' he said. 'Whatever's between me and her.'

Sarah started the car.

'You have more serious problems than that,' she said. 'One of them is trying to keep hold of your agency.'

On the ground floor of the agency, Stephen and Gordon were reviewing arrangements for the board meeting. Carol, had set out paper, sharpened pencils, agendas, bottles of mineral water, and glasses. Gordon, who had no faith in his subordinates, checked each item. Carol waited anxiously by the door.

'No place card for Simon Forbes,' Gordon said to her.

'I can't get hold of him,' explained Carol. 'I really have tried everywhere. I even rang his company in Melbourne. No one's seen him.'

'Simon Forbes,' said Gordon, 'is the senior director of this firm. Someone must know how to get in touch with him. Use what intelligence you have, girl. Ask – ask Alessandra.'

Carol turned to go.

'Wait a moment,' said Stephen. 'Make sure you don't tell Alessandra why you want Simon's address.'

'I won't,' said Carol, closing the door behind her.

'I don't trust her,' said Gordon. 'Sad to say, I don't completely trust any of them.'

Sarah was driving uncomfortably fast down the M4. David, who disliked being driven, was watching the cars she overtook.

'I do hold one high card,' he said. 'Managed to phone Simon Forbes before I left New York. He's been hiding out at his ex-wife's place. Hampshire, somewhere. I persuaded him to come to the meeting this afternoon.'

Sarah accelerated past a turbo Peugeot.

'You'll need any high cards you have,' she said. She leant over, opened the glove pocket, and took out a rechargeable Braun razor.

'At this speed,' said David, 'I'd rather you watched the road.'

Sarah passed him the shaver.

'Belongs to my absent husband,' she said.

David flicked the razor on and off. It was fully charged. He adjusted the mirror on the back of his sun visor and was about to start shaving. Then he paused.

'I still don't begin to comprehend what the board are thinking about,' he said. 'I'm giving the agency the basis of a whole global network. You've got Hamilton Forbes in London. Pater Paolozzi in New York – and all the subsidiary agencies round the world. West Coast, Manila, Tokyo, Sydney, Auckland, Hong Kong, Singapore, Delhi – lets you pick up the biggest of the transnational accounts. Globalisation: that's where the real money is in advertising.' He leant away from the passenger door as Sarah squeezed back into the fast lane. 'Given that – I simply don't understand why the board are challenging me.'

Sarah changed back into fifth gear.

'They're doing it, David, because you pitched for the government as a client – when you knew there'd be an election some time this year.'

'Look what a political account did for Saatchi's in 79,' said David. 'And in 83.'

'The trouble was,' said Sarah, 'you didn't bother to tell the board. Then you went to New York and bid for Pater Paolozzi, leaving us to put together the government presentation. Also without informing the board.'

David turned to face her.

'Do you know why I didn't tell them? Because this is Britain, God help us. You tell someone what you're doing, and what's the reaction? They say no. Automatic negative. In this country, it's a simple knee-jerk reflex. No. No. No.'

Sarah braked sharply as she came into west London traffic.

'Fine,' she said. 'You didn't tell the board, in case they said no. Well, now, someone has told them. Gordon's told them. And they may well be saying a final no, right at this moment.'

Stephen came out of the board room, walked along a passage, and entered Gordon's office.

'Apart from Simon Forbes and David Postgate,' he said, 'all the directors are in there.'

Gordon was sitting at the end of his office table. He was motionless. With his hands locked together, and his tonsured head, he looked like a figure from some early religious order.

'I should get in there and talk to them, if I were you,' said Stephen. 'Just in case the last two do arrive.'

'Give me ten seconds more,' said Gordon. His eyes were closed.

'Remember,' said Stephen, 'the three points I gave you. One: can't afford David's planned expansion. Two: can't manage the sort of transatlantic group envisaged. Three: can't accept David's deliberate deception of the board.'

Gordon nodded. Then he opened his eyes, stood up, and walked to the door.

'Best of luck,' said Stephen. When Gordon had left his office, Stephen went rapidly through the in-tray, and examined Gordon's diary.

Sarah stopped her car outside the agency so suddenly that David was thrown forward. He recovered himself, dropped the electric shaver back in the glove pocket, and got out of the BMW. He held the door open.

'You don't want to play Salomé? Wait till my head's carried out of the boardroom on a platter?'

'Tempting,' said Sarah. 'But I have to go home. According to the au pair, Daniel's not had the best of days.'

David paused before shutting the car door.

'Wish me luck.'

'You'll need more than luck with that lot,' said Sarah. She put the car into gear, waited until David shut the door, then pulled out into the traffic.

Sarah walked slowly up the path to her house. She stumbled over one of Daniel's plastic battleships; stopped to pick it up; then fitted her key into the door. Before she could turn it, the door was opened from inside. Daniel began to dance round her.

'Daddy's back-back-back,' he shouted. 'Daddy's back-back-back!'

Before Sarah could speak, her husband came out of the drawing room into the hall. Paul was a big man who looked as if he had been roughly, but skilfully, carved from weathered pine. He spread his arms wide; humorous, self-deprecating.

'Daddy's back,' he said.

Sarah stared at her husband. He had been gone two weeks; and she realised that, at some remote level, she had not expected him to return.

Daniel stood looking from Paul to Sarah. He hesitated, then rushed to his father. He put his arms around Paul's knees. Using one muscular leg as a pivot, he swung round and around.

Rose came into the hall.

'Excuse me –' she said.

'Daddy's back-back-back!' called Daniel.

'There was a gas leak,' said Rose to Sarah.

'Daddy can play Skyhawk a zillion times better than you.'

'The gas is off,' said Rose.

'There's no hot water,' said Daniel, delighted. Paul knelt down and began to whisper to him.

The hall telephone started to ring.

'And the gasmen have gone for the day,' said Rose. 'I was going to say – I can't really cook the risotto –'

Paul began to laugh. 'Feels like home,' he said. Then, to Daniel: 'Come and finish the game. I bet I beat you.'

'Can't we get the gas fixed privately?' Sarah asked Rose.

'I'll tell you what,' said Daniel to his father. 'We'll start a new game, and I can have a thousand points start.' They disappeared into the drawing room. The phone stopped ringing.

'I've tried about six firms,' said Rose. 'Five hours was the quickest.'

'I bet I get a zillion more points than you,' Paul called to his son.

'I bet you do,' said Sarah to herself. To Rose she said: 'Can you just go out and get something? Or make toast? Anything edible. And I need a drink –'

Rose disappeared into the kitchen.

The phone rang again. Sarah picked it up, listened, then said: 'Alessandra? Are you still at work?' She listened for a long time.

In the drawing room, Daniel said: 'I can have first go, can't I?'

'But I'll be watching you,' said his father. 'Like a hawk.'

On the phone, Sarah said: 'Alessandra – I can't believe he's asking this –'

Paul appeared at the drawing room door. He stood there, watching his wife as if she were a woman he had just met at a party. She said to him:

'With you in a moment.' Into the phone, she said: 'Alessandra, the answer is no. Absolutely no. No, I don't want to speak to David. I got him back for the board meeting – what more does he want? Tell him best of luck.'

Sarah put the phone down and called to Rose.

'Rose, love – second thoughts – could you go out and get some takeaway stuff? Chinese or something?'

'I hate Chinese!' shouted Daniel from the drawing room, where he was racking up huge scores on his computer. 'I really *hate* Chinese.'

'He should be getting ready for bed,' Sarah said to her husband. 'He gets very tired these days.'

'No hot water,' called Daniel, overhearing. 'No hot water! Can't have a bath!'

'You know, I miss this,' said Paul quietly. 'All of this. Even the domestic chaos.'

Rose came through the hall.

'Excuse me – do you know what sort of food you all want?'

Daniel dashed into the hall and upstairs.

'I'm going to get the other game. I'm tired of Skyhawk.'

'Will you – please – put your pyjamas on,' called Sarah. To Rose she said: 'I suppose – just standard Szechuan, or something. I can't really think at the moment.'

Rose was going out the door when Daniel ran downstairs, almost falling, and caught her on the doorstep.

'I know what I want,' he said. 'Prawn crackers. I really hate that other stuff, Rose.'

Paul watched Sarah.

'It doesn't change, does it?' He put a hand on her arm. 'You need a drink.'

Rose whispered to Daniel: 'Your Mummy said you had to put your pyjamas on.'

'I am going to,' said Daniel. 'But Rose – would you really get me a lot of prawn crackers? I don't like that other stuff, and Daddy doesn't like it – and Rose, did you know, Daddy says I can go and live with him. He's got a bath that squirts water.'

'You go inside now,' said Rose.

When Daniel came back into the hall, he closed the door very slowly and quietly. He could hear his mother and father in the drawing room.

Paul was making drinks.

'Still drinking Pernod? You haven't changed?'

'Haven't changed anything much,' said Sarah. 'Except I have to be a father as well as a mother.'

'You don't have to do that,' said Paul.

Daniel finished shutting the door. The latch clicked.

'Is that you, Daniel?' said Sarah.

'I'm putting my pyjamas on,' Daniel called from the bottom of the stairs. 'I'm going to.'

Paul brought Sarah her Pernod.

'Thank you,' she said. 'It's been such a day –' She looked at him as he sat down in what used to be 'his' chair. 'What do you mean, I don't have to be father and mother? You can't really be a father when you're living – where are you living?'

The phone in the hall started to ring. Paul listened, but didn't get up to answer it.

'Work still pursues you home?'

'I can't afford to be too casual about work,' said Sarah. 'This house has only the one income.'

She got up to answer the phone. It stopped ringing and she dropped back into her chair.

'I was thinking about that,' said Paul. 'Thinking: a lot of it was to do with me.'

'Your going away? Surely, all of it? I had no idea – till I found you'd gone –'

'Not that,' said Paul. 'I mean – what built up to it. You know, the way I get depressed about teaching, no one believing in higher education any more, the cuts, the way you spend all your time not doing your work, just trying to see that the bloody institution survives.' There was a pause, then he said: 'I must have been difficult to live with.'

Daniel, still dressed, appeared in the doorway and spoke to his father.

'I can't find my computer disc, with the Asteroid game.'

'Rose put all your discs in the blue room,' said Sarah. 'Now – pyjamas!'

Daniel backed slowly out the door.

'You don't have to be a teacher,' Sarah said to her husband. 'Giovanni said just the other day –'

'Please,' said Paul. 'I don't want to talk about Giovanni.'

The telephone in the hall began to ring again.

'If you could tell me why,' said Sarah, 'I might understand it. As it is, I'm lost. You say all the pleasure's gone out of teaching – you say you want to get back to what you were really wonderful at – actually doing designs, getting things made up the way you wanted them –'

'It's not as simple as that,' said Paul.

The telephone stopped ringing.

'But it was as simple as that. Giovanni said you could have all the facilities. You'd design what you wanted. Collection every season, if you like. His people manufacture – the workmanship in Milan's fantastic –'

'I know,' said Paul. 'I used to stay there.'

'Well – of course – you know. But really, he said he would have flown you back to Milan three or four times a year. You would have been marketed all over the world: Giovanni Vanucci shops everywhere. I had it all set up – I thought it was something any designer would give his eye teeth for. And then – you come home and say you don't want it. You're going on with teaching, which you hate.' She drew breath. 'I don't begin to understand it.'

'I'll go up and see Daniel,' said Paul.

'You can see Daniel in a minute. He's not going away: but you may be. Can you just explain to me?'

Paul paused at the door.

'Giovanni wasn't doing all that for Paul Copeland. He was doing it for Sarah Copeland, wasn't he? He wasn't putting the whole Giovanni Vanucci organisation at the service of an art teacher who hasn't done any real design for the last four years. He was doing it because I was your husband. It was a present for you – his attractive little thirty-year-old advertising genius in London. So this is the next stage –'

'What next stage?'

'You wouldn't just be buying me a house and a car. You'd be arranging my work as well. I haven't got quite to that point of desperation, Sarah. I may, but I'm not there yet. Given the choice of those two options, I think I'd rather stay and deal with my petty little art college politics.' He opened the door. 'Now – do you mind if I go up and see my son?'

'Giovanni liked your work,' said Sarah.

'Maybe he did. But what he really liked was you. I know what he was thinking. Pay off Paul – nice studio, guaranteed sales, let him play with his jewellery designs – and that might make up for whatever you do when you go to Italy. Wasn't that it?'

'Paul,' said Sarah, 'that's such a hurtful thing to say. I go to

Italy to get campaigns approved. The same way I go to Paris for Prisunic. And, if we're on that subject, I have never taken an art student to Venice, to stay in the Fenice –'

'Wait a minute –' said Paul.

'I've never even been to the Fenice,' said Sarah. 'I'd love to stay there, but I've never actually been invited –'

'Sarah: I said to myself before I came over, I'm not going to get into recriminations. I want to discuss Daniel –'

The phone began to ring again.

'Not going to get into recriminations,' said Sarah. 'Fine. Admirable. You'll just drop in on the wife you left, and suggest she slept with one of her Italian clients – then persuaded him to set you up with an international design contract, so she could keep on going to bed with him in Rome, or Milan, or wherever. Thank you very much. If that's your idea of a friendly, domestic evening, Paul –'

Sarah went to pick up the phone. It stopped ringing. She said:

'And what did you mean when you said you came to discuss Daniel?'

'Daniel?' said Paul. 'I just wanted him to come and stay with me. Not necessarily for good. Just for a while. I miss him, Sarah.'

'Daniel? Come and stay with you? So you're not coming back – Where would he stay?'

'I've got a place to stay.'

'Let me get this clear,' said Sarah. 'Having walked out of this house – without a word – left me to look after Daniel –'

'Come on. When have you ever looked after Daniel?'

The phone began to ring again.

'When have I looked after Daniel?'

'Be honest,' said Paul. 'You've had a nurse, or a nanny, or an au pair, or a mother's help, since he was three days old.'

'Well, while we're on the subject,' said Sarah, 'who's going to look after him when you're out? Have you got someone in mind for that?'

Daniel shouted from the stair landing.

'I can –' he shouted. 'I can look after myself!' He ran down the last flight of stairs. 'Daddy's got a house with a bath that squirts water at you –'

Sarah stood very still. She seemed to go pale. Then she sprang forward, seized Daniel by the arms, and shook him backward and forward.

'Will you,' she shouted, '*will* you – do what I tell you? Will you go up and get ready for bed? Will you? Will you? Will you?'

Daniel's head rocked backward and forward. His hair flew. Sarah let him go, and he stumbled. He stared at his mother, who stared back at him. Then he ran upstairs and locked himself in the bathroom.

Sarah turned to look at Paul. He too seemed transfixed. She made a slight gesture with her hands.

'I've never in my life –' she said. Then she went upstairs at a run, and rattled the handle of the bathroom door.

Rose came across the square with an assortment of Szechuan food. She was trying not to let it drip on her clothes as she unlocked the front door of Sarah's house.

Sarah was coming down stairs. She spoke to Rose as if continuing a conversation: 'Daniel. He's locked himself in the bathroom. He'll be all right.' She indicated the telephone, which was still ringing. 'Can you?' She went to the door of the drawing room and spoke to Paul.

'Don't delude yourself,' she said. 'You will be lucky if you see Daniel for an hour a week.'

Paul's intensity matched her own.

'On the contrary. I don't want to do this, but if I apply for custody of my son, I have a very good chance of getting it. I know there's a presumption in favour of the mother – but not when the mother's mistreating the child.'

Sarah said: 'Mistreating?'

Rose came to the door and said: 'Excuse me, Mrs Copeland –'

'Furthermore,' said Paul, 'the child's choice is taken into account. And Daniel's choice is quite clear. He wants to be with his father.'

Sarah stood still for a moment, looking at her husband. Then she turned to Rose and said: 'What is it?'

'It's your managing director,' said Rose. 'I'm sorry, but he says it's very urgent indeed.'

Hamilton Forbes and Kent was in partial darkness. In the huge, empty reception area, only a few lights had been left on. David Postgate looked out over it as he sat in his secretary's office. He waited. He had been waiting some time already. Then Sarah's voice came through the phone's speaker.

'David,' she said, 'this is the worst possible time to call. My husband's here for the first time in two weeks –'

David picked up the receiver and spoke.

'Sarah, you don't understand. I wouldn't have kept calling you this evening if it wasn't crucial for both of us. The meeting's still going on –'

'Where?' asked Sarah.

'In the board room.'

'Why aren't you there?'

'I've come up to Alessandra's office to talk to you,' said David. 'Listen, Sarah. I still don't know which way the board will vote. Could go either way –'

'What can I do about that?' she asked.

David looked across the vast shadowy space of the agency's reception area. There was no one in sight.

'The board want you to come in and talk to them,' he said. 'They want a second opinion as to whether we can keep our largest accounts with us. And whether we'll hold the political account. Who else can I ask? Gordon wants me out. Stephen – I never know which way Stephen will jump –' He dabbed at his lip, which was bleeding, with a white handkerchief. 'Let me put it this way, Sarah. If you can't come in this evening, that's your decision. But it is very finely balanced: me and Simon Forbes against the rest. I may very well lose my job – I'd say it was quite likely.'

'Where does that leave me?' she asked.

'After what you did today,' said David, 'it may leave you somewhere out in the cold. Listen. You must decide. I'll come out to reception in twenty-five minutes. If you're not there – well, I shall understand.'

He paused. Sarah said nothing.

'And I must get back to the boardroom.' David put down the phone and walked slowly down the stairs. Somewhere, in another empty office, a phone was ringing.

In Sarah's house, Paul was coming downstairs. His wife was putting on her coat.

'Rose is still with him, but he's asleep,' said Paul. He looked at Sarah's coat. 'You're not going out?'

'I don't think it's a good idea if we talk any more tonight,' said Sarah. 'We may say things that are hard to forget.' She picked up the keys of her BMW. 'Will you be here when I get back?'

Paul said nothing. Sarah waited, then went out, closing the front door quietly behind her. Paul opened the door and watched the car accelerate along the western side of the square. Then he closed the door and looked around the hall.

The phone rang, as it had been doing all evening. It was a highly contemporary phone incorporating an extensive electronic memory, a bank of pushbutton controls, and an answer machine. Paul put it on the floor and stamped on it. The ringing stopped. From the guts of the machine spewed yard after yard of recording tape. Paul picked up festoons of this tape and draped it around the hall.

Rose, coming down stairs, stopped to watch him.

'It's all right, Rose,' said Paul. I'm on my way out.' He dragged another skein of tape from the shattered machine.

'I just wanted to leave something for Sarah,' he said.

NINE

Two days later, at four in the afternoon, a limousine left Downing Street and drove down the Mall. The Prime Minister was on his way to request the Queen's dissolution of Parliament.

To most of the country, it was an unexpected decision. Only a few people knew the election's precise timing. Several of them were gathered at Hamilton Forbes and Kent, in the office of the managing director, David Postgate.

David had survived the board's attempt to terminate his contract. It was not a decisive victory, for the board refused to endorse his American takeover; but nor was it a defeat. David was still in place. He presided over the afternoon's political status meeting with an air of alert confidence; as if the events of the past forty-eight hours had never happened. Part of his mind, however, was actively engaged on them. He was deciding what to do with his deputy, Gordon Lochhead, who was now addressing the Minister of State for Army Affairs, summarising progress on the Party's advertising campaign.

'We, here,' Gordon was saying, 'have known, of course, for some time that Parliament would be dissolved this afternoon. Otherwise we could not have prepared the work which you, Minister, are about to review.'

Geoffrey Talbot, Minister of State, glanced ostentatiously at his watch.

'I shall be brief,' said Gordon. 'Let me just say that the fact of having a head start on the opposition parties makes it all the more urgent to maintain campaign momentum. Over the last few weeks, opinion polls have been – to put it mildly – less than encouraging –'

'We are very familiar with the polls, Gordon,' said Francis

Salk, who was sitting beside the Minister. 'The question is, surely, how to change them.'

'Exactly, Francis,' said Gordon. 'From today, we can go public with the election package that we have been preparing over the past weeks.' He indicated the advertisement roughs pinned around the walls of the conference room, and the cassettes of party election broadcasts which were stacked at the end of the table. 'We can now reach the British public with the work we have here. Work which, we trust, will be crucial in winning the present election.'

'I'll leave him in place for a while,' David decided.

Alessandra, David's blonde P.A., knocked on the door and entered.

'Message for Mr Salk,' she said.

Francis unfolded the note.

'PM's reached the Palace,' he said. 'Starter's orders. Let us have a look at this work which you say is bound to win us the race.'

'Stephen Hallam is going to take us through the opening stages of the campaign,' said David. 'Lights down, please.'

Before the lights were dimmed, David passed a note to Sarah, who was sitting two away from him. The note read: *We should meet. After the board meeting?*

Sarah read the note, then put it into her leather clipboard. She was well aware that Stephen picked up discarded communications. He was not ashamed of it; he had the notion that information equalled power – though, as Sarah had told him, he so far had a good deal more of the first than the second.

'We launch the election campaign,' said Stephen, as the lights went down, 'with an all-out affirmation of the government's commitment to the Health Service.' He used a keypad, and the screen at the end of the room filled with a close-up of an attractive young nurse. 'We have this staff nurse – Judy Axford – in our first broadcast. She is, of course, a real nurse, from one of our London hospitals. We hear her asserting that the National Health Service is, if you will forgive the expression, in good health.'

Geoffrey Talbot surveyed the enlarged image of the nurse.

'Important not to use actors in this business,' he said. 'Some difficulty over that in the last election.'

'There's no doubt that this woman is a staff nurse,' said Sarah. 'She has several years' experience. Helen Marriott and I researched her thoroughly. She camera-tested extremely well. All our voters' panels gave Nurse Axford a very high rating for warmth and credibility. In short, if she says the NHS is in good hands, she's believable.'

'We chose to start with the Health Service,' said Gordon, 'because our polls showed that this was a prime concern of undecided voters.'

'Who feel that the Sevice has been underfunded,' added Stephen.

'Misled by a lot of nonsensical statistics,' said the Minister.

'Indeed,' said Stephen. 'And, for precisely that reason, we shall saturate the print media with National Health advertisements. . . . Can we have the lights up again?'

Stan, in the control room, brought up the lights; Stephen indicated the full-page press advertisements on the far wall of the room. They were dominated by images of Judy Axford in her nurse's uniform.

'You will see that in print we follow through the theme of the young nurse,' said Stephen. 'We then go into the amount of money that's been spent on the Service – pay rises – new hospitals started – equipment ordered –'

'That, Minister,' said Sarah, 'is our first answer to those who say the Health Service had been seriously cut during your present term of office.'

'And, we think, a very powerful start to the whole election campaign,' said David.

Some time later, Nick Faulds came into the conference room. The progress meeting on the political account had ended some minutes earlier, but Sarah was still sitting at the table, with her leather clipboard open in front of her.

'Working?' asked Nick.

'For the moment, no,' said Sarah. With dismay, she noted

that her reaction to Nick was as unsettling as when he first came back from Barbados. 'Thinking. Has anyone told you, Nick, that you're losing all that tropical tan?'

'Any number of people,' said Nick. 'Once you get back here, it vanishes. I've come to tell you, it's Dee's birthday.'

'I know,' said Sarah. 'I just haven't had time to buy her a card.'

Nick perched himself on the edge of the conference room table.

'Buy her a drink,' he said. 'The whole department's gone down to the Blue Posts. I've been sent back to invite you.'

Sarah put finger and thumb around Nick's left wrist. They didn't meet.

'Do you mind? Coming back to look for me?'

Nick shook his head, and Sarah resisted an impulse to touch his hair.

'I wanted to see you,' he said. 'Look, if you can't face the whole crowd of them, would you rather go somewhere quiet? Hennessey's? The Greenhouse?'

'With you,' said Sarah, 'I'd love to. But tonight, no. Have to go home.'

'Still no Paul?'

'Still no Paul. He's been back to the house once.'

'And?'

'And,' said Sarah, 'it was like one of those endless dreams, where everything you do – whatever you do – it all comes out wrong. Unavoidably, disastrously *wrong*. Looking back, I think we were both trying to get things together again –' She paused. 'Just didn't work.'

Nick covered Sarah's hand with his own.

'Do you want to, sort of – tell me what happened?'

'Not much,' said Sarah. 'But I will.' She thought, then said: 'We just seemed to be helpless. Kept slipping into the past. Recriminations we didn't intend – We'd start to say something, and it came out completely different. Distorted. You know? It was like swimming, when there's something dragging you down. . . . As if there was something dragging both of us down. And – I suppose there was.'

'What was that?'

'Oh, nothing dramatic,' she said. 'Just nine shared years.'

Sarah gently removed Nick's hand, then stood and went towards the door.

'What about you? Heard from Sally?'

'Hasn't written to me,' said Nick. 'But Alessandra says she's flying home tonight.' He paused. 'She hasn't asked me to meet her.'

'No,' said Sarah. 'I imagine David will be doing that.'

In the early hours of the morning, Sally walked out of Heathrow's Terminal Three. David Postgate carried her bag. They walked sedately, like father and daughter, until they reached the car park where David had left his Ferrari Testarossa. Then Sally sprang at him. Unbalanced by the bag, he went backwards and almost fell.

'Oh, David,' she said, 'come on – put that damn bag down. I want to kiss you.'

David finally freed his mouth. He looked around the car park.

'No one's going to see you! Not out here,' said Sally. 'It's dark. Oooh, I have missed you.'

'But when you rang –'

'Oh, that,' said Sally. 'Well, I said that to make you feel better. You sounded so down. But, really, I didn't enjoy it over there; not after you left. Well, I did, bits of it, I mean, it was sweet of you, and I'm glad I got to know New York, but, oh, I really wanted to be over here, in bed with you. I kept thinking – what's happened with the board meeting – and then you called, and said you survived –'

'By the skin of my teeth,' said David.

'I really like your teeth,' said Sally, kissing them. 'But then you said there's going to be another vote in three weeks – and I was sitting over there in the Plaza, wondering – I was thinking: which way's it going to go? Is David really going to hold on to the agency, or is he just saying that to make me feel better? Is he still going to be my boss when I get back? Or just my lover?'

'Sally – do you want answers to any of those questions?'

'Yes. All of them,' said Sally. Then she broke away and ran to the Ferrari. She leaned on its low roof and watched David. She looked younger than his own daughter.

'No, sir. Actually, what I really want to do,' she said, 'is get in the car and kiss you properly. And a few other things.'

TEN

As David was driving Sally back from Heathrow, Nurse Judy Axford came out of the North London Hospital for Women. She was wearing her uniform; she had just come off night duty. She walked slowly across the street to a public phone box, and tried to put a coin in the slot. The phone was out of order. She said something under breath, and walked down the dark, rubbish-littered road until she found another phone box. This time it accepted her coin, and she dialled the number of Sarah Copeland's house. She waited. There was a high, humming tone and the phone was disconnected.

As Judy Axford was trying to phone her, Sarah was getting out of bed. For a few moments, she sat naked in an armchair, watching the lime trees in her garden move in the night wind. In her mind, she ran through the day's agenda, and rehearsed what she would say when she was interviewed for the post of creative director. Then Daniel called again, and she knew what had woken her.

Sarah put on a nightdress and went into the child's room. A tiny electric nightlight glowed beside his bed. She knelt down and cradled her son's small, hot body. For a moment he was tense; then, like a young animal, he burrowed his head between her breasts.

For what seemed a long time, there was silence. For the hundredth time, Sarah wondered what effect Paul's absence would have on their son. She bent her head to his. Daniel's breathing was easier. He lifted his head and looked around his bedroom.

'It was so burning in the tunnel,' he said. 'I want a drink.'

Sarah led Daniel down to the kitchen. He was still very quiet; and now he shivered occasionally.

'It'll be all right, my love.'

Sarah opened the cupboard.

'Would you like some cocoa?'

'Chocolate,' said Daniel. 'Made with milk.' There was a pause, then he said: 'It was in a sort of cave, like when we went down where they used to dig coal, except it was all slippery, so I couldn't stand up.

Sarah switched on the kettle.

'Try not to think about it, my love.'

'And there was this big person, he was lying down, holding my hand –'

'Was it a man, or was it a woman?'

'He was very big,' said Daniel, 'but he hadn't got a face, and he kept sliding back down, along the floor, and he wanted me to pull him up, but I couldn't, and he was pulling me down, and it was very hot, and then he pulled me over the edge, and I fell down for miles and miles –'

'– and then you gave that big jump in bed, and shouted –'

'– and you came and woke me up,' said Daniel. 'Why didn't Rose come? Rose always comes when I have a dream. Why didn't she come?'

The phone began to ring.

'Well, I think Rose was very sound asleep,' said Sarah. 'But she'll be getting up soon, because she wants to go before the traffic –'

'Does Rose's sister live in – Sussex –?'

Sarah gave Daniel his drinking chocolate.

'In Sussex. Where they've got a lamb, and a goat, and nine ducklings –'

The phone rang again.

'I don't like goats, because they smell. You should answer the phone. It might be Daddy.'

In a phone box on the Harrow Road, Judy Axford was leaning back against the door, and rubbing the left side of her forehead with one hand. She spoke slowly.

'Is that Mrs Copeland? I'm sorry to ring you so early in the morning – I suppose really it's still the night –'

'Who is this?' asked Sarah.

'Oh, yes. Sorry,' said Judy. 'It's Nurse Axford here. Judy Axford. The nurse in your advertisement about the Health Service –' She listened, then said: 'Yes. Good morning to you – but you see, that's what I was ringing about. I don't want you to use my picture.'

There was a silence. Sarah felt for a moment as if she were a child again, in a Kentish village, summoned by teachers for some unknown but undoubtedly dreadful crime. She put a hand against the wall to steady herself.

'Are you there, Mrs Copeland?' asked the nurse.

'I'm still here,' said Sarah. 'I'm just not sure I heard that right, Judy. I can't believe you're saying that. At this stage – when the election's just been announced – you're telling me you don't want the agency to use your image in our advertisements about the National Health Service. Is that what you're saying?'

'Well,' said Judy. 'Yes. That's right. You see –'

'Judy,' interrupted Sarah, 'you can't realise what you're doing. For a start, you are destoying my campaign. I don't have time to find anyone else and re-shoot the material. Secondly, it may be more serious than that. It may have very serious consequences for the government.'

In the kitchen, Daniel sat at the table, watching his mother talking on the phone. He was used to her being on the phone; when he thought about it, he imagined that everybody's mother had phone calls about their work in the morning and in the evening. He used his spoon to get the unmelted chocolate from the bottom of his mug. While he was doing that, Rose came into the kitchen. She was dressed, as usual, in jeans and a shirt. She carried the newspapers that had just been delivered. The headline of the *Mirror*, which was on top of the pile, read: Election! It's on!

'You didn't wake me when I had a dream, Rose,' said Daniel. 'And I decided. I'm taking all my battleships to Sussex, in case there's a fire.'

Rose bent down and kissed him; then she looked at Sarah, who was putting the receiver back on the wallphone.

'Sarah – are you all right? You look as if – someone's died–'

'Some thing's died. My National Health campaign.'

Sarah indicated a proof of the first National Health ad, which was pinned on the kitchen noticeboard. Judy Axford's image stared confidently back at her.

'She – the nurse – she won't let us use her picture.'

'When are you printing the advertisement?' asked Rose.

'Tomorrow,' said Sarah. 'At least, we were.' 'And I've just remembered, I have to look decent. On top of everything else, it's my interview day.'

'Who do you know that their bones broke?' Daniel called from the kitchen.

Rose found a Bruce Oldfield suit, already pressed, and passed it to Sarah.

'I didn't think they had interviews in your business?'

'They're not called interviews,' said Sarah, as she went up the stairs. 'There are, in quotes, informal chats with the top people. But it comes to the same thing – either they give you a place on the board, or they don't.' She came back down stairs and keyed Helen's number into the hall phone. 'And, Rose – before you set off for Sussex – can you get the gas people back? And do the window boxes – they look a touch jaded on the study side. And when you're driving, be careful of the Saab. It's got that turbo thing, frightens the hell out of you.'

'It frightens other people,' said Rose.

'That too,' agreed Sarah. 'I'll have to dash, if I'm going to do something about this damn nurse.' She went into her bedroom and started dressing. Rose came into the room carrying a shirt. From the phone's speaker came the sound of Helen's recorded voice, saying that she couldn't, just now, answer the phone.

Sarah said, more to herself than to Rose: 'Damn. Her machine's on.' She waited for a bleep, then spoke to answer-phone. 'Helen – it's Sarah. If you do get this, can you call in on your way to work? We have a major problem with the nurse in the National Health ads.'

Paul was sitting on a couch in the living room of Helen's flat.

He was wearing trousers and a shirt, and his legs were covered by a duvet. From the answer machine on the other side of the room, he could hear his wife's voice.

'I want to talk through whether we change the campaign,' she was saying. 'See if there's still time. I'll meet you either now – come round here – or we can have lunch later.' There was the sound of a receiver being replaced, and the machine cut out.

As the message ended, Helen appeared in the doorway. She was carrying her shoes.

'If you're in here, Paul, why didn't you answer the phone?'

'It was a message about your work,' said Paul.

'And it was from your wife,' said Helen. There was a pause, as she took in the state of his clothes. 'It's not that I don't sympathise, Paul. I know you're having a miserable time. When Ian walked out on me I was catatonic for weeks. But –'

'But –?' asked Paul.

'But you really can't just stay here like this.'

'I suppose you want your living room,' he said.

Helen sat down on the end of the couch and wriggled her feet into her shoes. She was somewhere between laughter and annoyance.

'Well – the room – that's part of it, I suppose. But really, it's the least of my problems. You seem to forget that Sarah's one of my closest friends. I knew Sarah long before I knew you. How do you think I feel – with her husband in my flat? She's wondering where you are – and you say I can't tell her. It makes me feel like – I don't know, a mistress.' She paused and thought. 'Certainly I don't feel like Sarah's friend.'

Paul began to fold the duvet.

'You don't feel like her friend. I don't feel like her husband,' he said. 'I told you what happened when I went to see her. I went to discuss the marriage. I wanted to be quite reasonable – admit there were faults on both sides, see what we could sort out – and you know what she did. She talked on the phone all evening. To bloody whatsisface. Your managing director.'

'To David.'

'That damn David Postgate.'

'You told me,' said Helen. 'Look – if there is a crisis at work – I must go.'

She went to the living room table and began to sort through her files of computer data.

'She talked to David all evening. I said: "Sarah, that's what it's about. That's why I left. You don't have a life outside work. There's no room for a marriage –"'

'You did choose the worst of times,' said Helen. 'David nearly lost his job that night. Sarah would have gone too.' She looked around the room. 'Listen. If you're staying, how about tidying up this place? And if anyone else calls, I'm on my way to the agency.'

Paul walked across to block the doorway.

'I thought we might work out a different arrangement here. I could contribute financially –'

'Different arrangement?' asked Helen. 'You and me? You mean you want to share the flat?'

Paul nodded.

'First, you really do have to settle with Sarah.'

'Always Sarah,' said Paul.

'You're still married to her,' said Helen. 'Maybe more than you think.' She put her hands on Paul's arms, and moved him gently out of the doorway. 'And, Paul – it's a bit personal – but how about having a shower?' She pointed towards the bathroom. 'Use whatever you want in there. No one'll interrupt you.'

Despite the motorway, Stephen arrived at the agency before either Helen or Sarah. He gave a passionless morning kiss to the beautiful Alessandra, who was covering reception for Jane, then went straight into Gordon Lochhead's office. Gordon was standing at the far end of the long room, looking out of the bay windows and down over St James's.

'I hear you have the minutes of the meeting. The board meeting,' said Stephen.

Gordon did not turn round.

'In the fullness of time, they arrived. Left hand side of the desk.'

Stephen picked a sheaf of typed notes out of Gordon's in-tray. He scanned them with professional speed.

'*Mr Postgate arrived some twenty minutes after start of meeting . . . lateness due to flight from New York . . .* da da-da . . .*board agrees to delay decision on bid for New York agency –*' He looked across the room at Gordon, who still had not moved. 'You know what David's done? He's screwed the lot of you.'

'By no means,' said Gordon. 'The board might still undo this New York nonsense –'

'AIDS might help your sex life,' said Stephen. He held up a promotional brochure for Pater Paolozzi, New York, which was clipped to the minutes. The brochure listed some of the agency's main branches: LA, Houston, Chicago, Toronto, Ottawa, Montreal, São Paulo, Buenos Aires, Sydney, Melbourne, Auckland, Singapore, and Hong Kong.

'Listen. If David's in London – telling them he's bought this truly global agency' – Stephen dropped the brochure into Gordon's waste bin – 'face it: we are out of the game.'

'That is unduly –' began Gordon.

'No,' said Stephen, 'believe me, it is not unduly. Gordon: as they say, so elegantly, in New York – you had just one chance to fix David's ass. That's when he was getting into Sally's. For two days, he's in the Plaza, he's in Sally, he's out of action.'

'Sarah brought him back to London –'

'Indeed. Sarah brought him back to London.' Stephen picked up the minutes, then dropped them back on Gordon's desk. 'Look at it. You and the board – you had David by the balls. You let him off the hook. Now – believe me – you ought to take the money and run. Put on your golden parachute. Take whatever staff you want; grab the big accounts; get out of this place.'

Gordon went back to the bay window.

'You still have this idea of a breakaway agency?'

'If you wanted, we could do it tomorrow. Lochhead and Hallam. Or Lochhead Hallam and Copeland if we went in with Sarah – We'd get it up and running, wait a couple of years, then go public. Make ourselves two or three million on the USM. . . . Short of selling State assets, few things could be easier.' He checked the time. 'Think about it.' He went to the door. 'I have a meeting with the said Sarah.'

As Stephen was going out, Gordon said: 'The board votes again in three weeks. I assure you – I can still ease David out of this agency.'

Stephen turned. He seemed about to say something forcible; then he changed his mind.

'Well. Make sure you have that sentence the right way round,' he suggested, as he went in search of Sarah.

Stephen went down blue-green staircase, and across reception. He waved to Jane, who was back on duty and talking to Carol; then paused, as he saw Sarah's secretary, Sally, come in from the street.

Carol had also seen Sally.

'You know,' she said, 'Sally never even *went* to Rome –'

'Ah. Sally,' said Stephen. 'Home from the honeymoon. You've been much missed. How was New York?'

'Now, Stephen,' said Jane.

There was a pause. Sally looked at Stephen, then at Carol and Jane. Finally she said: 'Everyone knows . . . about New York?'

'Unless we have any deaf mutes,' said Stephen. To Jane, he added: 'Seen Sarah?' And to Sally: 'Who has, incidentally, missed you very much. Not having another secretary.'

'Sarah's upstairs,' said Jane. 'Looking for that nurse.'

'I'll come up with you,' Stephen suggested to Sally. She shook her head and Stephen thought, not for the first time, how extraordinarily attractive she was. He wondered, also not for the first time, how David Postgate had managed to get her into bed. He spoke to her in a low, confidential tone.

'You remember the biblical king David? Old and stricken in years?'

'Please, Stephen,' said Sally. 'Not now. This is my first day back.'

'As I recall,' said Stephen, 'the good book says: they sought David a virgin – "and the damsel was very fair: and she cherished the king and ministered to him; but the king knew her not." The lift doors opened and he got in. 'You might learn something from looking at the Bible, Sally.'

In the conference room, Sarah, Linda and Helen were reviewing the National Health advertising, to see whether it would work without Judy Axford. The screen showed a huge close-up of the nurse, looking straight to camera. Sarah surveyed it without enthusiasm.

'The whole thing hangs on that woman,' she said. 'Take her out, and it all falls to pieces.'

'Legally,' said Helen, 'she can't do this. She's contracted to appear.'

Stephen came in to the conference room and closed the door.

'If you're talking about that nurse, she could make a great deal of trouble with the press,' he said. 'If we keep her to a contract she doesn't want to honour. I've told production to hold the press ads.' He looked at Sarah. 'Can we cut the woman out?'

'Means a complete re-shoot,' said Sarah.

'Complete re-*think*.' said Linda. 'We'd need a new concept.' She switched a video recorder to play. 'There's her section of the party political.'

A monitor showed Judy Axford speaking persuasively to camera.

'– I wouldn't say the Health Service has really been cut – it's more like pruning –'

'Can't lose her there,' remarked Sarah. To Stephen she said: 'This is impossible. The nurse goes – the whole National Health sector goes. We've got her in cinemas as well –'

Linda switched to back-projected film. The screen showed an even larger image of Nurse Axford. 'As a nurse,' she was saying, 'all I can say about the Health Service is . . . it's in good health –'

'All right, Stephen,' said Sarah. 'Tell me how we lose the nurse in that lot.'

'Rewrite. Re-shoot. No other way.'

Sarah stood and faced her account director.

'Fine. We scrap the National Health ads because' – she indicated the screen – 'a twenty-seven-year-old staff nurse has a sudden attack of conscience. It's absurd. The woman's legally contracted.'

'A contract,' said Stephen, 'is not going to stop her telling some friendly reporter that we ran these ads against her will. How's that going to look as a front-page story?'

'I can't really see any of the nationals wanting to embarrass the Prime Minister,' remarked Helen. 'Not with the proprietors we have now.'

'And do you really think,' Sarah asked Stephen, 'that I can take writers and art directors off the nuclear campaign? I can tell them, go on, do the Health Service again? That I can say: You've got twenty-four hours, starting from scratch? Press ads for Friday? TV for Tuesday?'

'It's possible,' said Stephen. 'Just possible.'

Sarah moved to the door.

'Dear God. In that time –' she enumerated: '– we also have to sell the bomb to the British public. We have to explain why unemployment's good for them – and then convince them the schools are OK, pensions are adequate, and the economy's basically healthy, despite the fact that the oil money ran away somewhere. Be serious, Stephen. The only way we save this National Health stuff is by getting that bloody woman to change her mind. Appear in the ads.'

'Meaning what?' asked Stephen.

'Meaning: you find where she's gone. I'll talk her round.'

Stephen followed Sarah out of the conference room.

'You assume that I couldn't persuade her – but you can?'

'It may be a matter of gender,' said Sarah. 'Some women don't fall for your masculine charm.'

'A minority.'

'But growing, Stephen,' said Sarah. She called to Carol, who was passing. 'Carol – has Sally come in?'

'She's in the creative department,' said Carol.

In the creative department, Nick came out of Mike Sutherland's office and almost ran into Sally.

There was an awkward pause: they had not seen each other since Sally walked out of Nick's flat, and out of his life, three weeks before.

'Well,' said Nick finally. 'Welcome back. How was – How was New York?'

'I was in Rome, wasn't I?' said Sally. 'Bloody ad agencies – the *gossip*.' She looked directly at Nick and said: 'I'm really sorry.'

'Sorry for what?

'Walking out on you like that. You knew I was over there with David?'

'Whole agency knows,' said Nick. Suddenly his tone changed. 'How could you do that – with *David*? The guy's so old. Must be like having it off with your father.'

Sally stared at him. It was hard to interpret the expression on her face.

'First Stephen – now you,' she said. 'Do you ever think I might have some feelings about David?'

She turned abruptly, went into the women's room, and shut the door. Nick was about to open it when Dee came past, carrying roughs of her unemployment ads.

'What's happened to Sally?' she asked.

'She's just done a quick bit of castration,' said Nick. 'Now, she's redoing her face. Do you know anyone who wants a room?'

'What are you on about?' asked Dee.

'Someone to take Sally's place. In my flat.'

'Oh, no,' said Dee. 'Leave me out of this one.' She went across the department to catch Sarah, who had just come up the stairs in animated conversation with Stephen.

'Don't give me game plans,' Sarah was saying. 'Just help me find the damn nurse. The hospital either don't know where she is – or won't say. Get your secretary on to it.'

'You could do the same with yours,' said Stephen. He indicated Sally as he went into his own office.

Sarah turned. She took the roughs that Dee offered without looking at them. Both women stood for a moment watching Nick. He had caught Sally's wrist as she came out of the loo, and continued their interchange as if there had been no break.

'What you're saying is – you'd give up three years of our life for some rich old man with a house in Hampstead –'

'David's not old,' said Sally. 'And it never was *our* life. It was me putting away your Yardbirds records, and you using the last of my cleansing cream.'

Sarah left Dee and went quickly across the department.

'Well, I've cured that problem,' said Nick. 'I just told Dee she could have your room.'

'My room? All my clothes are there –'

Sarah interrupted before Nick could speak.

'Now that you've finally come back,' she said to Sally, 'will you start using the phone?'

'I was getting your mail,' said Sally.

'So I see,' said Sarah. 'Right now, it's a missing woman we need.'

Sarah followed Sally into her office. She took a note from her clipboard and put it down in front of her secretary.

'This woman, Judy Axford, is an SRN: a state registered nurse. Works at North London Women's Hospital. She called me this morning, said she wanted out of the NHS ads – then disappeared.' She indicated two phone numbers. 'That's her work number. That's her home number. We already know she's not at her home address. Get on the phone till you find her. Get a messenger, tell him to bike round all the addresses she's used. Try her friends – try the nurses she's worked with. Say I want to talk to her – as in: have to. Otherwise, there's going to be some large blank spaces in the papers tomorrow.'

Sally was about to say something. She thought better of it, and picked up the phone. Sarah went round to her own office. On the way, she passed Nick, who was giving copy to Carol.

'That was a bit hard on Sally,' he said. 'When she's just come back.'

Carol went slowly towards the lifts, trying to hear Sarah's reply.

'And you were just having a friendly chat when I arrived?' asked Sarah. 'Listen, Nick: it may be different for you, but Sally and I have a strictly work relationship.'

'I'm not sure it is different for me.'

'Now Sally's finally back from wherever she was,' said Sarah, 'I want her working. Change of subject: what do you know about intermediate-range missiles?'

Nick was taken aback by this conversational shift.

'Well, now you ask,' he said, 'not a lot.'

Sarah extracted a Ministry of Defence document from her clipboard and passed it to him.

'Then read that,' she said. 'Ministry brief. You've got till three o'clock. By then I want some concepts. Convince the punters they need more American warheads around the country. Final question: have you sighted my elusive art director?'

'Warren?' said Nick. 'He went over to the studio. Said he was in search of the perfect back.'

In the stills studio, Warren was staring gloomily at a young model. The model looked nervously back at him.

'They're all in my book,' she said. 'That's all the shots I've got.'

Warren turned over the pages of her portfolio.

'No back shots,' he said.

Marika shook her head.

'It's a sportswear ad,' said Warren. 'We want your back. Turn around, take your shirt off, will you?'

She turned away and began to unbutton her shirt. Dee came into the studio and looked from the model to Warren.

'Sarah wants to know,' said Dee, 'one; do you have any ideas about contacting that nurse we used in the NHS ads? Two; aren't you supposed to be working with her? And three; where's the reference for the Russian tanks?'

'No to the first,' said Warren. 'I know, to the second. As for Russian tanks – I'm getting like one of those hydrangea-hat ladies. I'm starting to dream about Russian tanks. Five minutes – I'll come across and give you the pix.'

The model was now naked from the waist up. She had an elegant back, with three noticable marks at the base of her neck.

'What's that on your neck, love?' asked Warren.

Marika craned around, trying to see the back of her own neck. It went a gentle shade of pink, accentuating the marks.

'I think they must be – sort of, bites,' she said.

Warren pointed to a doorway at the left of the studio.

'Over there, where Dee's going. That's makeup. Go and ask for Fran. Get her to put some pan-stick on your neck. Then get Robin – wherever he is – to take some snaps of your back.'

The model began to put her shirt back on.

'And listen,' said Warren, 'if you're doing body shots, keep your dog tied up, my love.' He picked up his layout pad and followed Dee out of the studio.

In their shared office, Sarah was waiting for Warren; and, against her better judgment, thinking about Nick. She tried to invent some excuse for going across to his workspace, and was in fact on her way out the door when Stephen appeared. Feeling oddly guilty, Sarah retreated to her desk.

Stephen, who could be uncomfortably sensitive, watched her with interest.

'You look a mite uneasy, my dear,' he said. 'But we're not here to discuss your deeper feminine feelings, are we? We're here to discuss this missing nurse – in search of whom Annabel has been phoning the Health Authority. But the Health Authority do not give information about individual employees. You've got a bike messenger out?'

Sarah nodded. She pointed through a glass partition at her secretary, who was talking on the phone.

'And Sally's still chasing. So is Helen, I imagine.'

'Half the very expensive staff of this agency is looking for that nurse,' said Stephen. He moved away to find Gordon as Warren came into the office.

'We're late with the nuclear campaign,' said Sarah to Warren. 'We need three more full pages. Run in the national heavies.'

Warren sat down at his own desk, opened a layout pad, and waited.

'Where do we start, then?'

'We start from the assumption that people are worried about nuclear weapons,' said Sarah. 'The government's saying, let's accept that: let's not pretend otherwise.'

'Reasonable,' said Warren.

'Remember what the Minister said last Monday?'

'These days,' said Warren, 'I meet so many Ministers. Which one was this?'

'Minister for Army Affairs. Anyway: his line is we should demystify the whole nuclear business. Let's get out and sell the bomb. Same way you sell any other product. Facts, figures, prices, product benefits. Like a new car. Or,' – she indicated an advertisement for kitchenware on the magnet board – 'like a fridge.'

'Wasn't a fridge they dropped on Japan,' said Warren.

'They didn't need to sell it, either,' said Sarah. 'Just deliver.' She held up a blank pad and indicated spaces within its white rectangle. 'Why not have the whole Soviet arsenal at the top of the page? The lot. Headline: *Threat*.'

Warren lettered the word rapidly across the top of his layout pad.

'OK,' said Sarah. 'Then – just small pix – the Russian ICBMs.' She glanced at her copy of the defence brief. 'There's SS-11, SS-13, SS-17, SS-18, SS-19.'

Warren sketched in the missiles.

'Where do you get this stuff from?'

'I read the brief,' said Sarah. 'Then we've got the Soviet submarine-launched missiles. SS-N-5, SS-N-6, SS-N-8, SS-N-18, SS-NX-20. . . . That's, like two thirds of the page – let's see?'

Warren held up his rough. Sarah surveyed it. Sally tapped on the office door, came in, and waited to speak.

'Then, second headline: *Protection*. And a small cut-out shot, just one of our subs. Lonely. Lot of white space round it. And really dwarfed by this massive arsenal up above. With a caption: *The British nuclear submarine*.'

Warren sketched the vessel.

'American nuclear submarine.'

'Excuse me, Sarah,' said Sally, at the door of the office, 'but they still can't find the nurse –'

'One moment,' said Sarah. She was making notes. 'Then copy – on the lines of: Our nuclear submarine force is worth every penny –'

'Of twelve billion?'

'And a really strong tagline,' said Sarah.

'Eternal Peace?' suggested Warren, drawing tramlines of body copy.

'Keep trying,' said Sarah to Sally. 'Try her local post office. Try all the chemists: they know nurses. The police. Whoever. I do need to talk to that woman.'

Sally looked as if she were about to say something; then decided not. She went back to her own office. Sarah's attention shifted back to Warren.

'If it's not a personal question,' she said, 'What's the suit for?'

There was a pause. Warren looked down at ad rough, then said: 'Same reason as you, really.'

Sarah was wearing the Oldfield suit Rose had pressed that morning. She glanced at it, then back to Warren.

'You're in for my job?'

Warren nodded.

'The job I've been doing for the last three months?'

'You're only acting creative director,' said Warren. 'No one's put your name on the chair.' He waited for Sarah to say something. She didn't. 'No one even says the job has to be on the copy side. Could be art.'

'So?' said Sarah.

'So,' said Warren, 'I had a word with David. He said I ought to come in and chat about it.'

'I see, said Sarah. 'Well: thanks for telling me.' She looked in the direction of the managing director's office. 'And thank you, David.'

* * *

David Postgate was in a meeting with Geoffrey Talbot and Francis Salk. The three men were reviewing possible scandals which might interrupt the smooth progress of the election. It was not a relaxed occasion.

Francis Salk passed a photocopied report to David.

'I trust we can keep it out of sight,' he said. 'But this might – just might – cause a spot of bother with the media.'

David scanned the report rapidly, and read a sentence from its conclusion.

'A construction company in which the Junior Minister maintains, (through nominees) a considerable financial interest –'

'Parlett Construction,' said Francis. 'Puts up public buildings all over the country.'

'Nothing wrong with private enterprise putting up public buildings, surely?'

'Oh, indeed not –' began the Minister.

'– if only they stayed up,' said Francis. 'But one or two of these buildings have, in fact, come down without warning. Fortunately, also without loss of life. Not the best advertisement for Ministerial enterprise.' He retrieved his report. 'However, the PM's dealing with it. Out of our court. Now. Any other business?'

David indicated the roughs which Nick had earlier left on his coffee table.

'The Prime Minister suggested that you should look at the first nuclear ads.'

'Ah,' said Francis. 'Tiny hitch. As of eleven-thirty, there are no nuclear ads.'

'I'm not sure I understand,' said David.

'We seem,' said Francis, 'to have lost a quantity of fissile material. The stuff of which these weapons are made.'

'You're not serious?' said David. 'How can one *lose* fissile material?

'Oh, variety of ways,' said Francis. 'It can be mislaid – you know how careless these military men are.'

'Or the stuff may be there all the time,' said the Minister. 'But the bookkeeping says it's not. It may be stolen – the

Israelis apparently pinched a whole shipload of the stuff. It's the last possibility which rather weighs on the PM's mind.'

'Extraordinary,' said David. 'Exactly what does the PM think might follow?

'Most unwisely,' said Francis, 'someone gave Neville that book – what was it called?'

'*The Irish Atom Bomb*,' said Geoffrey Talbot.

'Indeed. Meant to be a bit of light reading: bog-Irish lad makes bomb in Kilburn bedroom. The lad tells Downing Street that we may lose a largish part of central London . . . Load of nonsense, really. But it's made the PM very touchy about this stuff going missing. So – for the moment, I fear – no nuclear advertising.'

David stood up and went to the door.

'The PM's own words were: put the whole business on the back burner. Not, I thought, the happiest of locutions,' said Francis.

David opened the office door and called to Alessandra: 'Can you get Gordon and Sarah down here? Stop whatever else they're doing. I want them now.'

Three minutes later, Sarah and Gordon were sitting in David's office.

'Ah,' said Francis Salk, 'How very nice to see you, Mrs Copeland.'

Sarah wondered, not for the first time, what it was in Salk's psyche that generated his vivid contempt for women.

'Now,' said the Minister, 'if you will seat yourself comfortably – I have a slightly awkward item of news for you. We are putting the nuclear campaign, as they say, on hold. I was telling David: we seem to have mislaid some fissile material.'

There was a pause. Then Gordon said: 'you're talking about – plutonium –?'

'Not yet specified,' replied Francis. 'At least not for our innocent ears. But, undoubtedly, one of the nastier transuranics.'

'You're saying – someone broke into a weapons store?' asked Sarah.

'I imagine something much less sinister,' said Francis. 'Probably lost count of how much they had. Great deal of this stuff around the country now, you know. In one form or another.'

'But – you do know where it was lost?'

'Who can tell? Nuclear explosives apparently have quite a short shelf-life. Have to be refurbished, or whatever the word is. So. One has all these nuclear convoys trogging up to Faslane, loaded with warheads. Then back to Aldermaston – melt them down – metaphorically speaking – drive them up to Scotland again –'

'Terrifying vision.'

'Oh, indeed,' said Francis. 'They tell me it can't happen, but I always imagine – one icy stretch up there in the north – convoy in road accident – then: pouf – no more wretched Scottish politics. Indeed, no more Scotland.'

'As a Scot myself –' began Gordon.

'Oh, not the whole country, Lochhead,' said Francis. 'Figure of speech. But, quite seriously: you go trundling nuclear bits and pieces all round the shop – no wonder some of the stuff goes astray.'

'You mean,' said Sarah, 'you've lost plutonium before?'

'Very seldom,' said Francis. 'And I'm told it always turns up. But – three weeks to polling day – the PM thought we could perhaps pause in promoting the bomb.' He indicated the advertisement visuals. 'These might – just might – be embarrassing.'

'You realise the amount of work that's already gone into this campaign?' asked Sarah.

'Won't be wasted, my dear,' said Francis. 'Like the poor, the bomb is always with us –' He glanced at his watch and signalled to the Minister. 'For rather the same reasons, when one thinks about it.'

Alessandra knocked on the door and entered.

'Sorry to interupt,' she murmured to David, 'but there's a message for Sarah that I'm told won't wait.'

'We must leave you anyway,' said Geoffrey Talbot. 'Due back at Downing Street.'

Alessandra crossed the room and said quietly to Sarah: 'They've found the missing nurse.'

'Where, in fact, the three of us have our next meeting,' said Francis to David.

Sarah followed Alessandra out of the office.

'If you'll excuse me,' she said to the Minister, 'I'll go and stop work on the nuclear ads.' When the door closed behind her, she said to Alessandra: 'You did say they'd found the damn nurse?'

'I did,' said Alessandra. She handed over a phone-message sheet. 'One of your bike boys found her at that address. But apparently she's only there till four o'clock.'

'Phone my office,' said Sarah. 'And tell Sally I won't be back till five. Tell Warren to hold the nuclear stuff.' She went down the stairs to reception at a run.

'I'll be out for the next couple of hours,' she said to Jane, who was behind the desk. Moments later, Nick leaned over the mezzanine gallery.

'Where was Sarah going?' he asked.

'No idea,' called Jane. 'But she won't be back for a while.'

Nick called a lift and rode it down to the car park.

Sarah's BMW was edging its way into the Jermyn Street traffic when Nick tapped on the driver's window. Sarah touched a switch and the window went down.

'I was going to ask you –' said Nick.

Sarah glanced at the dashboard clock.

'Ask me what?'

'Whether you'd like to have a drink with me when you come back.'

Sarah considered; then smiled. Nick reflected that she should smile more often. It brought an unexpected glow of warmth to her face.

'I'd love that,' she said. 'Where?'

'I'm at home,' said Nick. He tore a page out of his Filofax and wrote his address. Sarah glanced at it.

'Sally's not there any more?' she asked.

Nick shook his head.

'That's one thing you don't have to worry about.'

'I'll call you on the carphone when I'm back in the West End,' said Sarah, 'when I'm through with this nurse. But first, as Mrs Beeton says, I have to catch her.'

Nick stood back from the car. Sarah rolled up the window, waved, and pulled out into the traffic.

ELEVEN

At the agency, the day's work was ending. People were moving to the Blue Posts for their first serious drink of the evening. Among them was Warren, Sarah's art director. When he had the barmaid's attention, he said to her:

'Vodka. A large one.'

Dee came into the bar and looked around for Warren. She asked Carol, who was standing with Jane, near the door. Carol pointed to the bar, where Warren was in dispute.

'If I'd wanted a double,' he was saying to the barmaid, 'I'd've said a double, wouldn't I?' The barmaid waited, glass poised. 'I want a large one.'

The barmaid reached up and measured a third and a fourth shot of vodka into the glass, as Dee elbowed her way to the bar.

'And a spritzer for the lady,' said Warren, topping up his drink with tonic.

Dee picked up the glass and looked at it.

'Warren,' she said. 'How much of that is vodka?'

Warren retrieved his glass.

'My aim,' he said, 'is to achieve the thinnest possible meniscus of tonic. And let me tell you, young lady – before you start one of your temperance lectures – that if ever there was a time when I needed something stronger than orange juice, that time is now. You could say it is a special occasion.'

'What special occasion?' asked Dee. The barmaid put a spritzer down in front of her, but she kept her eyes on Warren.

'Celebration,' he said. 'I now have an excuse to get out of this place.' He touched his glass against Dee's, and swallowed half of his drink. 'So. A toast: To arseholes everywhere.'

While Warren was starting his evening, Sarah was parking her BMW in Parnell Road. The car looked grossly out of place.

None of the new prosperity that Sarah wrote about in her advertisements had reached this neighbourhood. It was going down in the world, not up.

Sarah sat for a moment, looking down the street. Though she wrote copy aimed at working-class housewives, it was not the sort of place she often visited. Trees had been planted in the pavements, but most were broken or dead. Old newspapers had been stuffed into wire guards around the tree stumps; and stayed there. Many of the parked cars were on blocks, and the tarmac was oil-stained. There were no children in sight.

Sarah got out of her car, checked the house number Alessandra had given her, and made her way through a small front garden. The path was crazy-paved. A BMX bike, without tyres, was chained to the steps. Sarah rang the door bell, then knocked. Noise inside the house stopped for a moment, then started again. After some time, Judy Axford opened the door and stood looking at Sarah.

'I wondered if you'd come.'

'It was hard work finding you,' said Sarah. 'Hospital didn't have your address –'

'I've moved,' said Judy. She was still in the middle of the doorway. 'Did it occur to you I might not want to be found?'

There was a pause. Sarah was, for once, unable to think of the right reply. Judy waited. Then she said:

'I'll put the kids in the other room. And the dog. Then you'll have somewhere to sit down.'

Some moments later, Judy called Sarah in. She stood in the tiny sitting room, trying to imagine what it would be like to live in such a place. Judy Axford was still in the next room, trying to quieten her children. Sarah cleared away toys and sat on the edge of an aged armchair. A striped cat calculated the distance to Sarah's knee, and whether it would be wise to jump. Five minutes later, Judy came back into the room and closed the door behind her. Noise from the next room diminished, but did not disappear. Judy sat down and brushed the hair back from her face. For a moment, she looked like a younger, but more worn version of Sarah.

'Tea?'

Sarah shook her head.

'Judy,' she said. 'I want to talk about these advertisements you're doing for us.'

'I'm *not* doing, Mrs Copeland.'

Sarah drew breath.

'I didn't come here to stand on legalities,' she said. 'But in fact you are effectively contracted to our agency. You did accept a fee. And you did agree to appear as a nurse in a number of advertisements about the Health Service.'

'I know. And then –'

There was a crash as a child fell against the closed door of the bedroom.

Sarah opened her briefcase and took out the proof of a full-page press advertisement. Under the headline *The National Health Service is safe in her hands*, a picture of Judy took up most of the page.

'You wouldn't believe,' said Sarah, 'the hours of time that went into this.' She held up the proof. 'We've had copywriters, art directors, photographers, production men, typographers – all working on it. Then there are the Party election broadcasts, in which you appear –'

'I thought of all that,' said Judy.

'On the film inserts,' said Sarah, 'we have had producer, director, very expensive crews, lighting, sound, makeup, editors – we have even had Cabinet Ministers checking rushes –'

Judy was trying to hear what was happening in the next room.

'You say all that –'

'Wait a minute,' said Sarah. She displayed the press ad again. 'This is in all the newspapers tomorrow. And on poster hoardings. Your picture. Right across the country. You simply can't change your mind now.'

Judy sat, looking at her hands, which were folded in her lap.

'I didn't change my mind now,' she said finally. 'You know that. I changed it yesterday. I couldn't get through to you till this morning.'

Sarah drew breath.

'I don't understand,' she said. 'Why did you do the ads in the first place?'

From the next room came an unearthly, high-pitched scream. Judy stood up and opened the bedroom door a few inches.

'Sharon!'

There was a moment's silence from the bedroom, then a sound of jumping.

Judy came back to her chair.

'Sharon's all right. She just likes the noise.'

There was another, louder, scream.

'Sharon ought to work for Roger Corman,' said Sarah quietly.

'What was I saying?' asked Judy.

'Why you did the ads in the first place.'

'I needed the money,' said Judy. 'Haven't you heard what nurses are paid?'

'What *are* you paid?' asked Sarah.

Judy leaned over and picked up the proof that lay on the arm of Sarah's chair.

'Put it this way,' she said. 'I don't know how much you get for doing these advertisements – but I should think you get in a month about what I get in a year.'

There was a long pause. Sarah sat, desperately wondering what might change the nurse's mind. Finally, Judy stood up and walked into the kitchen.

'I'll make that tea,' she said.

Sarah came to the door and watched. The kitchen was small, not much more than a pantry, and it opened off the living room. It reminded Sarah of the Kentish suburb where she grew up. She stood in the doorway watching Judy scrub tea stains from a cup.

'I can see you needed the money,' she said, breaking the silence. 'What I can't see is why you changed your mind about the ads.'

Judy poured boiling water into a teapot. The pot had feet on it. One of them was broken.

'They're closing my wing of the hospital,' said the nurse. 'I have to move to the Lister. Other side of London.'

'Dear God,' said Sarah. 'Closing.'

Judy brought tea into the living room.

'And you don't want to move?'

'It's not that I don't want to,' said Judy. 'I can't afford to live over there.' She indicated the noise in the next room. 'Not with them.'

'Oh, God,' said Sarah.

'And then, I told the other nurses I was doing the advertisements,' said Judy. 'They said – well, they said: You just can't do it. You can't be in all the papers, saying everything's wonderful, when they're closing the hospitals down.'

Judy pointed toward the next house in the terrace.

'My neighbour: she's an OAP. Can't get her hip done. Hasn't got a local hospital now – How could I face her, Mrs Copeland?'

Judy Axford picked up the advertisement proof. For a moment she studied her printed picture in silence. Then she handed the proof back to Sarah.

'I'm sorry,' she said. 'I can't do it.'

In the Blue Posts, Warren was on his third vodka tonic. Across the pub, in what was known as the inglenook, Stephen Hallam was sitting close to Alessandra. His arm was around her shoulders, but he was watching the door.

'Now this,' he said, 'should be interesting. Warren's infant – searches gin palace for drink-crazed Daddy.'

Warren's daugher, Kim, looked uncertainly around the bar. Carol pointed to where her father was sitting. Stephen watched Kim edge through the crowd of drinkers.

'Nice kid, that,' he said to Alessandra. 'What was I saying to you?'

'You were telling me how good I was in bed,' said Alessandra demurely. 'And that we should do it again.'

'What a memory,' said Stephen. 'It's all that dictation you take. And how do you react to my indecent proposition?'

Alessandra pushed back her mane of blonde hair.

'I don't think I told you. It wasn't so good for me.'

Stephen's expression changed. He looked like a patient who has consulted his doctor about headaches, and been told that he also has a malignant tumour.

'You mean – it wasn't good in bed?' he said eventually.

Alessandra nodded. 'The performance,' she explained.

Stephen detached himself from her, stood up, and leaned over so that his face was close to Alessandra's.

'Well,' he said. 'The Sarah Bernhardt of the bedroom. And, since we're playing true confessions, do you know what I really thought of you? That night?'

Alessandra shook her head.

'I thought you were a beautiful, ballbreaking bitch.'

Alessandra sat watching Stephen push his way out of the pub. For some time, she didn't move. Then she stood up, ordered a Perrier with lemon, and joined Jane and Carol.

Forty-five minutes later, Sarah parked her car in the darkness outside Hamilton Forbes and Kent. She was running toward the agency when Warren emerged from the Blue Posts.

'Sarah,' he called. 'Bone to pick with you.'

Sarah turned.

'Oh – Warren –' she said. 'Didn't see you.'

'No. You don't.' He kept pace with Sarah. 'Gordon says you're unhappy with my work.'

Sarah stopped on the agency steps.

'When did he say that?'

'This afternoon,' said Warren. 'Just before he fired me.'

'He – *fired* you? Gordon did?'

'Turned out they didn't invite me to talk about creative director, after all,' said Warren. 'He had a little surprise for the old man. A month to look round for something else. He said: somewhere that might suit me better.'

Warren led the way into the agency's reception. From his jacket pocket, he took a computer-generated organisation chart.

'Another little surprise. They gave me your new plan for the place.' Warren indicated an area of the creative department.

'And look: no Warren Greenbank. But then, as Gordon says' – he accurately imitated Gordon's Scottish accent – 'you can't expect Sarah Copeland to go on indefinitely, working with an alcoholic art director. Can you now?'

Warren was looking away from Sarah. She put up a hand and gently turned his face toward her.

'Warren,' she said, 'how long have we worked together? Nine years? Do you really think – after nine years – I'd help to push you out of this agency?'

Warren's colour was high. He stood breathing; then spoke.

'After nine years,' he said, 'if you really want to do something useful – why don't you get them to keep me on? After all, I hear they're putting you on the bloody board.'

He seemed about to say something else, but didn't. Sarah watched him leave reception. Then she turned and called a lift, just as her secretary came down the main stairs.

'Sally!' called Sarah. 'I thought you'd have gone. Seen Stephen?'

'He went out with Alessandra,' said Sally. 'Then came back and went up to Gordon's office.'

Sarah left the lifts, and started up the stairs.

'There's something I wanted to ask you about,' said Sally. 'Something personal.'

'Sally – this isn't the best of times –'

'It's about Nick.'

Sarah hesitated. Then she started up the staircase again.

'First,' she said. 'I've got to see Stephen. This whole government campaign's falling to pieces –' She paused at the door of Stephen's office and said: 'Like everything else.'

In Gordon's office, Stephen was circling the central table. He was treading the same path around and around it. Gordon was at his desk. With complete concentration, he was forming a triangle of blue paperclips. He did not look up as he spoke.

'David overrode my decision,' he said. 'Went against my advice. He's putting Sarah on the board.'

'More than he did for me, the bastard,' said Stephen.

'Possibly because you use that sort of language,' said

Gordon. He started a triangle of red clips. 'But the fact is, the balance of the board will change. Having that woman as a director makes things a good deal harder.'

Stephen stopped pacing and went over to the desk.

'Not harder,' he said. 'Bloody impossible. I told you days ago. You didn't get David out at the last board meeting – you're not going to get him out now. He's got more defences than a French fortress.' He looked down at the pattern on the desk. Gordon was filling in a red diagonal. 'Do you mind my asking what that is?'

'Flag,' said Gordon, starting on a second diagonal.

'You don't find it distracting?'

'Not in the least,' said Gordon. 'If anything, the reverse.' He began to fill in the red triangle. 'I imagine you are going to suggest, once again, that I should start a breakaway agency.'

One of the office phones rang.

'I'd suggest it again if I thought you'd listen,' said Stephen.

Gordon picked up the phone, paused, then said: 'I'll tell him.' He put down the phone and said: 'Sarah Copeland. Back in her office. Sounds unusually agitated. Wants to see you.'

'Better go and talk to the lady,' said Stephen.

Gordon called after him: 'Then come back, will you? We still haven't decided what we do about her appointment to the board.'

As Stephen came across the deserted creative department, Sarah was coming out of her office. She held a sheaf of National Health proofs. She indicated the photo on one of them.

'Judy Axford,' said Sarah. 'She won't do it.'

'The nurse?'

'The nurse in all our bloody ads. I couldn't change her mind. She's being moved to another hospital: they're closing the wing where she works and she can't afford to move. And she does not want her image used.'

'The miserable bitch,' said Stephen. He stood motionless for some moments, thinking. Then he started toward the stairs.

'Those ads are on the way to print. Gordon'll have to hold them.'

'Can't you?' called Sarah.

Stephen hesitated, then went on.

'Has to be Gordon. Don't go away.'

Sarah watched him out of the department, then took a lift back down to reception. Sally was sitting in a leather armchair, reading one of the listings magazines. In the huge chair, she looked very small.

'All right,' said Sarah. 'I've got to wait for Stephen. What did you want to tell me?'

Stephen went back into Gordon's office. The paperclip flag was finished. With intense concentration, Gordon was drawing out, on a yellow legal pad, possible power alignments in the newly enlarged board of directors.

'Putting Sarah on the board – that changes the whole thing –' he said as Stephen entered.

'Gordon,' said Stephen, 'can we come back to that?' He held up an advertisement proof. 'This nurse is in all our NHS ads. And the Party politicals. She's withdrawn permission for us to use her image. That photo. Plus magazine ads, posters, cinema, TV –'

There was a pause as Gordon surveyed Judy Axford's confident face.

'But – those ads run – tomorrow –?'

'Tomorrow,' agreed Stephen. 'National press.'

There was another pause.

'The nurse did sign a release?'

'They're closing her hospital wing,' said Stephen.

'The Health Authority must have something else for her.'

'On the other side of London. Says she can't afford to move.'

'But you said she signed a release?' asked Gordon. 'Legalities all tied up?'

Stephen nodded.

'We paid her full fee?'

Stephen nodded.

'Then the ads should run,' said Gordon. 'Very late to pull them out anyway.'

Stephen looked at his Rolex.

'Still could replace them. I checked with traffic. We might just do it.'

Gordon clenched his hands into fists and rested them on the corners of his morocco-leather blotter. He leaned forward over the desk.

'It's bloody ridiculous. The woman's absolutely in the wrong. Run them.'

Stephen moved to the door.

'You're sure?'

'We can't hold up a whole campaign because some little nurse changes her mind at the last minute.' He went back to his notes on the yellow legal pad. 'What do you think we're going to do? Have blank pages in all the morning papers – with an apology in the bloody middle: *Sorry. Woman's prerogative to change her mind.* What else do we run in the space? Pensions advertising – at the wrong end of the campaign? Nuclear weapons, when they've lost three kilos of plutonium? It's not on, Stephen. Legally, the woman's not got a leg to stand on –'

'I'll let traffic know we're going ahead,' said Stephen. As he went out the door, Gordon called after him.

'Then come back, will you? We still have decisions to make.'

As Stephen stood at the top of the main stairs to reception, he could see Sarah far below. She was talking to her secretary. Even from a distance, he could see it was not an easy conversation.

'I – I was sort of – involved – with David before we went to New York,' Sally was saying.

'By "sort of involved", you mean you were going to bed with him?'

Sally made a small movement of assent.

'I don't understand how you could do that,' said Sarah. 'David – David is a moral cypher.'

Sally was trying to keep her composure.

'He . . . he doesn't seem so to me.'

'And anyway,' said Sarah, 'I don't think you should be telling me this.'

'I haven't got anyone else,' said Sally. 'I can't talk to the other secretaries about – about the managing director –'

Stephen called from the stairs.

'Sorry to break in on your – little chat –'

Sally stood up hastily and pulled on her coat.

'Gordon cleared the ads to run,' said Stephen, as he came down the last flight of stairs. Sarah looked at him; not noticing that Sally had moved away.

'He cleared them? Did he understand –?'

'Perfectly. Said we were legally unassailable.' Stephen checked the time. 'I phoned through a clearance. They'll be on their way to print.'

'You don't think I should talk to Gordon?'

'Waste of time,' said Stephen. 'Deputy managing director's spoken. His decision. And if I can't change his mind, you certainly won't.' He watched Sally make a phone call from the reception desk, then turned his attention back to Sarah. 'I think, my love, you should say you've done what you can – and come for a drink.'

Sarah stood up and searched for her car keys.

'Thanks, but no thanks.' She found the keys at the bottom of her shoulder bag. 'This day's already lasted several months. I am going to do something that absolutely does not involve my mind.'

Stephen watched Sarah leave the agency, then walked across to Sally. He waited till she put down the phone.

'I do hope you're not rushing back to the bedsitter,' he said.

Sarah parked her car outside Nick's flat in Notting Hill Gate. It was a street that had gone upmarket fast in the last three years: old family houses converted into flats for people who were young enough to have no children, and old enough to have serious money. Dubonnet umbrellas flowered on patios. Elegant little trees grew in tubs, and you could buy fresh croissants at the corner; though not yet in New York's eighteen flavours.

Sarah found that she did not want to get out of the car. For a few moments she rested her forehead on the leather cover of the steering wheel. Then she picked up her carphone and called her son in Southease. She tilted back the car seat and waited for Telecom's aged machinery to make the connection between London and Sussex.

Rose eventually answered the phone. She sounded tired, and said that Daniel was asleep. For the first few hours after their arrival, she said, he had been profoundly suspicious of the countryside, and stayed in the farmhouse kitchen. Since then, a duckling had mistaken him for its mother, and followed him everywhere. He had spent the evening teaching the bird to swim. Eventually he had to be carried inside and up to bed.

Sarah put the phone down. Daniel was asleep in Sussex; he was not going to provide her with a way out. She sat for a moment longer. Then she said to herself: 'Come on, my lady. You either fish, or cut bait.'

In the bedroom of his flat, Nick was doing isometric exercises. Wearing only a pair of Levis, he was testing one set of muscles against another. He was a young man who took his body seriously. There was a film of sweat across his shoulders and chest. He watched his quartz clock and finished precisely at seven. Then he put on a digital tape of Mildred Bailey and began to feed a shoal of tropical fish.

The fish were in a huge tank along the eastern wall of the room. Together with framed posters for obscure rock bands, they provided the only colour in the flat, which was otherwise furnished in black, white and grey. The fish, though, were coloured more intensely than seemed possible for living things. Chasing food, they were a kaleidoscope of reflected light. Nick watched them entranced, as he did most evenings. Then came a knock on the door. He turned, looked again at the clock, put a Versace jacket over his shoulders, and opened the door.

'Sarah,' he said. 'I thought you'd forgotten.'

'Absolutely not,' said Sarah. She was carrying a package wrapped in black paper. 'It just took me a long time to deal with the nurse. Do you think I could come in? I feel a bit exposed, standing on a young man's doorstep.'

Nick stepped aside and Sarah went into the flat. For a moment, she stood and looked at him. Then, with her heel, she pushed the door shut behind her and held out the flat package.

'I brought a present for you. One of Rose's artworks.'

Nick began to take off the paper.

'The print that was in your office? It looked so good there.'

Sarah looked around the monastic room.

'It'll look better here,' she said. 'And also – I wanted to bring it –'

She paused. Nick looked up from the print; and understood.

'You wanted to bring it?'

Sarah spoke rapidly, as if a pause would force her to stop completely.

'– to be quite honest, I wanted to see you – because I just wanted to get away from anything to do with the agency – get away from this dreadful day, hunting for this nurse, get away from the *politics* – and because you didn't really invite me round just to drink a glass of wine, did you –?'

Nick shook his head. Sarah went close to him and took off the jacket he had slipped over his shoulders. She was still talking.

'– so, I decided – on the way here' – she hung the jacket over a bentwood chair – 'against all my better judgment – and any scraps of moral sense I may still have –'

Nick opened the door to the next room and Sarah said:

'I decided – I am taking you to bed.'

TWELVE

In the very early hours of the following morning, a faint light from a street lamp came through the slatted blind into Nick's bedroom. Sarah was sitting naked in Nick's bed. She listened to his even breathing, then leaned out of bed to pick up his T shirt from the floor. She buried her face in it, inhaling the smell of his body, then pulled the shirt over her head.

Nick woke.

'Sarah? What on earth are you doing?'

'Putting on your T shirt,' she said. 'I get cold in strange beds.'

Nick sat up and switched on an Italian lamp. He was wearing only a watch, and the tan had almost gone from his body. He leaned back, watching Sarah as she emerged from his shirt. Suddenly self-conscious, she began to laugh.

'The other thing I want is a paper.'

'Newspaper?'

On impulse, Sarah kissed him. Behind her back, Nick looked at his watch.

'Sarah – it's four-fifteen in the morning. Nothing's open.' He pulled away from her, and lay back with his hands behind his head. 'Do you do this to your husband?'

Sarah moved herself gently until she was sitting across Nick's hips. She put her hands on his shoulders and looked down at him.

'You're forgetting. I don't sleep with my husband. If I did – I probably wouldn't be doing what I'm doing to you now.'

Nick pushed upward into her.

'Double-edged compliment,' he said.

'My love, it wasn't meant as a compliment,' said Sarah. She concentrated for a moment on her physical response, and then said: 'You get those afterwards. Not before.'

Three hours later, Stephen Hallam was driving up the M25, and dialling Nick's number.

Sarah woke to the sound of the phone beside Nick's bed. She lay for a moment, staring at the unfamiliar room. Then she turned and ran her fingers down Nick's back as he dragged himself out from under the duvet. The phone stopped before he could answer it. Sarah curled herself round Nick's body, and pulled him back beneath the cover.

'I keep thinking Daniel's coming in,' she said.

Nick looked at her over his shoulder.

'Daniel?'

'My son,' said Sarah. 'Remember? You're sleeping with an errant mother.'

Nick glanced at the door, then back to Sarah.

'No one's coming.' He turned over and buried his face in Sarah's hair. 'Do you know the poem about the plumber?'

'Probably,' said Sarah.

'*– She said, Stop! Someone's coming! –*'

Sarah put a finger on his lips, and continued the rhyme.

'*Said the plumber, still plumbing,*
If anyone's coming
I think you will find that it's me.'

She ran her hand gently down Nick's body.

'Which reminds me,' she said.

The phone rang again.

By now, Stephen was off the M25, and caught in a west London traffic jam. He considered where Sarah might be. She was one of several people in the agency whose movements he followed with close attention. Finally, deciding that his original instinct was probably right, he put a Monteverdi tape into the car cassette player, keyed Nick's number into the phone again, and waited some time until he answered.

'Nick?' he said, 'Third time I've tried. Does your creative director happen to be with you?'

Nick looked down at his creative director, who was stretched face-down between his legs.

'Who is this?' he asked. 'Stephen?'

'If by any chance Sarah is in your bed,' said Stephen, 'you might suggest she has a look at the early edition of the *Messenger*. All right?' The traffic started to move again, and he put the Porsche in gear. 'Talk soon,' he said to Nick, and put down the phone.

'I heard that,' said Sarah to Nick. Her voice was muffled by the pillow. 'It's hard not to overhear conversations when you're lying underneath someone.' She moved herself out from that position and turned over. 'Would you be a darling, and go down and get me the papers?'

When Nick came back, Sarah was in the bathroom. She came out wearing Nick's gown, and curled up on the bed. She flipped expertly through a copy of the *Mail* until she came to the election advertisements. From the familiar layout, Nurse Judy Axford stared up at them with reassurance about the Health Service. Sarah turned the page so that Nick could see it.

'All our own work,' she said. 'Doesn't look too bad.'

Nick peered at the printing.

'If you don't mind very muddy half-tones,' he said.

Sarah wasn't listening. She was hunting through the pile of papers until she found the *Messenger*. When she did, she sat for some moments, looking at the front page. A banner headline read: *'No Cuts' Nurse Is Sacked.'*

Below the headline was a huge photo of Nurse Judy Axford and, inset, a smaller reproduction of Sarah's advertisement.

'Oh, dear God,' said Sarah. 'Tell me it's not true.'

Nick moved closer to her and looked at the newspaper.

'Somebody leaked the fucking story.'

'The nurse hasn't actually been sacked,' said Sarah.

Nick indicated the front-page lead.

'What are you going to do about it?' he asked. 'Complain to the Press Council? Write a letter to the editor?'

There was a silence; then he said: 'Heads will roll.'

'I wonder whose?' said Sarah. She was still looking at the front-page story. Then she dropped her own head on Nick's lap, and lifted her hair away from the nape of her neck. 'Would you like mine now?'

At Hamilton Forbes and Kent, Stephen had parked his Porsche and was on his way through reception. The Managing Director's personal assistant was also on her way to the lifts. She carried a huge bunch of irises.

'You never brought me flowers before breakfast,' said Stephen. He was referring to his brief affair with Alessandra; a liaison that he still hoped sometime to renew.

'These are a present,' said Alessandra. Her eyes, Stephen noticed, were a close match for the flowers. 'A present from Mike.'

Stephen entered a lift behind Gordon Lochhead, who had appeared from the direction of his office.

'Chivalry lives,' said Stephen to Alessandra. He pressed the Door Close button. Alessandra, who had paused to rearrange the irises, was left outside the lift.

As soon as the lift doors closed, Gordon produced a letter from the folder he carried.

'Something that might interest you,' he said. 'Had my reply from New York. Rather damning news of our Managing Director. Seems he was bidding up shares in that agency he bought.'

Stephen took the letter and scanned it.

'Insider trading?'

'Very much so,' said Gordon. 'And they take that quite seriously in the States. Several well-known financial figures now learning how to sew mailbags.' He retrieved the letter from Stephen. 'I shall need this. We may yet have David out of here.'

'I'll believe it when I see it,' said Stephen. 'When are we due to meet the Minister?'

'Ten minutes,' said Gordon. He came closer and lowered his voice. 'David was trying to keep me out of the meeting. I made it quite clear that I intended to be there. I said: Who do you think is running the political campaign?'

'Interesting question,' said Stephen. 'See you in David's office.'

David was already in his office. Three black leather chairs were drawn into a close grouping. David sat in one. In the others were the Minister of State for Army Affairs, and Francis Salk. Their conversation ceased when Stephen and Gordon entered the room.

'Do be seated,' said David. 'The Minister was just identifying one or two potential electoral time-bombs.'

'Principle of forewarned is forearmed,' said Geoffrey Talbot. He was watching Stephen stroke his hair into place, and deciding that he did not trust the man.

'We come back to these Parlett Construction buildings, I fear,' said Francis Salk.

'The ones which collapse without warning,' explained David.

'Mustn't exaggerate,' warned the Minister. 'Only two have collapsed. One being an empty school, somewhere outside Birmingham.'

From his briefcase he produced an internal Party report labelled *Parlett Construction: Summary of Findings.* He opened it to show a badly copied photo of the ruined school.

'Hardly sounds earthshaking,' said Gordon.

'I'm told it was,' said Francis. 'When the roof came in. But that is not our main concern.'

'Our difficulty,' said Geoffrey, 'is that all these edifices are built by one of my Ministerial colleagues.'

'Julian's family firm,' corrected Francis.

'Indeed,' said the Minister. 'Julian Parlett, of Parlett Construction. Only begetters of Paramor system building.'

'Surely the Minister's holdings must be held by nominees?' said David.

'Indeed they are,' agreed Geoffrey. 'Perfectly proper in itself.' He lifted the document from his briefcase, and let it fall back. 'But that does not change this rather damning report on the Paramor building system.'

'Under the right – or, more precisely, the wrong – conditions,' said Francis, 'several other Paramor System buildings may collapse. And, for some reason –'

'– no doubt perfectly legitimate,' said Geoffrey.

'– the responsible Minister has done nothing about the report. Or about the Paramor buildings,' said Francis.

There was a moment's silence in the office. Then Stephen said dryly: 'Time-bomb indeed.'

David was making rapid notes.

'Let me see if I have understood this,' he said. 'Since we may have to deal with the public-relations consequences. You suggest that one of our Junior Ministers has a financial interest in a building firm – whose buildings are likely to collapse.'

'Not likely, God willing,' said Geoffrey. 'Let us say: which *could* collapse.'

'Taking with them Julian's construction company,' said Francis.

'I find this harder and harder to believe,' said David. He turned to the Minister. 'You say that a report, spelling this out, has – for some reason – been shelved?'

Francis Salk spoke before Geoffrey Talbot could.

'I'm afraid there is an addendum. Jonathan Dacre, a fine old gentleman, is the Member for Leeds Centre. Ex-Services. Queen's Counsel. Board of various charities –'

'No political future,' added Geoffrey.

'Absolutely none,' said Francis. 'But this dear old buffer has got hold of that report. He is all too aware of the failings in the Paramor system.'

'And Dacre,' said Geoffrey, 'being Dacre, went straight to the Minister. Most intemperate: accused him of covering up the whole business.'

'This I could do without,' said Stephen.

'Indeed,' said Francis. 'We all could.' He indicated the report on Parlett Construction. 'Dacre, I'm sorry to say, has a copy of this little document. He is now threatening to make it public. Can you not see the headlines in the less submissive sections of the press? On the eve of poll?'

'Minister Puts Lives at Risk,' said David.

'Minister Suppresses School Safety Report,' said Stephen.

'To be fair,' said Geoffrey, 'Not all the Paramor buildings are schools.'

'No,' said Francis. 'I was forgetting. Some are clinics. One or two are old people's homes.'

There was silence. David made notes on his legal pad. Gordon and Stephen sat thinking.

'We must keep it in perspective, Francis,' the Minister said finally. 'PM's seeing Dacre today.' He indicated the report. 'Promising to act on this damn thing, moment the election's over. Appeal to Dacre's loyalty to the Party. Tell him he can't seriously contemplate this sort of hoo-ha – not a fortnight before an election.'

'Knowing Jonathan Dacre,' said Francis, 'that may be exactly what the old buzzard is contemplating.'

David dropped his notes into a desk drawer and stood up.

'I think, gentlemen, we should adjourn for breakfast,' he said. 'It is almost eight o'clock.'

'Feels a lot later,' murmured Stephen to Gordon as they made their way down to the restaurant.

THIRTEEN

Sarah was half-dressed, and alone in Nick's bedroom. She was doing her best to put out of her mind the front-page story of her National Heath advertisements. Instead, she tried for a moment to imagine how Nick lived when he was alone; or how it was when he lived with Sally.

She crossed the room to a wardrobe. It was full of expensively casual male clothes and, at the far end, a number of clothes that clearly belonged to a young woman.

Sarah took out a cream dress and held it against herself. It must have been bought by Sally. It was short: not much longer than the T shirt Sarah had worn in bed. She replaced the dress and was fastening her own stockings when Nick came in with coffee in green French cups. He put the tray down on a black laquered table.

'Time?' asked Sarah.

Nick consulted his watch.

'Eightish.'

Sarah finished fastening her stockings.

'Always a price for illicit sex,' she said.

'For you, it's free,' said Nick.

Sarah shook her head.

'I've just remembered: I had a breakfast meeting with the Minister.' She looked down at the newspaper. 'They'll have seen that. I really should be in at the execution.' She twisted her body, checking her stockings for runs. There was one. 'If I go now – do you mind? – I might just make the end of breakfast.'

At the agency, an extensive breakfast had been set in a corner of the restaurant. Stephen, Geoffrey Talbot, David and Gordon were eating enthusiastically. Helen, who had joined the group, and Francis Salk, both confined themselves to China tea.

'Apart from keeping fingers crossed, and hoping Dacre can be persuaded,' Francis remarked, 'there is a limit to what one can do.'

'One could,' suggested Stephen, 'plant a few stories. Member for Leeds Centre becoming tired and emotional – trouble with the Law Council – involvement with some lady – Then if he does start running round, spreading rumours about building firms –'

'Come on, Hallam,' said Francis. 'Who in their right mind is going to print planted stores about an aging backbench MP? From Leeds? In the middle of an election campaign? Now, if he had the lifestyle of some of our Members, it might be a different matter –'

Alessandra came across the restaurant. She came close to Stephen and said something about trouble with a client. Stephen dropped his napkin on to his plate, excused himself, and followed Alessandra out. Geoffrey Talbot turned his attention to Helen and David.

'What do you call it, again?' he asked.

'Compassion sector,' said David. 'A bit of trade jargon.'

Helen cleared away butter and marmalade. She spread out a computer-generated map, on which different sections of the country were printed in contrasting colours.

'The compassion sector, Minister, is the area shown in green.' Using a Mars pencil, she indicated swathes of colour. 'Here. Here. And in the university belt, across here. Attitudinally quite soft –'

'Going by yesterday's poll results,' said David.

Francis leaned over to see the map.

'Well,' he said, 'to quote Richard Nixon – if these chaps want compassion, perhaps we ought to give them compassion.'

The Minister put aside his kipper.

'Oh, come on, Francis. We went into this damn election, defenders of sterling, law-and-order, old-fashioned morality –' He gazed down at a hand-made, but rumpled, shirt. 'Doesn't quite fit with my bleeding heart. Wherever it is.'

From a stack of proofs on the table, David lifted out a copy of the National Health press advertisement.

'However,' he said, 'from today –'

'Exactly,' agreed the Minister. 'From today, we have your excellent advertising.' He leaned across the table and flipped through other proofs. 'National Health . . . New hope for pensioners . . . Nobody cares more about schools . . . Better news for the unemployed –' He looked at Helen, who was waiting to speak. 'Compassion writ large, is it not?'

Sarah had come into the agency, and taken a lift straight up to her office. There she collected a series of concepts that the Minister was due to take to the Cabinet strategy committee for approval. All promised a brighter future for old-age pensioners. The aged had so far given little support to the government.

On her way down to the restaurant, Sarah passed the third floor photocopying room. She was profoundly surprised to see Stephen doing his own copying. Normally, in such matters, he had a sharp sense of status. He was willing to use anybody's secretary if his own were unavailable.

Sarah paused at the door.

'Stephen! Strategy meeting finished?'

Stephen was reading the copies he had just made.

'It's breakfasting.'

Sarah glanced at the report lying on the photocopier. The words 'Parlett Construction' were typed on the cover. Without hurrying, Stephen turned the report face down. Sarah reversed it once more.

'Stephen,' she said. 'This is a confidential Party document – what are you doing? Copying it for the Minister?'

Stephen spoke without looking up from his reading.

'Cannot tell a lie, Sarah. I have borrowed this, for a few moments, from Geoffrey Talbot's briefcase.' With his finger, he marked a point on the page he was reading. 'Listen. I quote: "if the Member for Leeds Centre carries out his threat to communicate with Sunday newspapers, suggest responsible Minister should issue statement that Paramor report is already being implemented with greatest urgency –" Close quote.'

'I've no idea what you're talking about,' said Sarah. She picked up the original report and turned its pages. Then she said: 'Oh, no. they're building *schools* that – "that are liable to structural failure within the foreseeable future –"'

'In everyday language,' said Stephen, 'they collapse. But no one is to be told about this till after the election. Which is why I thought it might be useful to have a copy of the report.'

Sarah was torn between fascination with the document, and a sudden recognition of what might happen if they were found in possession of it.

'Stephen,' she said, 'you must be out of your mind. What if the Minister misses this? There'll be absolute hell to pay.' She pushed the report into Stephen's hands. 'We'll lose the account.'

Stephen collected his photocopies.

'They always used to tell me at school that knowledge is power. A copy of this opens up – all sorts of possibilities.'

Sarah backed toward the door.

'Well, here's a powerful piece of knowledge for you, Stephen,' she said. 'They find you with that, they'll roll the Secrets Act over you till you're flat as flaky pastry.' She pointed at the report. 'Put the bloody thing back.'

'I'm about to,' said Stephen. 'Do you want to keep *cave* outside David's door?'

'There is nothing I want to do less,' said Sarah, with emphasis. 'Sometimes, Stephen, I have real doubts about the balance of your mind.'

As Stephen departed in the direction of David's office, Sarah called: 'Did you show them the early copy of the *Messenger*?'

'There were other things,' said Stephen, 'on my unbalanced mind.'

Sarah came into the restaurant carrying her sheaf of concepts and a copy of the *Messenger*. The breakfast meeting, was, clearly, drawing to a close. Plates were spread with bones of kippers, the remains of croissants, and the crusts of wholewheat toast.

Francis Salk looked up from Helen's attitudinal map as Sarah sat down.

'Mrs Copeland,' he said. 'Pleasantly feminine, to arrive at the end of a meeting.'

'I'm sorry to be so late,' said Sarah. 'May I ask if anyone's seen this morning's *Messenger*?'

'Try not to, my dear,' said the Minister.

'Saw the midnight edition,' said Francis.

David was watching Sarah closely.

'Why do you ask?'

Sarah opened the newspaper and put it in the middle of the table, with the front page visible. Nurse Judy Axford stared up at them. Under his breath, the Minister read through the headline.

'*No Cuts Nurse Sacked.*' He looked from David to Sarah to Francis Salk. 'Now that,' he said, 'is not good news.'

While the breakfast meeting was working through the implications of the *Messenger* story, Stephen was in David's office returning the report he had borrowed. He unlocked the top drawer of David's desk, removed the Minister's briefcase and opened it. Though he knew it was unwise, he could not resist going through the Ministerial papers once again. He was reading a letter from the Chancellor about the possibility of engineering a run on sterling, when he heard movement in the outer office. Without undue haste, Stephen closed the briefcase, put it back in the desk drawer, relocked it, and returned the key to David's case. Then he left the room.

In the outer office, Alessandra was running an electronic search on her word processor. She looked up in surprise as Stephen came out of David's office.

'Stephen!' she said. 'Is David in there?'

'Any moment now,' said Stephen. 'In your absence – tending your irises – I am our manager's messenger boy.'

Alessandra expressed profound disbelief, but said nothing. She watched Stephen leave the office, then picked up the phone and called Sarah. There was no answer. Sally was not in yet, and Sarah was still in the restaurant, listening to Francis Salk.

'Someone here chose this ex-nurse,' he was saying. He rested one manicured finger on the press photo of Judy Axford. 'And someone else signally failed to keep her away from the press.' He turned and spoke directly to David Postgate. 'I think you should get rid of both of those people. That is, if you wish to continue working with us.'

Jane came in to the restaurant and spoke quietly to David.

'Excuse me,' she said. 'Downing Street asks if the Minister could return. It seems to be urgent.'

Geoffrey Talbot swallowed the last of his coffee, and stood up.

'I would guess,' he said, 'that the PM's had the newspapers.'

David walked out with the Minister to his waiting car. Sarah watched them go, then picked up the phone on the table and called the editor of the *Messenger*.

In the agency's reception area, Carol had stopped to talk to Jane. Jane was expert at wedging snippets of conversation between incoming phone calls.

'I mean, it's ridiculous,' Carol was saying. 'It's supposed to be a jazzercise class, and they give us Flight of the bloody Bumblebee –' She lowered her voice and looked busy as David walked through reception with the Minister and Francis Salk; then turned her attention to a young man, carefully unshaven, who was sitting in a cream leather chair in the reception area's small grove of potted palms.

'Who's *this*?' she asked. 'Oh, he's so *styl*ish. I could eat him.'

'I hope you don't mean that,' said Jane. She paused between calls, and looked where Carol was looking. Then she consulted her notepad.

'His name's Dusty Willith.' Jane spoke with a slight and intermittent lisp. 'I think he's Sarah's new copywriter.' She picked up the phone and listened. 'Gordonth chasing you.'

Warren's daughter Kim came through reception, late for work as usual. She glanced at the new copywriter, taking in the Comme des Garcons clothes and designer stubble.

'Poseur,' she muttered. With dignity, she went on toward

the lifts, passing Sarah and Nick as they came into reception to find Dusty.

Jane was taking an internal call.

'Gordon,' she said to Carol, when she had put the phone down. 'I really think you ought to go. He thounds madly ratty.'

'Bugger,' said Carol, departing. 'Some political cockup, and he blames it all on me.' She paused, looking back at Dusty, who was now talking with Sarah and Nick. 'Jane? Is he – straight?'

Jane, taking an outside call, nodded.

Nick could have told Carol that Dusty was, in fact, more interested in illegal pharmacology than in sex; but at the moment he was occupied with introductions.

'You do know Sarah?' he asked Dusty.

Dusty looked carefully at Sarah. He had an unexpectedly good eye for detail: among other things, he noted runs in each of Sarah's stockings, which were caused by her having worn them to bed the night before. It was not something she usually did.

'Dusty and I had a headhunting lunch somewhere. Before I hired him,' Sarah said to Nick. To Dusty she said: 'You described yourself as wasted. I wasn't sure whether it was physical, or just your talent.'

'*Neiges d'antan*,' said Dusty noncommittally. 'Hard to recall.'

Nick put an arm around his friend's elegantly clad shoulders.

'Come up to the famous first floor,' he said. 'Meet your new –'

'Chums,' suggested Dusty. He picked up his pink plastic case, and a copy of the *Messenger*.

'Workmates,' said Sarah.

Nick noticed the *Messenger*.

'But I wouldn't carry that particular paper, if I were you.'

As Nick was taking Dusty up to start work in the creative department, David Postgate was entering his PA's office. Alessandra was, as usual, on the phone.

'The message,' she was saying, 'is that all, repeat all, of the Health Service advertising is on hold. That's press, radio, posters, cinema. Can you read back and confirm?'

David waited until she had put down the phone; then asked: 'Still not through to the Prime Minister?'

Alessandra shook her heavy blonde hair.

'Keep trying,' said David. 'Don't hassle Lord Montfort, but do keep on to Downing Street.' He opened the door of his own office. 'It won't improve as the day goes on.' Then he came back to Alessandra's desk. 'And get Stephen Hallam down to my office.'

'He was in there a minute ago,' said Alessandra, watching with interest for David's reaction.

There was no outward reaction; but, whatever David was thinking, he said nothing more than: 'Get him down here again.'

On his way to David's office, Stephen passed Sarah on the stairs.

'Did you get that report back in the Minister's briefcase?' she asked quietly.

'What report?' said Stephen. 'Of course I got it back. You worry too much, my lady.'

'Just out of curiosity,' said Sarah, 'how did you know I was at Nick's place last night?'

'My dear, if you want a private love affair,' said Stephen, 'try Grand Central Station. Not an ad agency.' He gave his sudden vulpine grin, and went on down to David's office.

Once inside the office, his manner changed. The surface charm remained, but underneath it, Stephen was clearly uneasy. He refused David's offer of a seat. David himself was stretched in a black leather chair; he looked more relaxed than he had since his return from New York.

'No calls,' he said, into the phone; then, abruptly to Stephen: 'This National Health thing. Tomorrow, every national paper's going to have it. Television, radio, gossip columns –' Suddenly, he raised his voice. 'How in hell could we start an election campaign with an unemployed bloody nurse?' He paused and looked at Stephen, who said nothing. 'Particularly – *particularly*, Hallam – when we're telling the electorate that unemployment is no longer a problem?'

'David,' said Stephen, 'the nurse in our advertising' – he glanced at the copy of the *Messenger* on David's coffee table –

'is not actually unemployed. Her ward's closing. She was offered some other job. Trouble is, she can't afford to take it.'

David held up the newspaper.

'You think we should run more ads – explaining all this –?'

'The point is,' said Stephen carefully, 'by the time we knew about it, the campaign was ready to run.'

There was a pause. David watched Stephen.

'You . . . knew? You *knew* the nurse was out of work?'

'She phoned in,' said Stephen. 'She spoke to Sarah.' He adjusted his perfectly knotted tie. 'However, I am prepared to take responsibility.'

'Ah,' said David, drawing breath. 'Now we hear it. You knew. Sarah knew. Who else?'

'I'd really prefer to leave it there.'

David stood up and came closer to Stephen.

'Frankly,' he said, 'I don't give a brass fart what you prefer. This is my agency. I take on a political account, and we make a monumental balls of the first bloody advertisement. The Prime Minister's on the phone, threatening to move the account. Our share value's dropping. We are an industry joke. And I want to know why. Now. Let me ask you again. Who else knew?'

There was a pause, then Stephen gave a slight shrug, as if consigning himself to a fate more powerful than he.

'Gordon knew. It was Gordon who cleared the ads for press.'

David stood for a moment, working out the implications of what he had just heard. Then he opened the office door.

'All right,' he said to Stephen. 'You get out, while I hear what Gordon has to say.' As Stephen went through Alessandra's office, David said: 'However, I do want you back here in half an hour. With Sarah Copeland. By then, I shall have had a word with Gordon.'

Gordon was coming out of the conference room, at the end of a presentation for Honcho, a new chocolate bar produced by Fowler Rutherford Foods. Fowler Rutherford were one of the agency's largest clients. The presentation was designed to reverse what research had shown to be chocolate 'negatives': the fear of fatness, heart disease, and general degeneration. To counter this, Hamilton Forbes had put forward the concept of a slim, sexy chocolate eater; but Gordon felt that the client had not been entirely convinced. He was considering a new approach to Fowler Rutherford when Sarah emerged from the express lift. Gordon caught up with her outside the door of his own office.

'I have heard,' he said, 'that the Cabinet committee are reviewing us at this moment. There's talk of bringing Parr Sarris Bernstein back on to the political account.'

'Disaster.'

'Disaster for us,' said Gordon. 'Not for them. Whether it can be done at this stage, I have no idea.'

'The government account very nearly changed hands in the middle of the last election,' said Sarah. 'They ended up with two competing agencies, in mid-campaign.' She looked closely at Gordon. 'Was there something else you wanted to tell me?'

'There is,' said Gordon. 'About these National Health ads –'

'Yes?' said Sarah.

'I wanted to clear up the question of responsibility.'

'Responsibility?' There was a slight pause, then Sarah said: 'Depends on how you cut the cake, doesn't it? Helen found the wretched nurse. I wrote some of the ads. Warren wrote others. Stephen took them to the Cabinet committee – and you cleared them to run.'

Gordon glanced back at Stephen, who was still standing outside the conference room, talking to Vernon Waugh of Fowler Rutherford Foods.

'Stephen told you that I cleared them?'

'Of course he did.'

Sally came down the passage. She stopped a discreet distance away and waited for the right moment to speak. Gordon, clearly, had not noticed her.

'It was a very rushed decision, Sarah. Late at night. I was really concerned with something quite else.'

Sarah waited a moment, trying to assess what lay beneath Gordon's words.

'I make rush decisions,' she said. 'Some good. Some bad. They're still my decisions.' She looked at her watch. 'I gather we're supposed to be seeing David?'

'Before we do that,' said Gordon, 'I just wanted to say that you may view these things differently. Now that you're on the board. Now that you see the management situation. Realise the consequences.'

'Oh, I realise the consequences,' said Sarah. To Sally, she added: 'With you in one moment –'

'I'll be quite frank with you – I'd rather you didn't mention my part in clearing those ads.' Gordon paused. 'You may have realised that David wants my head on a platter.'

'And you his,' Sarah said quietly.

'Excuse me,' said Sally, moving closer. 'David's waiting for Gordon.'

Gordon was a man who believed that the best form of defence was attack. He brushed past Alessandra, who held a tray of coffee, and pushed his way into David Postgate's office. David, who was dictating into a miniature recorder, looked up to see Gordon produce the letter he had earlier shown to Stephen.

'From what I hear,' he said, 'you seem to have done some inside share dealing – apart from anything else that went on in New York.'

'Sit down,' invited David. He took the letter from Gordon, scanned it, and passed it back.

'Now,' he said, 'if this accusation were true – *if* it were true – what follows?'

Gordon was unprepared for the tenor of this response.

'I should have thought that was obvious,' he said. 'If it becomes public knowledge – that you were insider trading –'

'Yes?' said David.

'I really fail to see,' said Gordon, 'I really fail to see how you could continue.'

'Continue?'

'As managing director of this place. Or of the American agency.'

David eased himself out of his chair and approached Gordon.

'You know what happens in a wolf pack?' he asked. 'In case you don't, I shall tell you. What happens is this. Eventually, one of the pack-wolves challenges the leader. He takes a single bite at his throat: tries to tear out the jugular vein. Why only one bite? Because that's all there's time for. He opens up that vein, then he's the leader of the pack. Misses it: he's dead.' David held up a hand to prevent Gordon from speaking. 'Now. Think back to when I was in New York. And you tried to get me out of here. You missed the vein, Lochhead. Someone got hurt. Not I.'

Gordon moved toward the door. He indicated the letter he still held.

'This time –'

'I doubt it,' said David. 'Not this time; not any time.' His manner became gentler, almost persuasive. 'The trouble is, Gordon, you still live in an age when people pretended to worry about the way business was run. That was ten years ago. Now that concern is entirely cosmetic. It must be. There's too much money around to let ethics get in the way.' He came close to Gordon, and spoke confidentially. 'I'll tell you what will happen with us. They'll watch to see if I can make a global strategy work: if I can win this election, hold on to New York, expand into the Pacific. This they do care about. Make that work, and I'll push our share price through the bloody ceiling. Then, Gordon, believe me, you'll carry your lamp a long time before you find anyone worried about the ethics of what we're doing.' With the nail of his index finger, David flicked the letter Gordon was holding. 'Copy your letter. Send it round to the directors, the shareholders. See whether anybody's interested.'

Suddenly, Gordon seemed empty of energy. He stood, with one hand on the door handle, watching his managing director.

'You may find,' he said eventually, 'that the business community is not quite as amoral as you imagine.'

'I pray for that every morning, over my orange juice,' said David pleasantly. 'But don't go. The real business is just beginning.' He indicated that morning's copy of the *Messenger*. 'We are about to learn exactly who dropped us in this Health mess.' He picked up the phone and spoke to Alessandra. 'Call Sarah and Stephen, will you? Ask them to come down.'

It took Alessandra some time to find Stephen. He was leaning on the desk which had been given to Kim Greenbank, Warren's daughter. Kim was a tiny girl, dressed in layer upon layer of clothes. She was working on a finished rough of an education advertisement. Its headline read: *Teachers call them kids with special needs.* Under a picture of two leather-jacketed youths, Kim was lettering a tagline: *We call them thugs.*

'Nice bit of stuff,' said Stephen, indicating the ad. 'I gather your father's not at work today?'

Kim did not look up from her work.

'Dad's at home. He's sick.'

'In that case,' said Stephen. 'I have good news for you. Your Daddy suddenly rose from his bed, and walked. I gather, in fact, that he walked in the direction of Harman, Scott, French, an agency in need of a new art director. And who may not mind the fact that he suddenly lost his job here. So there's no cause for worry.'

Kim glanced at him, then went back to her work.

'You know every bloody thing, don't you?'

'Quite a lot,' said Stephen. 'And I have a new account which is targeted, as they say, upon angry and alienated young people. Such as yourself.' He gave his practised grin. 'Could you spare some time to tell me what it's like these days – walking on the wild side of life?'

Kim put down her Magic Marker. She looked at Stephen with a depth of understanding which, for a moment, disturbed him.

'All right.'

At that moment, Sarah came out of her office.

'We are summoned by David,' she said. 'It's time for the execution.'

While Sarah was on her way to David's office, Dee Vincent was searching the creative department for her. Dee had been infuriated by one of Mike Sutherland's political press ads. Over a photo of a young black model, the headline read: *To us, she's not black – she's beautiful.* Dee had taken the rough from Mike's desk. Now she was looking for Sarah, determined to have the campaign cancelled.

'Sarah's never here when you want her,' she was saying furiously to Sally.

'Sarah's in with David,' said Sally. 'Health Service stuff. It's really hit the fan.' She edged past Dee. 'I just have to catch Nick –'

'Tell me what I'm supposed to do about these ads –' said Dee; but Sally was gone. She caught up with Nick as he reached his own desk.

'Nick,' she said, 'it's just – my clothes are in your flat. There's a cream dress. Summer dress. And all the things in my room –'

'You want to collect them?' said Nick.

Sally nodded. There was no expression on her heart-shaped face.

'You do really mean it? About not coming back?'

Sally said nothing.

'I still have a spare bed,' said Nick. 'Or half of one that's not spare.'

'Oh, Nick,' said Sally. 'Don't do that. *Please* don't do that.'

When Sarah and Stephen entered the managing director's office, Francis Salk was there, as well as David and Gordon. The atmosphere was not comfortable.

'Sit down,' said David. 'To recap for you: Francis tells me that we may not keep the political account.'

'The Prime Minister,' said Francis, 'is chewing the very tasteless Downing Street carpet. And, as one of the people who recommended this agency, I am not in the highest of favour myself. I was just telling David, your agency's best chance –'

'Is to set our own house in order,' said David.

'It's an unexceptionable phrase,' said Sarah. 'What does it mean in this context?'

'I fear it means removing certain people,' said Francis. He indicated one of the cancelled NHS ads. 'Those responsible for this less than happy start to our campaign.' He checked the time on his Patek Philippe. 'I shall be back for the nuclear briefing. Always provided the PM agrees we are still working together.'

David stood up and went with Francis to the door.

'I'll see you out –'

'I would rather you settled this matter,' said Francis. 'As someone says, time may not be on your side. I'm sure that your delectable secretary will look after me.'

'I'm sure she won't,' murmured Stephen.

David closed the door behind the media adviser. He turned and looked at Gordon, Sarah and Stephen.

'To proceed,' he said: 'I gather Helen found this nurse, who's caused all the trouble. After that – who cleared these ads to run? Sarah?'

'I cleared them through my department.' She indicated the printed photo of Judy Axford. 'And when the nurse withdrew permission, I spent half a day trying to change her mind.'

'But you knew – before we went to press – that she hadn't changed her mind?'

'If I may say something –' said Gordon.

David made a silencing gesture. He continued to concentrate on Sarah.

'Yes,' she said. 'I knew she hadn't changed her mind.'

'And you knew she'd been made redundant?'

'Not redundant,' said Sarah. 'Nurse Axford eventually told me her ward was closing. Stephen and I discussed it. Then –'

'One moment,' said David. He turned to Stephen. 'Did you clear the campaign with anyone?'

There was a silence, finally and explosively broken by Gordon.

'This isn't an advertising agency,' he shouted. 'This is more like some disreputable Communist show trial. You want a public confession, don't you?'

David was unruffled.

'I have to give an account to the Prime Minister,' he said. 'You'll agree that it should be accurate?'

'All right,' said Gordon. 'All right. Well, you tell the Prime Minister this. Stephen came along to see me, late in the evening, when I was tied up with other matters. He gave me some story about this nurse. I asked if the plates had gone to press –'

'– they were, in fact, on their way,' said Stephen.

In Gordon, some final control seemed to snap. He rose half out of his chair and raised his voice further.

'Let me remind you,' he shouted. 'I am still a board director. I refuse to be questioned in this way. If we had pulled those ads, at that time, it would have been the most unholy mess.'

'But nothing, Gordon,' said David, 'absolutely nothing like the mess we're in now. Look. With unemployment as the electorate's primary worry, we start a campaign with an apparently unemployed nurse –'

'All right,' repeated Gordon. 'If that's the purpose of this little kangaroo court, yes: I said the ads should run.' He leaned back in his chair, breathing heavily. 'Then, about the middle of the night, I began to worry about the implications.'

'So?'

'So I rang Sarah, to check what the nurse said to her.'

'And?'

'Sarah wasn't home,' said Gordon. 'In the end, I called Stephen, to find out where she was.'

David turned to Sarah.

'Where were you?'

Sarah hesitated.

'I really think that's my business, David.'

'Not when I'm trying to hold this bloody agency together.' To Stephen he said: 'Where did you get in touch with Sarah?'

'It's all right, Stephen,' said Sarah. She looked at David. 'It's not something I usually do; and I'd rather it wasn't general knowledge – but last night I happened to be sleeping with one of my copywriters.'

'A male copywriter?'

'Yes,' said Sarah. 'If that helps, it was. A male copywriter.'

Outside the door, in Alessandra's office, Dee was holding the rough of the *She's not black, she's just beautiful* ad.

'Aly?' she asked. 'Where's Sarah?'

Alessandra indicated the closed door of the office.

'I wouldn't go in.'

'I would,' said Dee. 'I want to talk to her.' She showed Mike Sutherland's rough. 'Try and stop this shit.'

Alessandra drew an elegant finger across her throat.

'It's like that in there.' She pulled out a chair for Dee. 'Hang on. She'll be out soon . . . Dead or alive.'

Dee read the body copy of the advertisement for the fifth time that morning.

'I can't believe this stuff,' she muttered. '*Don't care what colour she is.*'

Alessandra looked up from her word processor. She was moving that month into a house Dee had bought, and she had a rather delicate request to make.

'Something different,' she said. 'I wanted to ask if it's kosher – when I move in your house – if I bring someone else –? Just for a while?'

Dee was still reading over the copy.

'*Not black. She's beautiful.* God help us.'

'His wife's just thrown him out. Must be mad,' said Alessandra. 'I mean' – she drew a reminiscent breath – 'he makes you feel like your hips came loose.' A brief circle of finger and thumb. '*Okay*, José.'

Suddenly alert, Dee looked up from the ad.

'Who are you talking about?'

'Mike,' said Alessandra. 'Mike Sutherland.'

'You want to move Mike into my house?' Dee pushed the advertisement across Alessandra's desk. 'Aly – didn't I tell you? It was your stud Mike that wrote this. This little pile of racist rubbish.'

In the creative department, Sarah's latest appointment, Dusty Willis, was surveying his surroundings. He had a considerable sense of satisfaction which, for once, was not chemically induced. Over three years in the business he had clawed his way up the agency ladder until, at the beginning of the year, he had been headhunted by HFK. Since that was where he already planned his next move, Dusty resisted only long enough to push his salary up to a figure that even he regarded as absurdly high.

Dusty now considered that he might be settled for some time; and set about furnishing his workspace to his own satisfaction. He was putting up an assortment of graphic images, and perching a small aviary of inflatable birds around the space. Then he set out the tools of his trade: electronic typewriter, felt-tip pens, layout pads and Polaroid camera.

Kim, working at the next desk, was a very different case. Kim was still at art school, and was doing work experience in the agency only because her father was an art director there. Nor was she sure that she wanted to be at Hamilton Forbes, for she strongly disapproved of political advertising.

Kim eyed Dusty from time to time with unquenched distrust as he settled in to his workspace. In appearance and general style they were oddly similar. This was not something which endeared them to each other. There was no exchange of conversation.

At the third workspace, Nick was reading the education section of the Party manifesto. From time to time, he swore under his breath. Finally, he stood up and walked around to where Dusty was fixing the last of a flock of parrots.

'What do you know about education?' he asked.

Dusty continued arranging his possessions.

'You mean, am I for it or against it?'

Nick showed the appropriate section of the manifesto.

'Serious business, my son,' he said. 'We are on compassionate ads. Higher pensions. Child benefit. Better schools –'

You're talking about this present moment in history?' asked Dusty, with interest.

'I'm talking about the next two weeks – up to polling day.'

Nick turned his attention to Kim.

'Come on. You're younger than us. What do kids want in school?'

'What I wanted,' said Dusty, 'was the girl in the next desk sticking her tongue in my mouth.' He thought for a moment, then said: 'Never happened.'

Kim indicated Dusty, and spoke to Nick.

'They're paying him for this?' she asked.

'Paying him?' said Nick. 'This man earns more than the Prime Minister.'

'Rightly so,' added Dusty. 'When did you last see the Prime Minister selling soapflakes?'

Kim came around the desk, to give herself a better vantage point. 'You want to know what kids need from school. I'll tell you what they need. They want to know how you get a job. What's going on up there, in the grey world. They need computers. They need teachers that get out of school once in a while – see what goes down.'

'Not so fast,' said Nick, who was making notes on a layout pad.

'Kids want books that aren't ten years old and falling to bits. They want –'

'Hang on,' said Nick. 'This could be a very type-heavy ad.' To Dusty he said: 'Give us a headline.'

Dusty's manner changed subtly. Now he was concentrating. He picked up his Polaroid camera and – before she could object – took a picture of Kim. He sketched in a rectangle on his layout pad, and surveyed the surrounding white space.

'Why don't we try –?'

With a Pentel, he began a swift, accurate lettering of a headline, talking as he worked.

'It's not what kids want. Kids don't vote. It's what their old mums and dads want.'

'And what they don't want,' said Nick.

Dusty finished the first section of his headline.

'So. Up here, we've got: *She learns Peace Studies. Famine Relief.* –' He paused. He took the print of Kim from his camera and gummed it within the rectangle he had drawn.

'You're not using my bloody picture,' said Kim.

Nick put a soothing arm around her.

'Example only,' he said.

'What else is progressive?' asked Dusty. 'Creative suffering?'

'Home sinus drainage,' said Nick. 'High-fibre sex.'

Dusty seized on this last suggestion.

'The wrinklies hate sex,' he said. He added to the headline: *Sex Education. And.* 'And what?' he asked.

'Lesbian rights?' suggested Nick.

'*Lesbian rights*,' agreed Dusty, finishing the headline. He indicated the photo of Kim. 'Then close-up of this really tacky kid.'

'Condescending prat,' said Kim.

Dusty was still working on his rough.

'Under the pic,' he said, 'you go for their hearts and minds – all your decent respectable dads –'

Dusty pointed out one of the framed photos he had just hung above his desk. It showed a tidily dressed man, wearing a hat, who stared out of his walnut frame with all the intellectual curiosity of a potato.

'Never forget the audience, they used to tell me. Here he is, our punter. Frederick James Baverstock, 11 Kitchener Terrace. Dad of the month. Reads the *Mail. Believes it*!! Now: what does he want for his little daughter, Stacy Baverstock? No fancy stuff is what he wants.'

Dusty lettered in a bold caption line under the Polaroid print. *Why can't they just teach her reading, writing and arithmetic?*

He put in tramlines to indicate body copy.

'Bit of yap here about permissive education – keeping up standards – what's wrong with the way schools used to be when Mum and Dad were growing up?' He lettered in a tagline. 'Then your compassion bit: we have our logo. Down here. And the punch line: *No one cares more about schools*.'

Sally came out of her office and stopped to speak to Alessandra. Alessandra was carrying several cans of film. She looked as near bad temper as her calmly beautiful face allowed. From some distance, she was watching Kim. Kim was still peering at Dusty's sketch.

'But the government runs education,' she said.

'No one knows that,' Nick assured her. 'They think it's those scruffy lefty teachers. Need smacking into shape.'

Dusty held up his completed rough and surveyed it.

'This would be for the lower middles. C-ones, C-twos. Full page in the *Mail. Express. Telegraph.*'

'*Telegraph's* not lower middle,' said Nick.

'Have you seen it lately?' asked Dusty. He was working again on his rough. 'You need to balance it up with some sloaney kid that wants hot and cold classics, oral French –' He looked around the department, searching for examples. He pointed to Alessandra.

'– someone like her –'

Nick looked in the direction Dusty was pointing.

'It's not oral French that Alessandra wants,' he said.

In the conference room, Linda and Helen were reviewing a videocassette and discussing Sarah. They had both known Sarah a long time; and Helen, at least, felt she had some right to assess her friend's life.

'I just mean, she might have picked on someone her own age,' she was saying. 'Instead of Nick.'

'Helen –' said Linda, rewinding the cassette.

'OK,' said Helen. 'You defend her. I mean, so do I. But really, what's a grown woman doing having a scene with Nick?'

'Trying to get her confidence back?' suggested Linda. She put the recorder on to play.

'I've heard a lot of things said about Sarah,' Helen remarked, 'but lack of confidence –'

Linda stopped the cassette, just as a line of tanks came over the horizon on the monitor screen. 'Why are you so upset about Sarah? Do you feel she's let you down?'

'Let me down?'

'Over the National Health business,' said Linda. 'I hear she told David that you found the nurse.'

'So I did,' said Helen. 'But who knows what'll happen about that? I'll deal with it when I have to.' She lowered her voice. 'No. I just think we all make too many excuses for Sarah. I mean, I've known her for ever. But when you hear what went wrong with the marriage – how Paul sees it – a lot of it's her. It's what someone said about Lincoln – "ambition like a little steam engine".'

'Helen,' said Linda. 'I can remember the end of your marriage. I seem to recall – you did the rounds. It's what happens. Happened when I broke up with Rachel.' She paused, then said: 'It's just a bit safer for us.'

'Being gay?'

'Being gay,' said Linda. 'But it's the same need, isn't it? You feel rejected. You want someone to show you you're still a desirable being. It's a sort of existential reassurance.'

'That's what Nick is?' asked Helen. 'Sarah's existential reassurance? I must have a coarse mind. I thought he was something much more basic.'

Unaware that she was the subject of discussion, Sarah was going back from David's office to her own. She dropped into her chair and began to go through the phone messages Sally had left on her desk. Then she became aware of someone standing in the doorway. She looked up to see Nick. She drew breath; then told herself sharply to stop acting like a teenager.

'Wanted to see you,' said Nick.

'I wanted to see you,' said Sarah, with more feeling than she intended. 'Also, I have a confession to make.'

Nick sat down in a lime-green chair, and waited.

'I have just had to tell a meeting of my senior colleagues that I spent most of last night in your bed,' said Sarah. She waited a moment, then asked: 'Do you mind?'

Nick glanced at the door. Sally was waiting to speak to Sarah. Her expression suggested she had heard what had just been said.

'I'll tell you the rest later,' said Sarah. 'Sally?'

'There was –' said Sally.

Sarah waited. 'Yes?'

Sally looked down at her notes. Eventually she said: 'Message from your au pair.'

Sarah sat up in her chair.

'Is Daniel –?'

'He's fine,' said Sally. 'The message is: he's back from the farm. He enjoyed himself. And this afternoon he and Rose are going to buy silverfish.'

'They can't be buying silverfish,' said Sarah. 'Silverfish are insects. It must be goldfish?'

Sally looked at her notes again.

'She said silverfish. And there was a call from your husband.'

'Oh, yes. What did *he* say?' asked Sarah.

'He said he was willing to meet you.'

'Kind of him,' said Sarah. 'Did he leave a number?'

Sally passed over her note of the telephone message, looked for a moment at Nick, and backed out of the office. Sarah missed the interchange of glances. She was staring at the number she had been given.

'That's – Helen's number –'

Nick turned back from watching Sally.

'What is?'

'The number my husband left,' said Sarah. 'The bastard. He's staying with Helen.'

Sarah picked up the phone and was about to key in a number when Gordon appeared at the office door.

'I'd like a word with Sarah,' he said to Nick. 'A private word.'

Nick stood up, collected his campaign notes, and went out the door. Gordon closed it behind him, and spoke to Sarah.

'David's letting Helen go,' he said.

Sarah put down the phone, which she was still holding, and looked at Gordon.

'He's firing her?'

Gordon nodded.

'Sacrifice to the Prime Minister. And – in his own words – he's considering your future.'

There was a pause. Then Sarah said:

'Gordon? Why are telling me this?'

'It's David,' said Gordon. 'He wants me to resign. He's got a resignation letter, typed, from me to him. But I'm not signing it.'

'You're not?'

Gordon shook his head.

'I know what David was doing in New York.'

Sarah glanced at her secretary, who was out of hearing, behind the glass wall of her office.

'You mean Sally?'

'Of course I don't mean Sally,' replied Gordon. 'What David does in bed is his own business. I mean that he was dealing up the shares in that agency he bought.'

'Pater Paolozzi,' said Sarah. She leaned forward. Her hair fell loosely around her face. 'I said, why are you telling me this?'

Gordon leaned on the desk. He looked exhausted.

'We don't have a very easy relationship. You and I.'

'That's a fair summary,' said Sarah.

Gordon's breathing was unpleasantly shallow.

'I thought you told David.'

Sarah waited, listening to the man's sharp respiration. Gordon indicated the National Health advertisements mounted on Sarah's magnet board. Each one was now cancelled with a broad red felt-pen cross.

'I thought you told him I cleared those damn things to run. However, I gather you didn't. It was Stephen.'

'What did you expect?' asked Sarah.

Gordon interlocked his fingers and brought his thumbs together, so that they were almost touching. Sarah remembered that her own father had used this way of calming himself. The memory surprised her: it was years since she had had that picture of him.

'What did I expect? I expected some loyalty, I suppose.' The thumbs were a hairsbreadth away from touching. 'I thought I could trust Stephen.'

'I should be at a meeting,' said Sarah.

'Wait,' said Gordon. 'That's not the end of it. Off the

record, I know some very damaging things about David. Two or three of us on the board could still get him out.'

Sarah, who had been collecting her papers, paused.

'We could keep Helen on the staff,' said Gordon. 'Bring Warren back.'

'It was you that fired Warren,' said Sarah. 'Not David.'

Gordon seemed not to hear.

'Further, we could safeguard our own positions.'

Sarah began to speak. Gordon stood up, leaned across the desk, and interrupted her.

'Personalities aside, it would be good for the agency. In management terms, David's out of his depth.'

'Gordon,' said Sarah. 'Sit down.' Gordon dropped back into his chair. She peered at him. 'Are you all right?'

Gordon tried to give an ironic overtone to the advertising industry's most damning confession.

'Getting too old for this.' He took several deep breaths. 'Do you want to meet me after work? Somewhere we can talk?'

Sarah's phone rang. She lifted the receiver and replaced it.

'You seem to be forgetting one or two things,' she said. 'I brought David back from New York to stop you pushing him out.'

'I'm aware of that,' said Gordon. 'But you can see the way he's going. He's getting out of your control. Out of anyone's control. So, change your mind. You're an intelligent woman.'

'Thank you,' said Sarah. She checked the time, then went to the door of her office. 'But even if I did change my mind – I don't know that I could turn around and put David out on the street –'

'Do you imagine he'd think twice about doing that to you?'

Sarah shook her head.

'I don't. But I have to live with my decisions. Not his.'

At Hamilton Forbes' production house, Linda and Dusty were in the control box of the smaller television studio. Through a glass panel, they could see the set. It was dressed to look like a comprehensive classroom. On the blackboard was the heading 'Peace Studies'; below it, a list of hints on the easiest ways of surrendering to an invading army. Some of these points had been rubbed off by the tweed jacket of a terrified teacher, who was cowering against the blackboard. He was cowering because two sturdy young actors, representing fifth-form pupils, were threatening him with violence. An assistant floor manager was rehearsing these lads in newer and more visually effective types of nastiness.

Dusty, who had recently come into the studio, watched this scene for a few moments.

'The education-isn't-what-it-used-to-be bit of the Party political,' said Linda.

Dusty watched the shoot for a few moments in amazed silence. Then he turned to Linda with a query.

'Have we still actually got the political account? After this National Health cockup?'

Linda shrugged.

'Sarah says, we go on as if we're keeping the account, until we know we're not.' She indicated the classroom set. 'And this, in case you're wondering, is an actual inner-city comprehensive school.'

'Ah,' said Dusty. 'I did wonder.'

'Picks up all the voter worries about education. You may have to do the related press ads.'

'I keep telling people,' said Dusty, 'this is my first day. What exactly is the message here? What am I telling the punters?'

Linda spoke to the AFM on talkback, then said:

'Basically, the message is: so-called progressive teachers produce pupils who grow up to devour their masters.'

'Never happened at my school,' said Dusty.

'Never mind your school,' said Linda. 'This is not the reality channel.' She indicated the studio floor, where rehearsal was ending. 'But this stuff goes down a treat in the popular press. They love it; red meat and drink to them. Sarah calls the whole thing the Myth of the Teenage Frankenstein.'

Linda left the gallery and went down on the floor before the shoot resumed.

Dusty scribbled down Myth of the Teenage Frankenstein. In his spare time, he wrote short stories. He had an idea that he might one day use it as a title.

Across the street from the agency, Sarah's husband Paul was sitting in the Firenze, nursing a capuccino. He was not drinking it; he was making it last until Helen came in. When she did, she was fifteen minutes late.

'I'm sorry,' she said. 'Meeting with –'

'Sarah,' said Paul.

Helen nodded and sat down. Paul turned her face, so that he could see her better.

'From what you said on the phone, it sounds like a difficult day. Coffee?'

Paul signalled to a waiter. The waiter looked in the other direction.

'It was a difficult day,' said Helen. 'I just lost my job.'

'Waiters go to training schools in avoiding a customer's eye,' said Paul. Then he stopped signalling, abruptly, and looked at Helen. 'Did you say you lost your job?'

'I did. We had an inquest over this so-called unemployed nurse. Gordon's fate is still being decided. Your wife seems to have come out smelling of roses. And David, after deliberating with the Minister, decided that the Party needed appeasing. So he's letting me go.' Helen framed the words carefully. 'His language, not mine.'

The waiter, now that he was no longer the object of Paul's attention, approached slowly.

'Sarah stays,' said Paul. 'And you go. Why?'

'If you want an uncharitable guess –' Helen glanced at the now-hovering waiter.

'Another coffee,' said Paul. 'Capuccino.'

'My guess is,' said Helen, 'David owes one to your wife. Doesn't owe me. And the Party's out for blood. They had to cancel all the National Health ads – take down the posters –'

Paul seemed more dismayed than Helen.

'Maybe Sarah could save your job? You say she's on the board.'

'Do you think she would?'

'She's a very close friend,' said Paul. 'That's what friends are for, surely?'

Helen looked at him.

'After you called today, and left my phone number?'

'Oh, God,' said Paul. The waiter came back with Helen's capuccino. 'It never occurred to me that she'd recognise it –'

'You really don't think, do you, Paul? Sarah calls me once or twice a day. Or did.' Helen tried her coffee. 'She's rather stopped since you walked out.'

'That was nothing to do with you.'

'That's not what Sarah thought,' said Helen. 'Not after she found out you were seeing me. And not seeing her.'

In the agency, Alessandra and Carol were bringing coffee for the day's last meeting about the National Health Service, to the managing director's office. Just before she returned to her own office, Alessandra was stopped by Mike Sutherland.

'Aly,' he said. 'I really need a word.'

Alessandra hesitated, then spoke to Carol.

'You go on in. Go *on*.'

Carrying her tray, Carol went reluctantly into David's office and closed the door behind her.

Mike took Alessandra's arm, to keep her from moving away. He was a squash player, with a very firm grip.

'That note you left me – are you serious?' he said. 'Dee won't let me come and stay with you – because of some bloody copy I wrote?'

'It's Dee's house,' said Alessandra. 'Ask her – if she'll talk to you. I've never seen her so angry. Now, would you let go my arm?'

Mike maintained his grip.

'I'm going to talk to Dee. Believe it or not, she's made a meeting about these silly little minstrel-show ads I wrote –'

'I have to go,' said Alessandra. 'There's a meeting in there, waiting.'

There was a sudden change in Mike's tone. He let her arm go.

'Aly, listen. Jess say's she's not coming back to me. I am actually on my own. I wanted to tell you: I really need someone.'

'I see,' said Alessandra. 'And that someone just happens to be me?'

Sarah was coming out of the conference room, leaving a briefing on nuclear weapons, which had been arranged some days previously by Francis Salk. The speaker was a retired colonel from the Institute of Conflict Studies. What he had to say was not cheering. He had also given the participants notes of various nuclear scenarios that the Institute foresaw. With professional speed, Sarah was now skimming through these prognoses.

Stephen, who had stayed in the conference room to speak with Dee, now emerged and headed for the lifts.

'That gathering,' he remarked in passing, 'told me rather more than I want to know about nuclear weapons.'

'Have you actually read these notes?' asked Sarah.

Stephen checked that he had his copy, and shook his head.

'More alarming than what the colonel just told us?'

Sarah went back to the briefing.

'Something he didn't say. We no longer seem to have much control over our independent deterrent.'

Stephen signalled to Warren's daughter Kim, who stopped and waited.

'Never was wildly independent.'

'Yesterday, Stephen,' said Sarah, 'I wrote three very plausible ads, denying that allegation.'

Stephen moved toward the lifts, and toward Kim.

'And why not?' he asked. 'If we can't change the world, we can at least console ourselves with plausible copy.' He held the lift door open for Kim, and followed her inside.

'Good news and bad news,' he said to her. 'I've just been told by an expert on nuclear weapons that some of us will survive the first few hours of a nuclear attack. The bad news is that your Dad didn't get his new job.'

'Does he know that?' asked Kim.

Stephen shook his head gravely.

'Don't tell him this evening. He'll find out tomorrow.'

Kim looked at Stephen without any warmth at all.

'I'm not going to see Dad this evening,' she said. 'I'm going out with you, aren't I?'

FOURTEEN

It was late in the afternoon. David Postgate was still exchanging phone calls with Francis Salk at Downing Street; still desperately trying to hold on to the political account.

The financial loss would not be significant. What worried David, at this stage in his expansion plans, was losing the most visible account in Britain; and the consequent damage to his agency's standing. That, in turn, would seriously affect the company's valuation.

A slide in Hamilton Forbes' share price would mean selling the New York subsidiary. David had no doubt that it would also abruptly end this phase of his own career. That was a possibility he did not yet care to contemplate.

Further down the agency, work still continued on the political account; but not all the agency's staff shared David's sense of urgency.

Mike Sutherland, for one, saw no reason to alter his usual routine. A little after five, he was striding through the creative department, carrying his squash gear in a new and expensive leather sports bag, decorated with coloured flashes. He caught up with Nick beside the lifts.

'Quick game of squash?'

'I'm working late,' said Nick. 'Telling the voters why unemployment's good for the country. To say nothing of their own spiritual growth.'

Mike jabbed several times at the call button for the lift.

'Come on, you bugger,' he ordered the lift. 'And waiting for Sarah?' he said to Nick.

A model dressed from head to foot as a pea pod came shuffling down the passage. The words Permafrost Peas were sprayed across her green breasts.

'What do you mean? Waiting for Sarah?'

The lift doors opened. Mike held the door for the pea pod, which shuffled into the lift. He winked at Nick.

'Well,' he said, 'there's Mrs Copeland. No Mr Copeland. Big empty bed. And a little bird tells me, she's been casting a hungry eye in your direction.'

The pea pod twisted round to see who was speaking behind her.

'Mike,' said Nick, 'Sarah Copeland is a mature woman. She's over thirty.'

Mike moved closer and lowered his voice.

'Come on,' he said. 'I've heard you say you'd be well pleased to get into Sarah's pants.'

The pea pod shuffled as far away as the lift allowed.

'Where do you get this argot?' Nick asked. 'Who uses the word pants?'

The lift stopped. Mike held the door open for the Permafrost girl.

'And if *she* wasn't in pod –' he said.

'Mike – that lady is my invention,' said Nick. He sang, a little out of tune: '*Permafrost Peas, Deep flavour-freeze* –'

The model, who was shuffling toward reception, paused, looked back, then continued on her laborious way.

'I'm afraid she may be frigid,' said Nick.

'*She's* frigid?' said Mike. 'You should have seen my first wife.' He went at an athletic run down the steps to the car park. 'I can handle cold, green women,' he called.

Carol, more than usually flustered, dashed across reception.

'Mike's not going home, is he?'

Nick pointed downward.

'He's going to knock the hell out of some unsuspecting squash player.'

'Oh, he can't,' called Carol. She too disappeared down to the car park, calling: 'Mike – don't go – they want you for a meeting!'

Nick, suddenly tired, went into the nearest kitchen to make himself coffee. Alessandra was already in there, tipping pills on to a saucer. She opened the refrigerator, took out a bottle of mineral water, and poured a glass. Nick watched with interest.

'I thought you only needed one pill a day?'

'It's not that sort of pill,' said Alessandra. She held up the packet: it was a remedy for travel sickness.

'Roads bad round Fulham, are they?'

Alessandra, carrying a glass and tablets, squeezed past Nick.

'They're for Sally.'

Now she had all of Nick's attention.

'Where's Sally going?'

'Nowhere,' said Alessandra. 'She gets morning sickness.'

Nick glanced at the clock. It was five-thirty in the evening.

'Is Sally –?'

'Pregnant,' agreed Alessandra. 'I thought – as the father – you'd know that.'

Sarah came out of the media department and into creative. She stopped at the door of Sally's office. Sally was sitting at her desk, apparently doing nothing. She was looking at her hands, which were small, with closely bitten nails.

'Sally – can I have those race ads?' asked Sarah. 'Quickly –?'

Nick came back in to the department, carrying his coffee, unemployment roughs, and point-of-sale material for Honcho chocolate. Sarah collected the disputed racial-harmony roughs, and turned away from Sally, to see Nick.

'I've got one last meeting,' she said. 'Trying to sort out these ads Dee's objecting to. Can I see you after that? Sixish?'

Nick hesitated. Sarah had an uncharacteristic sense of desperation, as if something she needed were slipping away.

'Meet you at the car,' she said. 'Please. We ought to talk about what's happening with us –'

Dee came through the department. Sarah gestured downward, to where the meeting would be held. Dee nodded, and went out in the direction of the lifts.

Sarah seemed about to say something else to Nick. After a

moment, she changed her mind, and followed Dee downstairs.

Nick watched her go. He went into Sally's office. She was taking a letter from her computer printer. Nick came close behind her, and put his hand on her stomach. He felt the flesh contract. Sally looked up at him.

'Aly told me,' said Nick. 'About my son.'

Sally seemed to be deciding among several possible answers. Finally, she said:

'It's David's baby.'

'Can't be,' said Nick. 'He's too old.' He sat on the edge of her desk. 'But I wondered: did you – did you start sleeping with him when you were still with me?'

Sally opened her mouth, but said nothing. Nick nodded slowly.

'You wouldn't have done that if we were married.'

There was a pause; then Sally said:

'Nick. We lived together three years – you never even suggested getting married.'

'I was immature.'

'You mean,' said Sally, 'you thought you'd meet someone sexier at the next party. Or the party after that.'

Nick took her hands, and stroked the bitten nails.

'I'm a changed man. Come and have a drink this evening. You might like the idea.'

'I'm not sure –'

'About the drink, or about marriage?' He picked up the letter Sally had taken out of the printer. 'What's *this*?'

'I'm trying to write a letter of resignation.'

Nick looked at Sally's narrow hips.

'But surely – you've got another six months –?'

Sally took a breath.

'You try and imagine what it's like,' she said. 'Working in an agency with two men who might be the father of your child.' She stopped, then added: 'One of them the managing director.'

'All right,' said Nick. 'Go on. Say it. "And one of them a junior copywriter".'

In Gordon's office, the meeting to discuss Mike Sutherland's ads had started. The advertising was designed to reassure racial minorities that the government had the best of ethnic intentions. Dee, however, thought the ads themselves were racist.

Being called back from his evening squash game had not improved Mike's temper.

'The government's going down in every poll we've had this week,' he was saying. He held up the rough he had done the day before. 'Which might be a good reason for getting these ads out.' He indicated the second rough, which told blacks that they were also British. 'Sitting in here, they're not going to change anyone's mind.'

'Those particular ads,' said Dee, 'never were going to change anyone's mind. Not in our favour, anyway.'

'All this may be academic,' said Sarah. 'After the NHS thing, we may not keep the account. The Prime Minister may bring Parr Sarris Bernstein back in.'

'Until the Prime Minister decides,' said Gordon, 'we continue.'

'In that case, we need to think about what Dee's saying. These ads may be wrong for their audience.'

'Not just wrong,' said Dee. 'Offensive.'

Mike stood up and rescued his roughs from the centre of Gordon's mahogany table.

'I can't see how you support that. The government wants to show it has nothing against coloured people.' He held up the first advertisement. 'So: it says, quite clearly – it doesn't matter if you're black.'

Dee stared at him. She seemed to be trying to formulate an acceptable sentence.

'But it does matter,' she said finally. 'It's important. It's what we are. We don't want to be told it doesn't matter.'

'Order,' said Gordon. 'Order, please.'

'You seem to enjoy being male,' said Dee to Mike. 'How'd you like to be told it doesn't matter to anyone whether you're a man or a woman?'

'This,' said Gordon, 'is not something we can resolve through emotion.'

Dee made a real effort at self-control.

'Mike – I can see you think your copy's very tolerant, and we ought to be grateful. I know you're not trying to be patronising. But whites can't write for blacks.'

Carol came into the office and waited for a chance to speak to Gordon.

'Try to be realistic, Dee,' said Gordon. 'The agency doesn't have any black writers.'

'And why not?' asked Dee.

Carol bent close to Gordon and whispered: 'David's waiting to see you. It's urgent. He says he has five minutes.'

Gordon heaved himself to his feet.

'Excuse me,' he said. 'Sarah, can you settle this? On the basis of effective advertising – and not simply some vision of the way we would like things to be?'

'I'll do my best, Gordon,' said Sarah, watching the dark-suited figure as he collected his papers and slowly left the room.

As Gordon walked round the mezzanine floor, he could see David Postgate below him, talking to Linda and Francis Salk. He paused, looking down. It occurred to him that his feeling for his managing director was more than a professional mistrust. It was a profound dislike, verging on hatred. And it came not just from a disagreement about the proper way to run an advertising business, but from something much deeper – a resentment of David's unearned gifts. David Postgate seemed to walk in endless sunshine. He had money and charm. He had every undeserved good fortune. But Gordon reflected, as he walked down the main stairs, there is always a term to good fortune. He believed that the golden weather might finally be ending for David.

If David had any such premonition, he showed no sign of it. He concluded his conversation with Linda, and greeted Gordon with unusual affability. Francis waited, watching the two men.

'Gordon,' said David. 'I thought you should know. The Prime Minister's been on the phone.'

Gordon waited.

'And we keep the account.' said David.

'Frankly, it's almost impossible to change at this stage,' said Francis. 'Happened informally with Neville's predecessor: switching advisers, in mid-campaign. But it's not something we could risk.'

David took Gordon's arm, and began to walk toward reception.

'However,' he said, 'we have agreed some changes. Helen goes. You will no longer be looking after the account.'

It took Gordon a moment to comprehend.

'You're saying I'm off the account?'

'Reluctantly,' said David, 'we have come to that decision. After all, as Harry Truman used to say, the buck must stop somewhere.'

Gordon was breathing quickly.

'You did that without consulting me?'

'Gordon,' said Francis, 'you must understand. It wasn't just the PM. With this unemployed nurse all over the media –' He spread his hands in a delicately fatalistic gesture. 'The Party's baying for blood.'

'And it's my blood they get,' said Gordon.

'Together with Helen's, I'm afraid,' said David. He turned to Francis, and indicated a black Daimler waiting in the street. 'Your car, I think.'

Gordon followed the two men through reception.

'I shall need to consider my position.'

David paused.

'I can see that,' he said sympathetically. 'Take your time, Gordon. Come back to me when you're ready.'

Then he and Francis moved on, deep in conversation. Gordon stood watching them go. He put out a hand and steadied himself against a pistachio-green wall. Dusty, on his way out of the agency, stopped to see if Gordon was all right. Gordon, suddenly aware of the young copywriter's scrutiny, turned and walked slowly back toward his office. Dusty went on through reception, pausing to speak to Jane at the desk.

'How was your first day?' she asked, putting two late callers on hold.

'Odd,' said Dusty. 'I think that's a fair description. For starters, I find the agency's lost the account I came here to work on.'

Jane put one of the outside calls through.

'The political account?' she asked.

Dusty, who was watching Linda, nodded.

'We haven't lost it,' said Jane. 'There was a call from Downing Street –'

Dusty looked at her.

'And you listened?'

Jane opened her green eyes as wide as they would go.

'Shameless,' said Dusty.

Linda paused at the desk.

'I'm going home,' she said. 'Rachel Hall didn't ring? The photographer?'

Jane gave no indication that she knew Rachel Hall, as well as being a photographer, was also Linda's former lover.

'No calls at all,' she said.

Linda waved and moved on toward the street. Dusty caught up with her.

'Would you like to come for a drink?'

Linda paused, and looked at him.

'You're new here,' she said finally. 'I might as well tell you: I'm – I'm a dyke.'

'I don't understand,' said Dusty, 'what has happened to the English language. When you ask someone for dinner, they assume it's indecent. Suggest a drink, and they think you want to get laid. What words do you use if you just want a glass of wine and a meal?'

'I'm sorry,' said Linda. 'I thought you didn't do that. Nick said you took most of your meals off a mirror.'

'And this is the man,' said Dusty, 'to whom I lent my Giovanni Vanucci jacket?' He took Linda's arm. 'Come on. I want you to tell me some gossip. I'm feeling very lost in this place.'

* * *

Inside the agency, Dee had finally emerged from her meeting about Mike Sutherland's advertisements for racial harmony. Nick caught up with her at the top of the central stairs. He looked at her closely; her dark skin was flushed.

'Hard day?'

'Not so much hard,' said Dee. 'Wasted, more like. Spent most of it stopping Sutherland telling us we're not black, we're beautiful. It makes the stuff he does for Scunthorpe beer seem tasteful.'

'Now,' said Nick. 'That reminds me. I thought we might give big Mike a new scenario. This, you understand, is a television commercial for the Seriously Strong Beer. You have this nuclear attack –'

'Not before the election,' said Dee. 'It's atoms-for-peace time.'

Nick shook his head.

'We tell him it's for next month – when we stop pretending bombs are harmless.' He stopped, halfway down the stairs, and sketched a picture in the air. 'OK: so in come the missiles. London totally destroyed. Except for this one bloke that survives, because he was down in the basement, feeding the ferret.'

'Not even Mike'd believe this,' said Dee.

'Don't overestimate him. So – bloke comes up, looks round. It's a wasteland. Flattened. Fire, smoke, ruins. All the makings of a nuclear winter. Pretty damn depressing. And he's desperate for food. Opens the fridge –'

Dee started down the stairs again.

'Don't tell me,' she said. 'He finds the world's last remaining bottle of Scunthorpe Six X.'

'Right. Whips off the top with his teeth – takes a swallow – looks out where the window was –'

'A vision,' said Dee, in gospel tones. 'Suddenly, there's flowers and trees growing up – all pure, primal colours – in among all the radioactive ruins of St Pauls –'

They went through reception, where Jane was finally closing down the switchboard.

'Now there's life and hope again,' said Nick.

Dee traced out a choral theme.

'I hear it. New World Symphony on soundtrack –'

'Then,' said Nick, 'you have your roller caption. Up comes the slogan: *Scunthorpe Six X. Even the Bomb looks Better.*'

Nick and Dee walked across reception in silence, contemplating this. Then Nick shook his head.

'Can't do it. Sutherland's eventually going to work out there wouldn't be anyone watching.'

'Pity,' said Dee. 'We'll try and find him something else tomorrow.'

She waved goodbye and went out to the street. Nick went the other way, into the agency bar. He passed Stephen, who was coming out with Warren's daughter Kim. He was adjusting her deliberately torn jacket.

'Even rebels can have style,' Stephen was saying. 'Look at Simon Bolivar. Sandino. Che Guevara.'

Gordon emerged from the express lift.

'Stephen,' he said. 'Come here a minute. I've been looking for you.'

Stephen looked from Kim to Gordon.

'Bit busy,' he said. 'Just on my way home –'

'Over here,' said Gordon. He waited until Stephen was a couple of feet away, then said quietly: 'He managed to hang on to the government. And he gave the PM my head. My head, on a platter.'

'You're talking about David?'

'I think you knew that,' said David. 'And he wants me to resign. I imagine he's told you?'

'Gordon,' said Stephen, 'believe me. I haven't talked to David.'

Gordon expressed profound disbelief. Kim, tired of waiting, moved away.

'Well, when you do talk to David,' said Gordon, 'you can tell him that I'm not resigning. I still have a place in this agency.'

Stephen began to edge away, in the direction of the disappearing Kim. Gordon seemed suddenly to notice her. He pointed.

'Is she – *Warren's* daughter?'

Stephen nodded.

'Helping me with a bit of research,' he said. 'I'm supposed to be looking after her.' He put a hand on Gordon's arm. 'We'll talk tomorrow. Decide on a strategy.'

Stephen went after Kim at a run. Nick, who enjoyed these small human dramas, went on into the bar. Alessandra, who had joined him, watched until Stephen and Kim were both out of sight.

'Interesting, isn't it?' she said. 'There's Stephen. And some others I could mention. The way *they* get older, and their girls get younger.'

'Alessandra, my love,' said Nick, 'you can't afford to work in an agency, and be censorious. Come on. Forget this depravity. Let me buy you a drink.'

Alessandra shook her head.

'Sally's over there,' she said. 'That's who you ought to be buying drinks for.'

Sarah was down in the car park, where she had arranged to meet Nick. Sitting in her BMW, she waited ten minutes, telling herself she was a fool. Then she walked slowly back into the agency. The reception area was empty. She went into the bar. Just inside the door, she met David.

'I thought you might like to know,' he said. 'We kept the account.'

Sarah was looking from one crowded table to another.

'I heard,' she said. 'I've uncrossed my fingers.'

David watched her searching the room.

'But I took Gordon off the political side.'

Sarah's attention came back to him.

'Then who's going to run it?'

'I was going to suggest,' said David, 'that we might. You and I.'

Sarah looked at him. 'I don't believe you said that. After this National Health mess? I thought you'd be cutting out my heart with an obsidian knife.'

'As I recall, even Abraham was only asked for Isaac.'

'Ah, yes,' said Sarah. 'And you've offered two. Gordon and Helen.'

Helen had just entered the room. Seeing that Sarah was with David, she changed direction, went to the bar, and ordered.

'Tomorrow,' said David, 'we'll sort out the political details.'

Sarah was looking away again. She had finally sighted Nick. He was sitting at a corner table with Sally. Their heads were close, and they were laughing.

David followed her glance, and indicated Nick.

'I see you've got competition.'

'I see you have too,' said Sarah. 'Assuming you're still interested in Sally.' She looked at David with genuine curiosity. 'Tell me. How do you feel about her?'

There was a pause; then David said:

'One's forced back on these banal phrases –'

Sarah waited.

'I suppose I would have to say that I'm in love with her.'

'How does that feel?'

This time, David did not hesitate.

'She makes me feel as if I were starting a new life.'

'You don't know how lucky you are,' said Sarah. 'Hold on to it.'

At the bar, Helen was saying, 'And I want a vodka tonic. I'll be back.'

She went across to where David and Sarah were standing. She spoke to Sarah.

'I need to tell you something.' Sarah seemed about to make some excuse, and Helen said: 'It's important.'

Sarah indicated one of the few free tables left in the bar.

As she moved away to collect the drinks she had ordered, Helen said to David: 'I've cleared my desk. If you were wondering.'

Sally had noticed Sarah.

'On the subject of fidelity –' she said to Nick, 'what about you and *her*?'

Helen went past, slightly spilling one of the drinks she carried. She put them down on the table where Sarah was already sitting.

'Your usual,' she said. 'It's my farewell.'

Sarah left her drink untouched.

'You're angry with me,' she said. 'I can tell you are.'

'Old friend watches while I'm given three days to get out of the agency,' said Helen. 'Watches David cut me off like a dead twig. Declines to take any responsibility herself. Why should I be angry?'

Sarah outlined a complicated pattern on the table.

'I can try and get the board to bring you back.'

'But let's not hold our breath,' said Helen. 'After all, you said that to Warren – and what have you done? Nothing. There's the guy you worked with for nine years, put out to grass. No one saw you fighting for him.'

Sarah was very quiet.

'There was nothing I could do about Warren.'

'So I gather,' said Helen. She willed Sarah to look at her. 'I sometimes wonder: does it mean anything at all to you – the time we've spent together? Warren – you – me?'

Sarah started to say something, and Helen interrupted.

'You know, I can remember – when you started at Doyle Dane – we were sharing the flat – and you didn't even know an onion had to be peeled before you cooked it.'

'Oh, come on,' said Sarah.

'In fact,' said Helen, 'you never did cook, did you? Used to live on toast. You worked all the time, even then.'

'Wasn't just me,' said Sarah.

Helen seemed not to hear.

'I remember the day you came home: said you'd met this wonderful young designer. We got drunk, didn't we? And I met your beautiful young man.'

'You said –'

'I said she's not your sort, Paul. She's far too ambitious for you –'

'You were envious,' said Sarah. 'Actually, I was wondering if – somewhere in this tirade – you might mention Paul.

Otherwise, I was going to mention him. He finally left me a phone number today.' She watched Helen's face. 'A number I knew very well. It was yours.'

Helen finished her drink. Then she said:

'Sarah – he was just terribly depressed. Asked me if he could stay a few days. I said yes. He's been sleeping on the couch in the living room.'

'My husband,' said Sarah. 'Sleeping on your couch.'

Helen said: 'You don't have to believe it. I don't, at the moment, care very much whether you do or not.' She drew breath. 'And I don't actually think, Sarah, you're in a position to judge anyone else's private life.'

'Just what does that mean?' asked Sarah.

'It means, you didn't sleep with Paul for three months –'

'He told you that?'

'You certainly didn't. And then, a week after he leaves, you're in bed' – Helen pointed across the room at Nick – 'with the toy boy. You can't say there's any great moral dimension to that.'

'Well, at least Nick's not married.'

'Oh, come on,' said Helen. 'It isn't exactly Heloise and Abelard, is it? You know you could walk right across Nick's mind, and you'd never get your feet wet.'

Sarah was clearly more hurt by this than either she or Helen expected. With an edge of guilt, or desperation, Helen found another angle of attack.

'And Paul,' she said. 'Paul worries about what you do' – she indicated Nick again – 'when you're with him. Paul worries about what's happening to his son. In the middle of your little love affair.'

The mention of Daniel refocused Sarah's attention.

'Paul worries about *his* son? He talks to you about Daniel?'

'Of course he talks about Daniel,' said Helen. 'He talks about him obsessively.'

'But not to me,' said Sarah. 'Paul came in once – smashed the phone – went away – never said another word about Daniel. I've no idea what he wants –' She looked closely at Helen. 'But you know. Don't you?'

It was a while before Helen said anything. When she did speak, she sounded suddenly exhausted.

'Yes,' she said. 'I know what he wants for Daniel.'

The two women sat, as if spent. Sarah did not take her eyes off Helen's face. Then Helen said:

'He wants you to give him up.'

FIFTEEN

Late on Tuesday evening, two days before the election, Sarah was driving home. She was listening to political bulletins on her car radio.

On the whole, the news was good. The government was climbing in the opinion polls. Commentators agreed that the National Health Service debacle had faded from public attention. It had been replaced by bitter arguments between the Prime Minister and opposition spokesmen over defence and unemployment. For this, Sarah felt nothing but relief. The country was saturated with her pro-nuclear advertising; and she had managed to extract from the Prime Minister a powerful, televised speech on his Party's employment plans, and Cabinet's humane concern for the unemployed.

'We may,' said Sarah to Rose, who opened the door, 'we may be out of the wood with this damned election. Has anyone arrived?'

Rose shook her head.

'We're finishing the food in the kitchen. The caterers have come –'

'You're wonderful,' said Sarah. 'I'll go and change. Shouldn't be more than twenty people – it was very short notice.'

It had been very short notice indeed. On impulse, that afternoon, Sarah had invited those working on the political account back to her house for drinks. She did it partly for reasons of morale. A month's ceaseless work on the campaign had brought everyone to the edge of exhaustion. Unexplained quarrels flared and faded. As she went upstairs, Sarah thought it was worth seeing if she could get at least her own staff mixing socially again.

* * *

In the kitchen, Rose was arranging food the caterers had brought, and adding specialities of her own. Loving summer fruit, she bought huge bowls of raspberries. Daniel had positioned himself at the end of the kitchen table, where he could unobtrusively help himself to them. At the same time, he was watching his mother's latest Party Election Broadcast on the kitchen television. Rose, whipping meringue mixture, also kept an eye on the screen.

It had just changed from graphics – which showed that rising unemployment figures concealed a downward trend – to a closeup of the Prime Minister. He looked, Rose thought, much older than when she had seen him, four years earlier, at an election rally in Birmingham. The last term of office had clearly taken its toll; but he spoke with much of his earlier energy.

'Yesterday,' he was saying, 'I was accused of ignoring unemployment. Ignoring unemployment. And I have to say to you – that is the most scandalous nonsense. In the years that I have been your Prime Minister, I have worked unceasingly – *unceasingly* – to reduce unemployment – to provide genuine jobs for the people of Britain.'

Sarah came into the kitchen. She had changed into a grey dress that Vanucci made specially for her. She hugged Daniel, and removed his hand from the bowl of raspberries.

'You're not looking at me,' said Daniel. 'You're looking at the television.'

'Your Mummy made that programme,' said Rose.

'For my sins,' said Sarah. 'I have now seen it, in the editing suite, something like thirty times.'

'Then I don't see why you want to watch again,' said Daniel. But he knew his mother would.

'No one,' said Neville Henderson to camera, 'and let me repeat: no one – feels more deeply for the unemployed than I do.' He paused dramatically and Sarah counted to four under her breath, then signalled an imaginary camera crew for action.

'But let me also remind you,' said the Prime Minister, 'that I would be doing no favour to the unemployed if I said to them–'

Sarah turned down the sound on the television. In the sudden silence, the doorbell rang. Daniel went to answer it. Sarah spoke to Rose.

'Do you think we've made an honest man of him?' she asked. 'Never mind what he's saying – is that the face of a Prime Minister from whom you'd buy a used car?'

Rose looked at the Prime Minister's face. He was still silently speaking on the screen. Whether or not it was honest, she thought, it was certainly not the face of a man in the best of health.

A subtitle flashed up below Neville Henderson's face. It read: *By Raising Wages, We are Pricing Ourselves out of Jobs.*

'Is it a cheap car I'm buying from him?' Rose asked Sarah. Before Sarah could answer, Daniel ran back into the kitchen. He was followed by Stephen Hallam, dressed even more elegantly than usual. Stephen glanced at the television, and picked up a glass of wine from the side table.

'Your son admitted me,' he said to Sarah. And to Rose: 'Remember we go to the polls on Thursday. That was a very tepid response to our leader – after all we've done for him. More precisely, after all Sarah's done for him.'

'Modulated his voice,' said Sarah. 'Slowed down his delivery – rewritten his speeches – schooled him in sincerity –'

Stephen moved to the television, and spoke to Rose.

'You see what I mean? In election week, we expect a more enthusiastic reception from you.'

A subtitle flashed on to the screen: *As the Economy Revives, Unemployment Drops.*

Stephen turned up the television sound again. Neville Henderson said: 'Give us another term. Let us finish the job we started. The economy will revive – you and your families will watch unemployment coming down!'

The Prime Minister waved regally to an unseen, but rapturously cheering, crowd.

Rose was putting meringues in the oven.

'He's got an enthusiastic audience,' she said. 'Unless it's a tape?'

The doorbell rang again. Daniel grabbed a handful of berries and raced out to the hall.

'Daniel!' called Sarah. 'Don't you dare drop raspberries on the carpet! And it's time you were in bed.'

Stephen opened his briefcase and took out a provincial paper, the Brighton *Evening Argus*. He indicated the Prime Minister's image, which was still on screen, and spoke quietly to Sarah.

'Henderson may be in trouble. Salk brought in the Brighton rag.'

He opened the paper and read:

'Brighton Fire Disaster. Deaths in Smoke-Filled Veterans' Home.'

'I don't begin to understand,' said Sarah. Through the folding doors she could see Carol, Linda, Alice and Dusty entering her drawing room. Rose was offering them drinks and canapés. 'What has a fire in a veterans' home got to do with the Prime Minister?'

'This particular veterans' home,' said Stephen, 'was a Paramor System building. Put up for the Brighton Council by Parlett Construction. You do recall Parlett Construction? The family firm of Julian Parlett – one of our less likeable junior Ministers?'

'Dear God,' said Sarah. She took the paper and scanned the article. 'Tell me it's not true. Tell me there's a mistake somewhere.'

'I fear not,' said Stephen. 'Salk and the Minister have been closeted most of the day with various members of the inner Cabinet. All trying to decide what to do about this little story.' He indicated the drawing room, which was rapidly filling with Sarah's colleagues. 'But we should try not to seem over-preoccupied with it. You should attend to your guests.'

Stephen and Sarah moved slowly into the drawing room, where Carol had just discovered that it was the twenty-fifth birthday of Dusty Willis, Sarah's newest copywriter.

'It's never your birthday!' Carol was saying.

'It's all true,' said Jane. 'The man's twenty-five years old.'

Dusty was adjusting the music to his taste, but also attending to the conversation around him.

'It feels like fifty,' he said. 'Today, I made a resolution. I am taking care of my body. I hope to age gracefully and, in the fulness of time, become a patriarch. An earth-father. From this moment – or, more precisely, from six o'clock this morning – I decided I can live without pharmacology.'

'Dusty,' said Linda, who was listening. 'This is election week. Think of the unemployment you'll cause.'

Sarah followed Stephen slowly down the length of the room, greeting new arrivals and seeing that they were supplied with drinks. In the bay window, she paused and spoke again to Stephen, who had kept pace with her.

'And what about the backbench MP?' she asked. 'The one who was threatening to leak the report on these buildings? The report you copied, in fact.'

'I've recently been reminded of him,' said Stephen. 'Reminded by Francis Salk. The MP is Jonathan Dacre.'

'Dacre,' said Sarah. 'Don't recall the name.'

'You may remember him all too well before long,' said Stephen. 'He is Member for Leeds Centre. And, apparently, the powers that be in the Party, are asking very much the same question as you. What about Jonathan Dacre?'

'Gentlemen: the question is: what are we going to do about Jonathan Dacre?' said the Minister of State for Army Affairs. He was sitting on the edge of a leather armchair in the Wellington Room at Party headquarters. With him were Francis Salk and David Postgate. All three men gave the impression that they would much rather be elsewhere. They had been discussing the Parlett Construction Company for several hours, and still had not decided how best to keep its affairs private for the next two days.

'It does always come back to Dacre,' said Francis. 'It's quite possible to keep the press quiet, but the mind of man has not yet devised an effective way of silencing Jonathan.'

'If Dacre does as he suggests,' said Geoffrey, '– if he tells the press that a Cabinet Minister and a Prime Minister suppressed a report on faulty buildings –'

David and Francis waited.

'We shall be held responsible,' Geoffrey concluded. 'Publicly responsible, for the deaths of' – he picked up the *Argus* – 'these five men.'

'Six,' said Francis. 'Another of the old sods died in hospital. He was seventy-three. In bad health.'

'Can't have expected him to live, surely?' said Geoffrey.

'They didn't,' agreed Francis. 'But it doesn't make the public relations task any easier.'

'I thought the Prime Minister had seen Dacre?' said David. 'Pointed out that he was jeopardising the Party's chances of re-election –'

'Oh, indeed he has,' said Geoffrey. 'Neville had a chat with Jonathan. Jonathan agreed to keep quiet for a week. That is part of our problem.'

'Jonathan now tells us,' said Francis, '– and the old boy has a rather Shakespearian turn of phrase – he now tells us he has blood on his hands. Had he not agreed to keep quiet, this thing in Brighton might not have happened. Jonathan will – I quote – be silent no longer.'

'He'll have to be kept silent,' said the Minister.

'Otherwise,' said David, 'I would think we are going to lose the election.'

Mike Sutherland was driving Alessandra to Sarah's party. Alessandra looked more than usually lovely in a fitted, black dress without a back. Mike was paying her a dangerous amount of attention, given the speed he was travelling. Suddenly, he signalled left, pulled in, and parked. Alessandra looked at him, puzzled.

'We said we'd be at Sarah's by nine.'

Mike ran his hand down Alessandra's naked spine.

'Let's make love,' he suggested.

Alessandra peered out at the traffic pouring past.

'On the Liverpool Road? Are you serious?'

Mike began to slip her dress from her shoulders.

'It can be done,' he said. 'These cars are too low to look into.'

Alessandra removed his hands. She surveyed the pedestrians walking past, bent to the night wind.

'What about jockeys? Dwarves? Persons of restricted growth?'

Mike looked like a small, thwarted boy. He put the ignition key back in; but Alessandra stopped him from starting the car.

'Mike,' she said, 'I've been meaning to ask – did you ever have a conversation with your wife? Before she left – did you ever talk to her? I mean, when you weren't in bed?'

In the darkness of the car, Mike stared at her.

'Did you ever talk about Woody Allen? Tom Waits? Anything like that?'

Mike restarted the car.

'My wife? Conversation about Tom Waits?' He pulled out into the traffic. 'You had to defrost the bitch before she'd talk at all.'

In the Wellington Room at Party headquarters, the meeting on the Parlett Construction scandal was finally coming to an end.

'Time we went our separate ways, gentlemen,' said the Minister.

'May I just see that I have it clear?' asked David. 'You, Minister, are going to suggest the strong possibility of libel suits to the various editors of the national papers?'

'Not at all,' said Geoffrey Talbot. 'Most inappropriate for a Minister of the Crown. The good Lord Haston will make that suggestion, in appropriately minatory legal language. When I ask him to. And the libel suits will be in Julian Parlett's name. If anyone can afford to sue, Julian can.'

'Does Julian know this?' asked Francis.

'Not yet,' replied Geoffrey. To David, he said: 'Now, to recap: we want no connection – absolutely no connection – between one of our Ministers, and these damned card houses he keeps building.'

'I thought,' said David, 'I had the impression – the Minister severed all connection with the company?'

The three men moved toward the door of the Wellington Room.

'So he has,' said Francis. 'So he has. And so, if the time comes, we must continue to insist. However – nominee holding or not – our Julian still has a few million pounds in Parletts. And the wretched business – as well as putting up these sadly temporary constructions – it still bears his name.' He looked gloomily at the rain falling on Priory Square. 'Whatever the legalities, that is not going to look like the white unspotted snow. Not a couple of days before an election.'

In the hall of her house, Sarah was closing the door behind Mike Sutherland and Alessandra. There was a palpable tension between them.

'Are you two all right?'

'Oh, fine, Sarah,' said Alessandra. 'Full of lively conversation. Ready for verbal intercourse with anyone.'

The doorbell rang again. Rose took coats, then led Mike and Alessandra through to the drawing room. The drawing room was now crowded. A liberal supply of alcohol had eased some of the pre-election stress.

'Thank God,' said Sarah to herself, and opened the front door on her latest visitor. Nick stood shivering in the unseasonable cold.

'And they call this a summer election,' he said.

Sarah took his coat, and ran her hands up the nape of his neck, to where the hair began to curl.

'That makes up for the weather,' said Nick.

Sarah bent her head close to him.

'Just before you start partying,' she said, 'can I tell you something about whatever sort of relationship we have? For example: that it does not include you getting out of my bed, and playing innocent games of she-loves-me, she-loves-me-not with Sally.'

Nick turned and looked at her. Then he pointed toward the square.

'Sally wanted a lift,' he said. 'She's in the car.'

'That's what I mean,' said Sarah. 'Ten years ago, I might have enjoyed this sort of romantic drama. Competing with my secretary for some blue-eyed boy. But not now.'

There was a knock at the door. Sarah opened it again, to find Sally on the step.

'I was in the car,' said Sally. 'Lost a lipstick –'

Sarah looked at her secretary, and said nothing. Sally became uncertain.

'It is tonight –? Drinks –?'

Sarah stood aside to let Sally in.

'Oh yes,' she said. 'It's tonight. Has the makings of a jolly little knees-up.'

David Postgate drove straight from Priory Square to Barnsbury. He was trying to work out, as he had been all day, some way of keeping the scandal of Parlett Construction quiet until after the election.

At Sarah's house, he forced himself to put the matter out of mind. He reminded himself that he was approaching forty; that he had resolved to relax. Also, he wanted to see Sally. He was always surprised to find just how much he wanted to see Sally.

Admitted by Rose, David stood at the door of Sarah's drawing room. Amid the music and conversation, no one had yet noticed his entry. He listened to a conversation on his left, trying to make sense of it.

Carol was saying: '– so we asked him. We said: "How did she get the job, then?"'

'I go: "I suppose she slept her way to the top?"' said Jane. 'And he goes: "So far, love, she's only slept her way to the middle."'

Linda's lover Alice, a tall, blonde barrister, was standing listening.

'Aren't men such bitches?' she said.

On the far side of the room, Sarah came in from the kitchen, carrying food. Stephen moved to her side.

'Something else I wanted to mention.'

'Stephen,' said Sarah. 'This is supposed to be a social

occasion. Where you talk to people, drink a lot of booze, and have very good fun. I'll come back to you.'

David had finally seen Sally. She was sitting on the far side of the room, with her small hand trapped by Dusty. He was saying: 'You have extraordinarily cold, sensuous fingers. Might I read your palm?'

Nick was talking to Alessandra, but keeping an eye on Sally and Dusty.

'He's a fetishist. He'll have hold of your hand all evening.'

'At least,' said Sally, 'it's attention.'

Dusty claimed to have given up cocaine, but seemed not to have the same inhibition about alcohol.

'Thank you,' he said to Sally. 'Come through with me to the kitchen.'

Nick watched them go, then spoke to Rose, who was offering him a plate of dolmades.

'What's it like?' he said. 'Working for Sarah?'

Rose thought for a moment about her answer. Two mornings before, she had found Nick naked, and sound asleep, in an upstairs bedroom. Clearly, he was more than just a junior colleague to Sarah.

'What's she like to work for?' said Rose. 'Interesting. Sometimes a bit sad – with no husband –' She watched Nick. 'You know her better than I do.'

'It doesn't follow,' said Nick. 'I know people who sleep together – they say it's easier than having conversations.'

On the other side of the room, Sarah was watching Nick, but talking to David.

'You've just come from seeing the Minister?'

David nodded.

'I gather from Stephen it's getting worse –' said Sarah. 'This bloody building firm the Minister owns – How did the meeting go?'

David finished his first drink, and looked around for another.

'Awful,' he said. 'In the end, I made a break for it. Left Salk to deal with the latest crisis.'

'And Geoffrey?' asked Sarah.

David took a second glass of wine from the tray of a nervous young man with a shaved head.

'Geoffrey was extraordinary. Seems to think that because his Cabinet colleagues have swept all the political scandals under the carpet for the last four years, they can do it with this one.'

'And can't they?' said Sarah. She indicated the kitchen doorway, where Dusty was standing, with Sally's hand still trapped in his. 'Come through to the kitchen. There's some mulled wine, to help this so-called summer.'

David tried not to look at Sally as he went past her.

'I sincerely hope they can sweep it under the carpet,' he said. 'But what you can do in four years, and what you can do in forty-eight hours, are entirely different things.' He exchanged his burgundy for mulled wine. 'People may have short memories – but longer than that.'

On the other side of the huge kitchen, Dusty was introducing Sally to Buddhist philosophy.

'You see it as a choice between two men,' he was saying. 'That's why it's difficult. The answer is not to regard it as a choice at all. Regulate the flame of desire downward, until you don't want either of your lovers. Till you don't desire any man.'

Sally said: 'Dusty: you're drunk.'

'Or you could take men out of the equation altogether,' said Alice.

David could hear only fragments of this conversation. Beside him, Sarah was warming more mulled wine.

'You don't think we can keep the Parlett business quiet?' she asked.

David shook his head.

'The whole thing's about as watertight as a colander. It may yet blow the whole election campaign apart.'

Alice came back into the kitchen, looking for two more glasses of mulled wine. In passing, she glanced with interest at Dusty. He was absently spreading cooking salt in a line along the bench, and dividing it into sections with a gold American Express card.

'David – you've met Alice?' said Sarah. 'Alice is a barrister. And Linda's friend.'

Alice took her wine.

'I love that use of friend,' she said. 'As in: I'll take this through to my friend.'

Alice left the kitchen. Sarah noticed what Dusty was doing.

'Dusty,' she said, 'not in my kitchen.'

Dusty looked away from Sally, and down at the salt.

'Ah. Sorry. Only salt. Strictly therapeutic.'

Dusty scooped the salt into his hand, tipped it into the double sink, beckoned to Sally, and walked out of the room with her. Sarah watched David watching Sally go. Finally, he turned away.

'If this Paramor business does leak,' he said, 'we have to find a way of diverting public attention.'

'There's a limit to what an ad agency can do.' said Sarah. 'It takes a while to change headlines – if it does get as far as headlines.' She pushed her hair back from her face. 'David: do you think we could work this out in the morning?' She led the way back into the noise of the drawing room. 'This little occasion was supposed to give us a few hours away from the election.'

At the far end of the drawing room, Stephen Hallam watched Sarah and David come in from the kitchen. Then he turned back to Gordon, who was talking earnestly to Nick.

'I thought I could reform our agency,' Gordon was saying. 'Stephen persuaded me otherwise. So, if we are starting a new agency –'

'– and we are –' added Stephen.

'– the time is now,' said Gordon. 'Hamilton Forbes has been badly hurt by all that National Health nonsense. Clients feel the political account's edging them out. Several are ready to move. So we need your decision. Otherwise, we'll simply look for another copywriter.'

Stephen looked toward Sarah, who was working her way down the room.

'Or, perhaps, first thing in the morning,' he said to Nick. 'Working breakfast, perhaps? Eight o'clock in the Firenze?'

Before Nick could reply, Sarah had taken Stephen's arm.

She pointed at a very young girl in torn clothes, leaning against the white marble fireplace.

'Who on earth brought Warren's daughter?' asked Sarah.

'Ah, Kim,' said Stephen. 'She's my guest, Sarah. You might say – I'm in loco parentis.'

'Well, you're about the right age,' said Sarah. 'But what happens if her actual parent arrives?'

Number Ten Downing Street is, of course, much larger than it looks from the outside. Over the years, the house has been expanded in every possible way. Much of the expansion has involved burrowing underground; and in one of these underground rooms Francis Salk was now sitting. The long table in front of him was bare, except for two telephones and a small, expensive Panasonic tape recorder. He looked up from the machine as the Minister of State for Army Affairs walked into the room. The Minister was clearly not pleased.

'Francis,' he said, 'it is almost two in the morning. I had managed to get home from our last meeting. I was, in fact, on my way to bed.'

'As was I,' said Francis. He indicated the machine in front of him. 'Until the messenger brought this tape.'

Geoffrey Talbot sat heavily down on the far side of the table and massaged his face with his hands.

'One really can't do this twenty-four hours of the bloody day, Francis.'

'We've both had to come back,' said Francis Salk. 'Some things, unfortunately, won't wait.' He ran the cassette back to start. 'This went out an hour ago. Broadcast by one of the Brighton radio stations. A station which, I'm told, has been taking an uncomfortably close interest in this damned old people's home.'

'About which we are all trying to forget,' said Geoffrey.

'Indeed,' said Francis. He switched the recorder to play. Both men sat listening to the light, female voice of a local newsreader.

'This,' she said, 'is Radio Southdown: news on the hour.'

'You are not going to like this,' said Francis.

'The disastrous local fire in the West Park Veterans' Home could have been prevented. That is the claim of a currently anonymous civil servant. In an exclusive interview, he told Radio Southdown that he personally prepared a damning report on the Paramor building system – the system which was used to construct the now-destroyed West Park veterans' home. That report was passed to the Minister responsible over six months ago – and disappeared. More news of the Paramor scandal, on this station, tomorrow. . . . Now, cricket: and, in the West Indies –'

Francis switched off the tape and sat looking at the Minister.

'You're right,' said Geoffrey finally. 'I don't like it.'

'No mention of Julian yet,' said Francis. 'No mention that we might be involved. Or the PM.'

The Minister picked up a phone and keyed in a number.

'This Radio –?'

'Southdown,' said Francis.

'One of ours? Or is it commercial?'

'Commercial, I'm afraid,' said Francis. 'Easier with the BBC. You're calling Haston?'

Geoffrey Talbot was listening to an unanswered phone.

'Providing,' he said, 'providing I can get the noble lord to leave his ermine-trimmed bed.'

In Barnsbury, Sarah's party was coming to its close. She stood at the front door of her house, bidding farewell to the dishevelled Kim. Tired, and more than a little drunk, Kim looked even younger than her nineteen years.

'Thank you for coming,' Sarah said to her. 'Stephen knows the way to your father's place.'

To Stephen, she said more quietly: 'And if you're still in loco parentis – I hope you know what the parental role involves. And doesn't involve.'

She watched the two of them walk out to Stephen's Porsche; his arm round her thin shoulders. Then Alice was at the door. She seemed quite unaffected by the party; she was, Sarah thought, the only woman who looked as elegant now as when she arrived.

'We must go,' said Alice. 'Linda has a shoot at some unearthly hour in the morning.'

'Sarah knows,' said Linda. She was putting on her coat. 'Sarah arranged it.'

'To each her own,' said Alice. 'And I have a court case.' She enfolded Sarah in a cool embrace. 'Let me check that legal bit tomorrow morning for you. I'm no expert on child custody. But maybe we could meet for lunch?'

'That would be wonderful,' said Sarah. 'Just in case Paul does get difficult about Daniel –' She switched on the drive lights. 'Get her home safely, Linda.'

'I have my own interest at heart,' said Linda.

Behind them, in the hall, David was speaking to Sally. Sarah reflected that it was only when he spoke to her secretary that David was ever tentative.

'Sally,' he was saying, 'I wondered – can I – could I give you a lift anywhere –?'

'Thank you,' said Sally. 'But I'm staying with Alessandra. She could take me –'

Sarah turned.

'Alessandra's gone,' she said. 'Had a considerable falling out with Mike.'

Sarah watched with interest the reaction of her managing director, and her secretary.

'Oh, I missed it,' said Sally. She moved closer to David. 'Is Fulham on the way?'

Sarah answered for David.

'I'm sure it is,' she said. 'To somewhere.'

The only one of Sarah's guests who did not leave was Nick. He had retired to Sarah's kitchen where he sat, on a stool, leaning back against the door of a Provençal linen press. He looked exhausted.

On the opposite side of the kitchen, Rose tipped three soluble aspirin tablets into a glass, then opened the fridge and filled the glass with carbonated mineral water.

'You didn't answer my question,' she said.

Nick was yawning massively.

'What question?'

'How you felt about your work?'

'Do you mean selling soap?' said Nick. 'Or selling politics?

Rose brought the dissolved aspirins across the kitchen, and offered them to Nick.

'Selling us a new government.'

'Actually,' said Nick, 'we're trying to sell you the old one. Repainted.' He emptied the glass, and put it down on a marble worktop. 'I suppose I feel the same way as you do about being an au pair.'

'Mother's help,' said Rose.

'Mother's help. You get on with it, as well as you can, because it lets you do something you think's worthwhile. Your printmaking.'

Rose resisted the temptation to put her arms around Nick. She decided that he was well aware of his power to arouse maternal feelings.

'And what do you think's worth while?' she asked him.

Sarah appeared at the kitchen door and stood for a second, watching. Then she said: 'Rose, you were wonderful with the food. I didn't think people would stay so late. Could you do one last thing: look in on Daniel on your way up to bed?'

Rose picked up her copy of *Leaf Storm*, and edged past Sarah.

'Of course. But we would have heard him if he was awake.'

Sarah looked after Rose as she went upstairs, and then surveyed Nick.

'You look as if you should have been asleep hours ago,' she said. 'What would you like to do? Stay?'

Under his fading tan, Nick was pale with tiredness.

'I have a breakfast meeting,' he said. 'Should sleep.' He made his way toward the door. Sarah blocked his path. She had her hands behind her back and was digging her fingernails into her palms.

'Tell me, Nick, what am I to you?' she said. 'Am I your boss? Your occasional lay? Or what?'

Nick leant against the architrave of the door and looked at Sarah.

'I think I'm puzzled by you.' He paused and thought. 'A bit – frightened, I suppose.'

'Frightened?' said Sarah.

Nick closed his eyes, as if to shut out her reaction to what he was saying. 'The first time I came here – for the night – I cleaned my teeth about five times. Put on pine-scented deodorant. I never use deodorant. I thought, what *is* this? What am I doing – all this squeaky-clean bit?'

'And then?'

'Then I parked, down the end of your street. I just sat in the car, thinking: Why me? Why Nick Faulds? You must know dozens of men, your own age –'

'My own age,' repeated Sarah.

'I listen to different music, go to different clubs,' said Nick. 'I thought, why did she choose me?'

Sarah ran a finger down the side of Nick's face, from eye to mouth.

'Were you worried it might just be your body? You mean you never picked anyone up because she had a good body? But women mustn't do that, must they? No nice bit of ass for us.'

There was a pause. Nick had opened his eyes and closed them again. Then Sarah said: 'If it helps at all, I went through the worst couple of days of my life, before I came to bed with you. Paul was gone – I had all that to deal with – morally, I didn't like myself at all – and the only thing I could think about was your damn wrists.'

Nick opened his eyes and looked down at his wrists. Striped shirt sleeves were rolled halfway up his arms; the tan was deeper there.

'Wrists,' said Sarah. 'Let the symbolism fall where it may – that's what I thought about. When I was working with you that day – it was absurd – I actually had to get myself away. Got in the car, turned on the radio, and – my God, the pop songs were meaningful. I'm listening to this bubblegum, and it sounds like Anna Karenina, set to music. I thought, this is all I need. I'm a mother, with a missing husband, trying to get the government back in – and then I have my first major attack of adolescence. The way some women get migraines.'

Sarah put her hands on Nick's shoulders; but she stayed at arm's length.

'If it's any help,' she said. 'I do know other people with beautiful bodies. I don't feel this way about them. Not at all.'

Nick looked at her.

'When I did get to bed with you – it actually was wonderful.'

Sarah nodded slowly, remembering.

'It was. But the way you look tonight – there's a spare bedroom upstairs.'

Nick pushed himself upright.

'I have this breakfast meeting –'

'Sure,' said Sarah. 'So do I. I'm suggesting we get some sleep.'

SIXTEEN

The next morning was the morning before polling day. At three minutes past eight, Alessandra Castorina was listening to the radio news in the reception area of Hamilton Forbes and Kent. Jane, who was behind the reception desk, watched Alessandra switch the machine to record the bulletin.

'D'you mind?' she said. 'David wants this.'

The BBC announcer was saying: '– and it was one of these Parlett Construction buildings which collapsed last week, after a disastrous fire in Brighton –'

Jane stopped sorting the morning's mail.

'Why on earth are you recording that?' she asked. 'What hath it got to do with us?'

Alessandra was monitoring the recording.

'Don't know yet.' She pointed an elegant, silver-nailed thumb upward, toward the management offices. 'But it's making some of them mega-nervous.'

While she was speaking, Warren's daughter Kim had come into reception. She stood watching Alessandra and Jane.

'Carol says you went out with a reporter. From the *Messenger*.'

Alessandra switched off the tape recorder, and turned to look at Kim.

'You're early,' she said. 'I thought you usually came in about ten?'

'You never know where they've been, journalists,' said Jane. A light was flashing on the electronic switchboard in front of her. She picked up the phone and said: 'Hamilton Forbes and Kent, good morning. How can I help you?'

Kim said: 'A reporter.'

Alessandra thought for a moment.

'Ian Someone. It was a while ago . . . Ian Cassen. Why do you want to know?'

Kim took a bundle of A4 paper out of plastic bag she carried. On the back of it, she wrote the name in fibretip. Then, without answering Alessandra's question, she went toward the door of the agency.

Alessandra called after her: 'He's married.'

'Aren't they all!' said Kim as she went out to the street.

At seventeen minutes past eight, Sarah walked up the steps of Hamilton Forbes. She felt terrible. She had a slight hangover. She had slept badly, knowing that Nick was in the bedroom next door, and that she had promised to let him sleep. And she felt even worse when she reminded herself that she was losing sleep over one of her junior copywriters. It had not been a good start to a crucial election eve.

Sarah was about to open the glass doors of the agency when Stephen came out. He was running. He stopped so violently that he almost fell.

'Have you seen Kim?' he asked.

'I've just this moment arrived,' said Sarah.

Stephen was about to resume his dash to the street, when Sarah stopped him.

'Listen,' she said. 'There's a political volcano about to blow – this Parlett business – and what are you doing? Chasing a kid you spent last night with –'

Though it was not a warm morning, Stephen was sweating.

'I didn't spend last night with Kim. Silly little bimbo ran off. Early hours of the morning.' He checked that Alessandra was not close enough to hear. 'And she must have been through all my papers. Took that report out of my flat.'

'Kim? Took a report?' Sarah suddenly realised what Stephen was talking about. 'The report you copied? The one you took out of the Minister's case?' She paused a moment to consider the implications, then said: 'You haven't got the bloody sense you were born with, have you?'

'I'll do the recriminations myself,' said Stephen. 'Walk with me to the car park.'

Sarah hesitated, then went back the way she had come.

'Kim left a note,' said Stephen. 'Little bitch can't spell, but the gist of it was, she's going to give the report to the press.'

'The day before polling day, the papers find out the Prime Minister is implicated in seven deaths,' said Sarah.

'Screw the Prime Minister,' said Stephen. 'I could go down for this. She'll tell them where it came from.'

They entered the car park. Sarah followed Stephen to his Porsche.

'I might say, fooling around with Kim, you deserve whatever you get.'

'I'd rather fool around with a funnel-web spider,' said Stephen. He stopped by the car, searching for his keys. When he spoke, his tone had changed. 'Sarah,' he said, 'I know you don't particularly approve of me – and, believe me, I see your point of view. There are times when I don't particularly approve of myself. But just try to understand what makes one act like this.'

'Satyriasis?'

'I'm serious,' said Stephen. 'Think what it's been like for me – never going beyond account director. Watching you come into the agency a year later: then getting on to the board. Are you surprised I fool around a bit?'

'Surprised, no.'

'All that would go,' Stephen said, 'if I had something real to do. That's why it's vital I get my own agency off the ground. Do that, I can use my energy on something worthwhile. Get Gordon out of David's reach – stop David pulling his limbs off, one by bloody one – get Helen working again –'

'Talk about your plans later,' said Sarah. 'What do you want me to do now?'

Stephen climbed into his car.

'Please,' he said. 'Just cover me till I get these bloody papers back. Otherwise I'm in every sort of trouble.'

'You and the Prime Minister,' said Sarah, watching the Porsche accelerate out into Jermyn Street.

Sarah walked more slowly back into the agency. Gordon was waiting for her by the express lift.

'You've heard the morning news?' he asked.

Sarah nodded.

'I would think,' said Gordon, 'that if this Parlett business gets into the papers today, it will undoubtedly be a vote-loser. May be a massive swing of uncommitted votes. The inference will be – damning report, on a company in which a Minister has a financial interest. Report suppressed by second Minister.'

Sarah tried to interrupt.

'Gordon –'

'With the eventual agreement of the Prime Minister,' said Gordon. 'As a direct result, lives have been lost. That could lose us the election.'

The lift doors opened.

'I'd got so far in my thinking,' said Sarah.

'And if the election's lost – there must be changes here. We can't keep a managing director who gambles like that – and loses.' He shook his head. 'David will go.'

The lift stopped at the third floor.

'I disagree with you on almost everything, Gordon,' said Sarah, 'but I do know you wouldn't do that. You wouldn't watch the Prime Minister – the Party – go down; not for some agency game you're playing. Stephen might, but you wouldn't.'

Gordon seemed about to say something, then stopped himself. He went into his own office. Sarah waited a moment, then opened the door to the creative department.

On the far side of the department, Dee and Dusty were already working on law-and-order concepts.

Dusty was scanning a full-page press rough.

'On this ad,' he said, 'they don't want pictures of police? Who do they want? Eeyore and Piglet?'

Dee was sorting rapidly through a library file of police shots.

'There's a lot of people,' she said, 'they see pix of riot squads – law and order's not the first thing comes into their mind.' She held up a photographic enlargement of a constable on a local beat. 'Why don't we use one of these nice old bobbies? You know. Big grin, pointy hat.' She held up another picture. 'The sort your Mummy said you could ask the time.'

'These days,' said Dusty, 'wiser to buy a watch.'

Sarah was on her way to speak to Dee, when she was intercepted by Sally.

'Linda called,' she said. 'First thing this morning. And there was Honcho Chocolate – director wants to know if he can move the shoot?'

'Uh huh,' said Sarah. 'They've got an area launch. Call him back, tell him.' She tried to gather her thoughts. 'Did you hold the nuclear weapons ads?'

'They can run in the evening papers,' said Sally. 'If we clear them by ten.' She checked her notepad. 'Mike's having a day off.'

'Because Alessandra dropped him,' said Sarah. 'and he finished my tequila. Get on the phone, remind Mike it's polling day tomorrow. Tell him to get in here, whatever his head's like. With him,' she added, 'it won't make too much difference.'

Sarah turned to Dusty, who was standing beside her with a sheaf of roughs. 'Still fretting about law and order? I'll be with you – five minutes –'

Sally looked up from a note she was making.

'David says the meeting's at nine. And to tell you it's not a colander; it's a sieve. Said you'd understand.'

'Unfortunately,' said Sarah, 'I do.'

Sally indicated Sarah's office.

'And there's someone waiting. An American. *Molto* charming. Called Larry Secoli.'

'Who the hell's Larry Secoli?' said Sarah.

Larry Secoli was a tall, grey-haired man, dressed in a style that was conservative, but not quite British. He looked more like an Ivy League academic than an advertising man. He was sitting in Sarah's lime-green chair, with his feet on her metal desk. He was watching the news on her miniature television.

'The Prime Minister, at his morning news conference, said he had no knowledge of an allegedly critical report on the building firm Parlett Construction,' said the newsreader. He looked briefly down at his autocue. 'But a member of his own party – the backbench MP Jonathan Dacre – later said that he personally discussed the report with the Prime Minister –'

Larry Secoli noticed Sarah standing in the doorway of her office. He switched off the set, leant further back in her chair, and looked at her amiably.

'Seems no big deal,' he said, indicating the television.

'I imagine that's what they said on the *Titanic*.' Sarah came into her office and stood by her desk. 'I'm Sarah Copeland. Owner of that chair. May I ask who you are?'

The stranger held out his hand.

'Larry Secoli. Creative Vice President, Pater Paolozzi.'

'Of whom?' said Sarah.

'The agency your boss bought. In New York. He asked me to fly across: maybe give you a little assistance.'

Sarah said: 'Do you think I could sit down there?'

'Sure,' said Larry. 'Your desk.'

With unshaken affability, Larry Secoli eased himself out of Sarah's chair. He moved around to the room to perch on the facing desk – which belonged to the absent Warren. Sarah sat down in his place.

'Now,' she said, with emphasis. 'Let me get this clear. David Postgate asked you to fly across from New York to' – she put the words in verbal quotes – 'give me some assistance?'

Larry Secoli was not affected by irony.

'That is right,' he said. 'Strong finish to the election campaign. Ease your man back into Downing Street.' He paused, and then said modestly, 'I guess they told your boss: told him when he came over.'

He began to sort through the roughs which covered Warren's desk.

'When he came over – they told David what?' asked Sarah.

'Oh,' said Larry Secoli. 'I guess, told him I'm the guy that elected Ronald Reagan.' He looked up from the roughs, and smiled. 'Just between us, I'd say, it's an exaggeration.'

* * *

Five minutes later, Sarah walked in to David's office. David was on the phone. Francis Salk was already installed in a leather armchair. He had come straight from Downing Street to discuss the latest revelations in what the press was now calling Parlettgate. All the morning papers were spread on the coffee table in front of him. He glanced at Sarah, then went back to the early edition of the *Mirror*.

'Look at this,' he said. 'Second page lead. I quote: " – a Junior Minister in the last government is now said to have a large financial interest, held by nominees, in the controversial Parlett Construction firm – "'

'Excuse me, Francis,' said Sarah.

David put down the phone and spoke directly to Francis.

'They do say the Minister's not directly involved with the firm.'

'If I could interrupt –' said Sarah.

Francis glanced at Sarah, but answered David.

'To most people,' he said, 'if it walks like a duck, and it quacks like a duck – it's a duck. Financial interest is financial interest. Especially if it's counted in millions.'

Sarah walked across to David and stood in front of him.

'This is urgent, David,' she said. 'And it does have a bearing on what Francis is saying.'

David waved toward one of the leather chairs. Sarah stayed standing.

'I'm effectively running the political account,' she said. 'I need to know who's in charge.'

Francis Salk had temporarily abandoned the papers.

'Who else?' he asked.

'This morning,' said Sarah, 'I find an American in my office who says he's Vice President of Pater Paolozzi –'

There was a peremptory knock at the door. David glanced at it, then back to Sarah.

'Creative Vice President,' he said. 'Larry Secoli.'

'Whatever,' said Sarah. 'Now. This man says he's offering me assistance – which I neither need nor want – and he has some crazy scheme for distracting attention from this business.' She indicated the story Francis had been reading in the *Mirror*.

'How?' asked Francis with interest.

'By concocting – as far as I can understand – a foreign-policy crisis.'

There was another knock. David murmured an apology, got up and opened the door.

Francis Salk said: 'We may, in fact, need some sort of diversion quite badly. What has your American colleague in mind?'

At the door of his office, David was confronted by Gordon and Alessandra. Clearly they had been in dispute.

'She sends me,' said Gordon, 'this ridiculous memorandum –'

'I told Gordon you were in a meeting –' said Alessandra. 'And I told him he hadn't been invited.'

David spoke with benign warmth.

'Gordon: my responsibility. Thought you were no longer involved. But if you do have the time –' He stood aside from the door. Gordon, wrongfooted by this turn of events, came cautiously into the office, nodded to Francis Salk, and took his seat. He was followed by Larry Secoli.

Larry, by contrast, seemed entirely at ease.

'This is your strategy meeting?' he asked David. He indicated the sheaf of papers he carried. 'I made some notes –'

David came back into the office and made introductions.

'Larry Secoli from Pater Paolozzi in New York.' To Larry he said: 'Sarah Copeland you already know. Francis Salk is the Prime Minister's media adviser – and Gordon Lochhead is one of our board directors.'

'Deputy managing director,' said Gordon.

'Of course.' David picked up the internal phone and called his personal assistant in the outer office. 'Alessandra: no calls. But phone around, see if you can find Stephen Hallam. Tell him we have something of a political crisis, and he is now' – David checked the time – 'more than ten minutes late.'

Stephen Hallam, at that moment, was in the offices of the *Daily Messenger*, looking for the photocopies which had disappeared from his flat the night before. Using all his charm, he asked one of the newspaper's receptionists whether she had seen a young girl called Kim Greenbank.

She gave him a stare of profound uninterest, and shook her head slowly.

'An art student,' said Stephen. 'About twenty. Wears layers and layers of clothes.'

The receptionist glanced down at her own clothes, which came from Next for Women.

'We wouldn't have anyone like that here,' she said. 'Sir.'

In David Postgate's office, Sarah said to Larry Secoli: 'But this is just absurd. It's bloody ridiculous.'

'I think we should let Larry finish,' said David. 'You said yourself, if this business keeps leaking there's no easy way to bury it.'

'Believe me,' said Francis, 'we have tried the usual things. Threat of legal action, Official Secrets, chats with the great and good – but we have to face the fact: there are times when the British press can't resist nibbling the hand that feeds it. We may have Parlettgate stories across the board on polling day.'

'How many of these old fellows did you say died?' Larry asked.

'Fortunately,' said Francis, 'not many. But it may be argued that there's a principle involved. In the area of foreknowledge and fatal risk. Tell us the rest of your diversionary notion.'

Larry stood at the end of the table and rested his hands lightly on it.

'Just let me give you all a little background,' he said. 'Right up to Grenada, Ronnie Reagan is down there. On . . . the . . . floor.' He enumerated on his fingers. 'What did we have? For starters, we have high inflation, we have unemployment, we have the deficit, we have the Pentagon so corrupt it makes the Mafia look honest – and we have Ronnie Reagan on twenty-eight, twenty-nine per cent popularity. Lowest-rated President since Truman. Then the White House calls us – calls us at the ad agency – and they say Listen: We have this plan. You do the ads. We plan to kick shit out of some little island down the Caribbean –' He turned to Sarah. 'You'll pardon my language.'

'Which message,' said Francis, 'you received enthusiastically.'

'Absolutely not,' said Larry. 'I have to tell you that I am a registered Democrat. No way do I think we should send in Marines – waste some bunch of blacks that's just sitting down there cooking coconuts. Or whatever they do.' He showed a contemporary attitude poll which he had brought in with him. 'Also, my analysis: post-Vietnam, I thought, this is an electoral disaster. Look at these attitudes. Grenada, in my reckoning, has to be about as popular as nuclear waste.'

David was examining some of the advertisement proofs that Larry had put on the table. He looked up.

'But it worked?'

'I have to tell you, gentlemen,' said Larry, with quiet emphasis, 'it worked like a dream.'

Larry took one of the ad proofs back from David. The picture showed a small, gift-wrapped island. The headline read: *Grenada.* Below the picture was a bold sub-headline: *For the Russians, it's a gift.*

Larry held up the advertisement.

'We ran a whole series like this. Right through the media – press, TV, radio, name it. Saturation. Then another set, that says: 'Welcome to the Communist Caribbean.' 'Aeroflot to the Bahamas' –' he showed a fourth proof. 'Then the ethnic one. Jewish.' He read the headline aloud. 'So now I want to go down the Caribbean, I should get my visa from the KGB?'

'Very New York,' said David.

'We had something a little stronger on the West Coast,' said Larry. 'Then, OK, Ronnie puts in the troops. And I have to say that I was wrong: for the voters, it is pure magic. Seventy-four per cent approval rating.' To Sarah, he added: 'We're not talking morality here. We're talking votes.'

'I understand,' said Sarah.

Larry addressed the group generally.

'There's a punchline. After Grenada, Ronnie's walking on water. Never mind the Contras are running drugs, the deficit's going through the roof, never mind Star Wars won't work – he's the Teflon President.'

'Wasn't there another foreign policy diversion?' asked Sarah. 'In Tehran?'

Larry was not disturbed.

'Oh, sure. He blew it. That one, they handled their own PR. Down in White House basement. Never came near us. So, sure. Look what happens. Proves my point.'

Gordon spoke for the first time.

'We hardly have time to invade islands, Mr Secoli. Tomorrow, we go to the polls.'

'No need to invade,' said Larry. 'Communist threat's all you need. They want one of your islands. Your government refuses to be blackmailed. Strong stand. Patriotic appeal. We get the story out to the media – tomorrow they'll be hunting Argies. Cubans. Whoever. Listen: papers love a war. Tits and ass rolled into one; hot fudge topping on it.' He turned to Sarah. 'You'll pardon me.'

'I've got work to do,' Sarah said to David. 'I have ads to get out for tomorrow.'

'And precisely which of our possessions might the Cubans attack?' asked Francis.

Larry produced a map.

'This little island right here, sir. Name of Diego Garcia.'

Alessandra tapped on the door, then entered:

'Excuse me. Downing Street for Mr Salk.'

As Francis moved to the desk to take his call from the Prime Minister, Gordon spoke to Larry.

'Forgive my ignorance. What is Diego Garcia?'

'British possession. Indian Ocean. We have Cuba attack Diego Garcia – we get the story right across the media – I mean, soup to nuts – then maybe, *maybe*, we can turn this thing around.'

Sarah was on her way out of the office.

'You do realise the distance between Cuba and Diego Garcia?'

'Look at the distance, Cuba to Angola,' said Larry amiably. 'Plenty of Cuban army up there.'

'And you don't think anyone would check this story?'

'Check it how? There's no flights to Diego Garcia. It's a

military base: you folk moved out all the natives, put them on some other island. Time anyone gets down there – your election's over.'

'Wonderful,' said Sarah. 'I'm going to do some real work.'

Francis Salk had finished his phone call.

'Our friends in Downing Street are not uninterested in this notion,' he said to Larry. Then, to David: 'And the reason for that is Parlett Construction. The whole thing is leaking uncontrollably.'

For the rest of the day, Sarah tried to put Larry Secoli out of her mind. It was not easy. He moved into an empty office next to hers and comandeered a secretary from Mike Sutherland. Whenever Sarah passed his office, she could hear him on the phone, detailing the Communist threat to Diego Garcia. Sarah would go back to her own office, close the door, and concentrate on the final wave of law-and-order advertisements for polling day.

The agency had decided, several weeks earlier, on a simple typographic message. It read:

If you want law and order,
you know who to vote for.

For once, there was no Party logo. Just the slogan in bold upper and lower case on a plain white ground.

The simplicity of the layout was matched by saturation coverage. Poster sites across Britain were being prepared for it. There were full-page advertisements in every publication that came out on polling day. If anyone missed the message it would not be the fault of Hamilton Forbes and Kent.

Within the agency, the election team was working with exhausted efficiency. After a month's non-stop concentration on the account, they had the reflex coordination of a sports team at the end of a long tour. Creative, media, production and planning departments meshed with unusual ease. The adrenalin of the closing campaign kept them working long hours, but it produced less than usual panic.

Nevertheless, Sarah became increasingly depressed as the day went on. She had a gut feeling that all this effort was wasted; that they would not get the government back. References to the Parlett Construction scandal were appearing right across the political spectrum of the press. The threat of libel action, reinforced by phone calls from Lord Haston's office, ensured that references to the Prime Minister remained oblique. But Sarah knew that if even one paper published the full story, it would dominate all the polling-day headlines. And she knew that one paper was indeed planning to run the full story. The *Daily Messenger* now had a copy of the suppressed report on Parlett Construction. This Sarah learned from Stephen Hallam.

Stephen came back to the agency at the end of the afternoon. He said he had eventually found Kim – but several hours too late. By then, Kim had carried out her threat. She had handed over to the *Messenger* the photcopies she took from Stephen's flat.

'So what have you done about it?' Sarah asked him. 'Apart from destroying yourself – you realise you could destroy the government?'

Stephen had entirely lost his usual composure.

'I'll tell you what I've done about it,' he said. 'I talked to Francis Salk. Bloody drama queen. You should have heard what he said to me.'

'I can imagine,' said Sarah. 'But what did he do?'

'When he calmed down,' said Stephen, 'he phoned the Prime Minister.'

'Henderson's in Birmingham,' said Sarah. 'Going to make this last big speech. I've just seen the news –'

Stephen nodded.

'He's on his way there. Francis called his plane. PM apparently said: Get on to Tim Hall. Tell him to talk to the *Messenger*. After all, he owns the damn paper.'

'Tim Hall's not in the country,' said Sarah. 'He lives in some tax haven.'

'He has a phone,' said Stephen. 'Francis got him on the line. Hall was holding out for some sort of honour; Francis said he couldn't promise –'

'Hall won't get any gongs if the government goes out,' said Sarah.

'I gather that's what Francis told him,' said Stephen. 'So Hall talked to the *Messenger* – put the owner's point of view.' He looked at his watch. It was seven o'clock. 'I've got to go down there now. See what the editor's decided.'

When Stephen left, Sarah switched on the miniature television monitor she kept on her desk. The creative department was emptying. She acknowledged those who stopped to say goodbye to her. She went to the door of her office when Nick passed, walking with Sally. Otherwise, she did not shift her attention from tiny cube of screen in front of her.

Nick and Sally walked down the main staircase together. Nick had kept his distance from Sally since she walked out of his flat – and since she had told him that she was pregnant with David's child; not his. Sally had been far more hurt by his coldness then she ever expected. She, in turn, avoided Nick. But now she wanted to talk.

'Yesterday,' she said. 'David took me back to his house.'

'This I don't want to know,' said Nick. Then he said: 'Where was his wife? The kids?'

'Kids are at boarding school,' said Sally. She paused while Alessandra went past them. 'His wife was there.'

If Sally had been hoping for Nick's full attention, she had it now.

'You're saying – David took you home – to see his *wife*?'

Sally nodded.

'He'd told her about me. Wanted us to meet. Before he started the divorce.'

'Jesus,' said Nick. 'Plain Hampstead folk.' He looked around the reception area, checking that David was not in hearing. 'What was the wife like?'

'What are those dogs that love you to bits?' asked Sally.

'Spaniel?'

'She was like an old spaniel. She's called Flora. No, Fiona. Ever so nice. You must be Sally, she goes. I've heard so much about you from David – Dear God, I thought, what *have* you heard?'

Nick waved goodnight to Jane at the reception desk. He stopped just inside the street doors.

'And then?'

'Then I thought – Oh, no, Sally – can't do this. There's this nice old spaniel, giving me Earl Grey tea, waiting for me to go off with her husband, like she was sitting by her plate, watching another dog eat her munchies –'

'Another bitch,' said Nick, so quietly that Sally missed it.

'I just thought: I can't do this,' said Sally.

Nick opened the glass doors for her.

'Have you told David?'

'Not yet,' said Sally. 'But I'll have to, won't I?'

In her office, Sarah was still watching the television monitor on her desk. News bulletins were now covering the Prime Minister's arrival in Birmingham.

Pictures showed Neville Henderson's black Daimler parked in a crowded square. In the background was the most hostile crowd Sarah had seen in the present campaign.

A television reporter was saying: '– and here in Birmingham, the Prime Minister had a far from friendly reception when he arrived this evening. But, on his way to the Chamberlain Hall, Mr Henderson had this to say –'

The screen changed to a shot of Neville Henderson about to get into the back seat of his limousine. His face came into close-up. He looked more tired and strained than Sarah had ever seen him. His speech was unclear. She bent forward to catch his words.

'Let me tell you this,' the Prime Minister was saying, into a waiting microphone. 'They may not all be shouting in the streets here – but I know we have a lot of loyal supporters in Birmingham. And in the Midlands –'

A burst of heckling drowned Neville Henderson's next words; but it seemed to arouse a trace of his old spirit. He began to shout toward the microphones.

'And to those who think law and order can be defied – I

would say, Think again. The rule of law holds in Birmingham, as it does in the rest of the country –'

The Prime Minister climbed into his car, and the door was closed on him. Sarah watched as the black car forced its way through the hostile crowd. Then she switched off the set and sat for a while, in the now empty department, staring at the blank screen. She was still sitting there, in half darkness, when Gordon Lochhead came into her office. Uninvited, he sat down and began to talk.

'You will be pleased to know, Sarah, that I am on my way out.'

Sarah watched him, and waited.

'He destroyed me.'

'I suppose you mean David?' said Sarah.

Gordon nodded.

'He had the locks sealed on my office. I brought clients back from lunch, and Carol told me that I could no longer get in to my own room. She said David claimed that some money was missing. Until he cleared the matter up, no one was to go in there.' He paused. 'I am deputy managing director of this agency. Or was. And in front of Vernon Waugh and Brian Hesketh he made me look like an embezzler.'

'You were trying to shift their account to a new agency,' said Sarah. 'Stephen told me. Someone must have told David.'

Gordon smoothed down what remained of his hair.

'It was still an utterly ruthless thing to do.'

'Gordon,' said Sarah, 'it comes with the territory. Last month you were trying to put David out on the street . . .' She paused, then said: 'What did you mean – you *were* deputy managing director?'

'I simply resigned,' said Gordon. He pushed a typed letter across Sarah's desk. 'That's what I mean. David was waiting for me. With that American fellow. I was in a blind rage –'

'While David was cool and charming?'

'He was. Eventually, he said: If that's really how you feel, Gordon, should you stay here? Wouldn't it be better for all of us if you looked around?' Gordon indicated the letter Sarah was holding. 'He had that all ready for me. I was so bloody angry –'

'That you signed it,' said Sarah. She switched on her desk lamp and scanned the typescript. 'Dear God. "– rights only to a standard pension".' She looked up. 'I know we don't always see eye to eye, Gordon – but that was a very expensive gesture.'

David Postgate was no longer thinking about Gordon Lochhead. He and Larry Secoli were watching the late evening election news bulletin. The television screen showed Birmingham's Chamberlain Hall. Around it, lit by street lamps and police lights, there was a full-scale riot.

The television presenter's voice was strained.

'According to latest reports,' he was saying, 'the Prime Minister has been trapped here in the Chamberlain Hall, Birmingham, by this violent crowd which has surrounded his final election meeting – and our reporter is there, in the centre of the city –'

Using a remote-control keypad, Larry Secoli switched a videorecorder to run and lowered the television's sound. The telephone rang. David picked it up, listened, then said: 'Yes. We are watching. Can I come back to you?' He put down the phone and thought for a moment. Then he said to Larry Secoli: 'You are serious about this?'

Larry was still watching the rioting crowd on screen.

'I still think,' he said, '– I have this feeling – we just might make it to the wire.'

David picked up an internal phone.

'We'll have to bring in Sarah Copeland.' He began to key in Sarah's extension; then paused. 'I gather she didn't go with your earlier plan? The invasion of Diego Garcia?'

'She did not,' said Larry. 'Most emphatically did not.'

David indicated the television.

'But you want to try this?'

Larry switched the tape counter to zero, and nodded.

David said into the phone: 'Sarah. I've got something urgent.'

* * *

Four minutes later, Sarah came into David's office. She looked exhausted.

'David,' she said, 'I have to say that from where I sit, everything's urgent. And I am on my way home.'

David pointed to the television.

'Have you seen this?'

Sarah shook her head, and dropped into a chair, watching the screen.

'Apparently the Prime Minister's been trapped by a crowd –'

'Real mean,' said Larry, without turning round.

'In Birmingham?' asked Sarah.

'The Party's not universally popular in the Midlands,' said David.

The news bulletin ended. Larry ran the vidoetape back to the start.

'So?' said Sarah. 'They'll send in a riot squad. They've been training them for years.'

There was a moment's silence. Larry turned to face Sarah. Then David said: 'Larry's idea is: we should keep the police away for a while.'

Larry switched the tape to play. David pointed at the Chamberlain Hall which was once again in the centre of the screen.

'The Prime Minister's in there. Larry says, leave him there a while.'

'Say the cops can't get to him,' said Larry.

'We brief Downing Street,' said David. 'They brief the media.'

Sarah sat still, considering the possibilities.

'You'd leave the man in the middle of that crowd?' She looked from David to Larry. 'Apart from the ethics of it – surely that can't be safe?'

'Security tell us he's actually in no danger,' said David.

Sarah looked back at the screen.

'What about Henderson's state of mind? With all that going on outside?'

'What about his state of mind when he goes down the tubes

tomorrow?' asked Larry. 'When all the headlines say he's tied up with these old guys that died in the fire? You think he's going to thank you for that?' He pointed to the television. 'Now – we leave him in the crowd a few minutes longer – leak the story – this has to be front page tomorrow. All the papers. Lead item, TV news. Knock that building business right out.'

Sarah checked the time.

'I don't like it,' she said. 'Could we catch the morning papers?'

'Still time,' said David. 'You can see the headlines: *Rioters Threaten Prime Minister's Life*.'

'I guess that's better than: *Prime Minister Implicated in Fire Deaths*,' said Larry. He turned back to the television screen, on which he was replaying the riot. 'Then we get the guy out of there. Really dramatic rescue. Mounted police – snipers –'

'No snipers,' said David. 'They kill each other.'

'And run the story right through tomorrow,' said Sarah thoughtfully. 'Right through polling day.'

'Sympathy vote,' said Larry. 'No question.'

'Make it a real old-fashioned law-and-order election.'

Larry switched television channels and found more coverage of the Chamberlain Hall.

David put down the phone and watched the screen.

'We just have to hope,' he said, 'they don't stop that riot.'

SEVENTEEN

Later that night, Sarah was lying with her back to Nick, curled into the curve of his limbs. She suspected he had come home with her only because Sally had some mysterious appointment of her own; but Sarah was not in a mood to care. For a while, after they made love, she stayed awake, wondering how much longer the liaison could last. She no longer pretended to herself that it was anything more than a sexual relationship; but she also knew she had no wish to be a single, celibate woman. She turned and put her arms around Nick, considering whether the sex was as good as it had been. She was still testing that proposition on her body when she fell asleep.

In the early hours of the morning, the phone woke her. Sarah freed herself from Nick, picked up the receiver and listened. It was David Postgate.

'We have the Prime Minister out,' he said.

'I've been asleep,' said Sarah. Behind her, Nick stirred, turned.

'You should be so lucky,' said David. 'I haven't got home yet. But Henderson's out of the Chamberlain Hall.'

The television pictures came back to Sarah.

'Out of the riot?'

'Indeed,' said David. 'Wonderful coverage. He's now in hospital – somewhere in Birmingham. Not injured. Resting.'

'David,' said Sarah, 'it is the middle of the night. Why are you telling me this? Why can't I read it in the papers like everyone else?'

'Because it's not the papers we're concerned about,' said David. 'It's television. Prime Minister's appearing live on the eight o'clock news. We're bringing him back from Birmingham. And Francis thought that you and he should write the PM's speech. Nothing political, of course. Above

Party. Magnanimous. Concerned only with the healing of the nation. Maintaining law and order.'

'Television news on polling day,' said Sarah.

'Exactly,' said David. 'Worth its weight in votes. Besides killing that other little story – but –'

'But what, David?'

'We do need some words from you. Very soon.'

'Dear God,' said Sarah. 'When? And how many minutes air time?'

'Three minutes, maximum,' said David. 'And we need a draft by' – he paused – 'it's four now – we shall need it in a couple of hours. Francis and Montfort will meet you at Priory Square. Say six-thirty. We'll fax the speech to Birmingham. They'll get the PM up at six, fly him down here – he can learn the words on the plane.'

'That means doing a draft now,' said Sarah.

'I'm afraid it does, my dear. Which is why I called you.'

'God damn you,' said Sarah. 'If ever I needed sleep, I need it tonight.'

She put the phone down and lay still for a few moments, thinking. Then she turned over and gently ran her hands down Nick's body. It was warm, and soft. He woke.

'I thought I heard the phone,' he said.

'I know what sort of father you'll be,' said Sarah. She stretched herself across him. 'Never hear the child.'

Nick yawned.

'Don't insult me,' he said. 'You've done that once tonight.'

Sarah lay still.

'How did I insult you?'

'Falling asleep when I was inside you,' said Nick. 'No one's ever done *that* before.' He shifted his body underneath her. 'Don't do it this time.'

Sarah detached herself.

'There isn't a this time, my love.' She eased herself out of bed. 'I have to write a short but touching speech for the Prime Minister.'

* * *

At ten past six, Sarah's son Daniel was standing beside her bed. Moving quietly, he shifted a chair, climbed on it, then on to the bedside table. From there, he looked down. His mother was nowhere to be seen; but a man was on her side of the bed. He was asleep, on his back, and breathing heavily. Daniel held his nose, as if he were diving into a swimming pool. He judged the right spot on the duvet, and jumped. He landed on the lower part of the man's stomach, rolled off, and stayed to watch what happened.

What happened was that Nick sat up, bent his head to his knees, and tried to force air back into his lungs. Finally, he looked round at Daniel, though he still could not speak.

'What's your name?' asked Daniel.

'*Bastard*,' said Nick. It was the first thing he was able to say, and he said it with emphasis.

Daniel moved away, to the far edge of the bed.

'Well, Bastard,' he said, 'where's my Mummy?'

There was a long pause, while Nick looked at Daniel, and breathed. Then he said: 'You'll have to find Rose. Sarah's gone out.'

At about the time Daniel found Nick in her bed, Sarah was parking her BMW in Priory Square. She put a typed draft of the Prime Minister's speech in her shoulder bag, locked the car, and ran up the steps to Party headquarters.

Although it was just after six, the building was alive with activity. Sarah was met in the entrance hall by the Prime Minister's political adviser, Lord Montfort. Though he was not yet forty, Hugh Montfort was tipped as the next Party chairman. Sarah hoped the guesses were right. She had considerable admiration for the man. Even at this hour in the morning, he managed to look calm and rather elegant. It was more, Sarah felt, than she could say for herself.

'Mrs Copeland,' said Hugh Montfort, 'I am glad you could get here. I wondered if you had seen the papers.'

'This morning,' said Sarah, 'I've not even seen my son. Nothing but the screen of a word processor.'

Like a magician with cards, Montfort displayed the newspapers he was carrying. *The Times* lead was *Prime Minister at Risk in Birmingham Riot*. The *Mail* said *SAFE! PM Freed by Riot Police*.

'Lead story right across the board,' said Montfort. 'Not a word about the other business.' He opened up the Mail to one of Sarah's full-page advertisements. On a white background was the simple message:

> If you want law and order,
> you know who to vote for.

'The riot last night, and these advertisements today,' said Montfort. 'Could hardly have been a happier conjunction – if you had planned the whole thing.'

He opened a door into the Wellington Room. The Minister of State for Army Affairs for was already installed, behind an immense leather-topped desk.

'I thought we might retire in here,' he said. 'Ten minutes peace and quiet. Make sure we all agree on what Neville is going to say to the media this morning.'

Almost exactly ten minutes later, Linda Prentice came into the room.

'Minister,' she said. 'Lord Montfort – Francis Salk phoned. He wants to know if you've finished the speech. We have to fax it through to the PM, before he flies back from Birmingham.'

'Have you heard whether he can read?' said Montfort.

Sarah looked curiously up from the corrections she was making to her draft, and waited. Linda shook her head.

'Pray God,' said Montfort.

Geoffrey Talbot spoke directly to Linda.

'I'm the delay. Just asked Mrs Copeland to change a paragraph.'

'Give me three minutes,' said Sarah. 'Last changes. When's the Prime Minister's plane?'

* * *

At Birmingham airport, the Prime Minister was being helped to a seat in his plane by Sir John Fellowes, his personal physician. As he sat down, Francis Salk put a rug around his knees, and on it a copy of *The Times*. Neville Henderson looked down at it. Clearly he was trying to read the headline. His glasses slipped off and fell to the floor. Francis picked them up and hooked them back over the Prime Minister's ears. He and Sir John Fellowes exchanged glances, out of Neville Henderson's sight.

'We are waiting, I assume, for the draft of his speech,' said Sir John.

Francis Salk checked the time.

'Which should be here,' he said.

Next door to the Wellington Room, where Sarah had re-written the Prime Minister's speech, was the much larger Blenheim Room. The Blenheim Room was used for the Party's news conferences. It was dominated by a raised dais. Behind that were floor-to-ceiling drapes, the shade of which was changed according to the gravity of the session.

In front of this dais, Sarah and Linda were having a low-toned discussion about how best to light the Prime Minister, for the morning's televised news conference.

Geoffrey Talbot and Lord Montfort entered at the far end of the room.

'Excuse me,' said the Minister to Linda. 'This is rather urgent –' To Sarah he said: 'Mrs Copeland – the Prime Minister has landed at Northolt. We have had a call from his car. Neville's coming straight here' – he checked the time – 'wants to go through his speech with us. Parts of it he's finding difficult.'

'Difficult?' said Sarah. 'Minister, you saw that speech. It's four minutes. Words of one syllable –'

The Minister was not listening. He was speaking urgently to a Crown messenger, a small elderly man who clutched a briefcase as if it had become part of his physical being.

Sarah shrugged, and turned back to Linda.

'The lighting,' she said. 'We should try it on – someone.'

She turned to the Prime Minister's political adviser. 'Lord Montfort – would you, please, sit up there on the dais for a moment. You're going to be Prime Minister.'

Hugh Montfort hesitated for a moment, then seated himself in the Prime Minister's chair.

'And who, pray, pulls my strings?' he murmured.

'OK,' said Sarah to Linda. 'He's Henderson. Tell them, light him so we can actually see the suffering. Valley of the shadow bit.' Linda began to move toward the door. Sarah called after her. 'Not sick. Troubled. A descent into hell.'

The Minister came back toward Sarah and Montfort.

'Not the best of news,' he said. 'Another call from the car. From Sir John Fellowes. Prime Minister's doctor. He's suffering – some memory loss. Neville, that is.'

Sarah and Lord Montfort looked at him.

'Memory loss?' said Sarah finally. 'That's –' For once she seemed at a loss for an appropriate phrasing. 'Minister: you must realise – we can't put the PM on national television if he's – if he's had a stroke.'

'Stroke,' said Talbot, 'was not the word his doctor used.' He looked at Lord Montfort. 'But we do need a decision.' He indicated the adjoining Marlborough Room, from which came the sound of numerous voices. 'Half the national press out there now. Most of the television. Can't keep them waiting much longer.'

At the back of Party headquarters, facing away from Priory Square, the Prime Minister's Daimler had just parked. Neville Henderson was escorted into the building, with his advisers grouped around him like a bodyguard.

Once inside, Geoffrey Talbot drew Francis Salk and Sir John Fellowes aside.

'I have now had three phone calls,' he said. 'None of which told me exactly what's happened to the Prime Minister.'

Francis nodded to Sir John Fellowes.

'You must ask the physician.'

'It's my opinion,' said Sir John Fellowes quietly, 'that the Prime Minister last night suffered a minor CVA.'

'I don't know the term. CVA?'

'Cerebro-vascular accident,' said Francis. 'I've managed to understand that.'

'You'd probably call it a slight stroke, Minister,' said Sir John Fellowes to Geoffrey Talbot. 'Nothing major. There's a little attendant receptive – and rather more expressive – dysphasia. Some agnosia.'

Geoffrey indicated the increasingly restive crowd of reporters in the huge Marlborough Room.

'Sir John,' he said, 'much of the national press is in there, waiting for the Prime Minister. Could you just tell me, in English, what happened to him?'

Sir John seemed to be seeking words that the Minister might understand.

'Receptive dysphasia,' he said, 'is the brain's inability to receive messages accurately. Expressive dysphasia – inability to say quite what you want. Agnosia – recognition difficulties.'

'You're saying – he can't –?'

'I am not giving an opinion,' said Sir John, 'on what Neville can or cannot do. I will say that, in my opinion, he should not be here. But: I can do no more than advise. My patient is a very determined man.' He moved into the Blenheim Room, which was now set up and lighted for television. 'Who should not be out of my sight.' He lowered his voice. 'And who is still, for better or worse, our Prime Minister.'

Six minutes later, the doors of the Blenheim Room were still closed against the press. The Prime Minister was seated on the dais; and Linda was bending over him, like a nurse with an elderly patient.

'Prime Minister,' she said, 'if we may – we would like you to wear a very small radio receiver. In one ear.'

Neville Henderson peered up at her.

'Radio? In my ear?'

Linda displayed a tiny earpiece.

'Just like this, Prime Minister. Then – if you forget any part of your speech – Mrs Copeland can prompt you.'

There was a silence.

'Prompt?' said the Prime Minister. 'So silly, you know. Really can't recall a thing this morning. What does that mean, exactly? *Prompt*?'

In the tiny room next door, Geoffrey Talbot, Francis Salk and Sir John Fellowes were still assessing the risks of putting the Prime Minister on national television.

'And it's your medical opinion, Sir John,' the Minister was saying, 'that the Prime Minister can safely do this?'

'Not at all,' replied the physician. 'I have already said that, medically, the Prime Minister should be resting. But he has, in fact, been telling me since six o'clock this morning that he was going on television. He thinks it may turn the tide. Win the election.'

'For better or worse,' said Geoffrey, 'Neville may be right.'

'That remains to be seen,' said Francis Salk. 'But we can hardly take him off screen now.'

He indicated the television monitor on the far side of the room. It now showed the scene in the next room. A wide panning shot swept across the mass of technical equipment, the assembled newsmen and women who had finally been ushered from the Marlborough into the Blenheim Room. The camera swung to the huge dais. Finally, it showed the figure of the Prime Minister, flanked by his deputy, Rupert Dalton, and his political adviser, Hugh Montfort. Between them, the Prime Minister looked aged and suddenly frail.

'By the look of him. I should be in there,' said Sir John Fellowes. He left the Wellington Room abruptly and, a moment later, appeared on the televsion screen, standing discreetly at the back of the stage, behind the Prime Minister.

Geoffrey Talbot and Francis Salk moved across the room, for a better view of the monitor. Sarah was already seated in front of it, watching the screen intently. In one hand, she held a radio microphone; in the other, a copy of the speech she had written for the Prime Minister. He was now in close-up, and did indeed look as if he had travelled through some valley of the shadow.

Waiting for Neville Henderson to speak, Sarah tried to imagine the millions of people throughout Britain who would be watching this edition of the morning news. It would be their first sight of the Prime Minister who, they had been told, was nearly killed the night before. Sarah wondered what they would make of his appearance on screen this polling day morning. She wondered how it would affect their voting intentions.

Now, and with some difficulty, Neville Henderson was speaking to camera.

'I do not intend,' the Prime Minister was saying, 'to dwell on my own experience over the past twenty-four hours. Nor, on this election day, will I draw any political conclusion from what has happened –'

At the agency David Postgate was sitting in his office, watching a television screen with a concentration that equalled Sarah's. He was staring at a small bubble of saliva on the Prime Minister's lip.

'– whichever Party we support,' Neville Henderson was saying, '– whichever Party we support – I am sure that we will agree on one thing . . . we will agree that –'

Henderson paused and stared, for a moment at the camera. In front of the monitor, David had bitten his own lip deeply enough to draw blood. Absently, he blotted it with a lawn handkerchief, one of a set Sally had given him in New York.

'Ah, come *on*, will you,' he said to the screen. 'We set this up for you, Neville. Now, for Christ's sake, *talk*.'

In the Wellington Room at Party headquarters, Sarah was speaking urgently and clearly into the microphone.

'– we cannot live in a country –' she was saying. She watched the televised image of Neville Henderson.

'– we cannot live in a country,' he said, 'where – where our lives are not safe, where –'

'Our liberty –' said Sarah into the microphone.

'– where our liberty is not secure,' said the Prime Minister.

'Please – just another thirty words, Neville,' murmured Francis Salk, standing behind Sarah.

'– nor does one mis – mis –

'– nor does one misguided –' said Sarah.

The Prime Minister visibly concentrated.

'– nor does one misguided crowd represent the country,' he said. 'We are, at heart, a peaceful –'

'– a law-abiding –' said Sarah into the mike.

'– a law-abiding people,' said the Prime Minister. 'We respect law. We want order.'

'I cannot stand this,' said Geoffrey Talbot. He turned away from the monitor Sarah was watching. On it, the Prime Minister was frowning at camera as if he had momentarily forgotten where he was. Then he spoke.

'And whatever Party we support, if we work together as a nation – if we work together, we can have those things that we all value –'

'– peace, law, and order,' said Sarah urgently.

There was a pause. Across the country, millions of viewers waited.

Suddenly, the Prime Minister spoke strongly.

'We can have the thing we really value,' he said. 'We can have peace. We can have law. We can have order.' He looked at the camera with his old authority, then gave the slightest acknowledgement to the wave of applause, led by Lord Montfort, and echoed by the reporters below him.

In the Wellington Room, Sarah sat back from the screen, and looked at Francis Salk.

'Don't ever do that again,' she said. 'Do not ever put a post-cardiac Prime Minister on national television.'

'We may never have another chance,' said Francis.

Geoffrey Talbot had turned back to watch the television screen, on which the Prime Minister was being helped from the dais by Sir John Fellowes.

'Post-cardiac or not,' he said, '– we may at least have kept him in office.'

EIGHTEEN

That polling day, after the Prime Minister's early morning speech, was one of the longest and emptiest times Sarah could remember. It was like the school speech days of her childhood in Kent, when time seemed to stop altogether. She was beset by a hundred irrational fears.

Work was also Sarah's answer to private panic; but today she was unable to work. Nothing more could be done on the election campaign. For better or worse, that die was cast. She had done all she could. The Prime Minister dominated the morning headlines, and the news bulletins. The speech had been hesitant, but perhaps all the more moving for that. All that remained was to wait for votes to be cast and counted. Then she would know whether or not her words – the Prime Minister's words – had won the nation's heart. She would know whether she had done enough to get the government back.

Throughout the day, Sarah tried to work on other accounts. Her in-tray held a huge backlog of urgent material, put aside during the last days of the election campaign. But she found it impossible to concentrate. It was now clear that Warren was not coming back to the agency; and, today, Sarah was sharply aware of his absence. She wondered whether she should have fought harder to have him reinstated. With one part of her mind she knew Warren was coming to the end of his creative career; in other ways, she badly missed their working partnership.

By the end of the afternoon, Sarah had stopped even pretending to work. She left St James's, drove back to Barnsbury, and cast her vote. By the time she returned to the agency, the working day was almost over. Restaurant and bar were being decorated for an election party. Sarah, looking at the balloons and streamers, wondered whether in the end they would have anything to celebrate.

When Sarah finally returned to her own office, the creative department was almost empty. Only Sally and Nick remained. They were absorbed in what seemed an uncomfortably intimate conversation. Sarah felt a resurgence of suppressed jealousy – an emotion she once swore she would never experience.

From the far side of the room, Sarah weighed up her secretary's advantages. Sally was young. She had a delectable body, wonderful dark eyes, a luxuriant cloud of hair. On the other hand, she was naive, she read nothing but women's magazines, and she had no political skills. Outside the bedroom, any intelligent man would get tired of her within weeks. Or so Sarah had always assumed. She was just reviewing this conclusion when Sally looked up, and caught sight of her. She touched Nick's arm gently, and came out of the office.

'Sarah,' she called, 'your au pair phoned – seemed a bit worried –'

Instantly, Sarah's anxieties were overlaid by fears for her son. She picked up the nearest phone and keyed in her home number.

Rose answered almost immediately.

'Oh, Mrs Copeland,' she said. 'It's all right –'

'What is all right?' asked Sarah. 'Where's Daniel? Is he there?'

There was a pause, then Rose said:

'He's not. He caught the bus. It really wasn't my fault, Sarah. He went upstairs – and said he was going to play with his battleships –'

Sarah sat down on the edge of a desk, and tried to breathe evenly.

'Then what?'

'Then he must have come downstairs, and gone out, and caught a bus. Your husband rang and said Daniel came to his art school.'

Sarah breathed out.

'So he's home again. Paul brought him home?'

'Well,' said Rose, 'he's not at this home. He's in the flat, with his father – and your friend. Mrs Marriott.'

'My friend Mrs Marriott,' said Sarah. 'You mean Helen.'

'I was going to drive round there,' said Rose, 'but I wanted to talk to you first.'

'I'll go and get Daniel,' said Sarah. 'You stay where you are. Make him something to eat. See if you can do that without disaster.'

Twenty five minutes later, Sarah parked her car in front of Helen Marriott's flat in Primrose Hill. She left the car without locking it, and banged on the brightly-glossed door of the flat. The door was opened by Daniel. He stood looking up at his mother, trying to see who was standing there in the darkness. All Sarah's fears fell away.

'Oh, Daniel,' she said. She knelt down to take him in her arms. Daniel dodged skilfully, and dashed up the hall.

'Run, run, as fast as you can! You can't catch me –' he shouted. 'I'm a gingerbread man!'

Sarah stood for a moment, trying to control herself. Then she slammed the front door shut with all the energy she could gather. The shock of its closing brought her husband out of the living room, and into the hall, as if he had been shot there from a cannon.

'What the hell was that?' he said. Then: 'Sarah. What are you doing here?'

'I might ask: what are *you* doing here?' said Sarah. 'What's my son doing here?'

Helen appeared from the living room. Her calmly beautiful face fuelled Sarah's anger.

'Sarah,' she said, 'come in. Daniel's quite all right –'

Sarah walked slowly down the hall.

'I can see he's all right,' she said. 'I just want him home.'

Paul led the way into the living room. Daniel was nowhere to be seen.

'Sarah, listen,' Paul said. 'Daniel says he doesn't want to go back with you. He came here entirely of his own accord –'

'He came to your college,' said Sarah. 'He didn't come here. He wouldn't know how to get here. He didn't even know you were staying with Helen – till you brought him back to this place.'

Helen seemed to have been in tears.

'Sarah,' she said, 'it's not going to help. Talking like that.'

'Oh, *help*,' said Paul. 'Now, we mustn't expect help. That is not my wife's metier. Constructive criticism, maybe. As in: Paul – are you really intending to be a teacher for the rest of your life? I didn't marry an art teacher, Paul. I married a designer –'

'You were a wonderful designer. In those days.' Sarah looked after Helen, who had gone into the kitchen and switched on a cafetiere.

'I don't want coffee.'

'Ah. In *those* days,' said Paul. 'I still had a pair of balls, didn't I? And all the creative juices flowing.' To Helen he said: 'You wouldn't have known us then. I was the money-earner. Used to fly across to Milan – before I became a "teacher" – before I started teaching design, instead of doing it. And, of course, before I started driving my wife's seriously expensive cars – living in my wife's seriously expensive house –'

Helen looked from husband to wife.

'I thought we were discussing Daniel?'

'I don't think Paul was,' said Sarah.

'Oh, no,' said Paul. 'Far from it. I was talking about sex and money. Scylla and Charybdis of the marriage bed. Those two rocks that rip apart many a Dreamsuite double mattress' – he looked at Helen – 'a brand that my wife advertised – and even bought – in our early days together –'

'Paul,' said Sarah.

'– when we still imagined we'd grow old in a grey olive grove, on a red Tuscan hillside,' said Paul. He grinned. 'You wouldn't believe: we even had designer dreams. In those days.'

Sarah was looking at her husband as if she had never properly seen him before. Suddenly, she moved from her chair and stood close to him. She moved her hands towards his face. Expecting attack, Paul turned his head away. Sarah cupped her hands under his chin, still scrutinising his face.

'I thought that you were the sexiest man I'd ever met,' she said. Then: 'I do still want to talk to you.'

Helen looked from wife to husband.

'Well, you're a busy woman, Sarah,' said Paul. 'All those meetings –'

'I've time to talk,' said Sarah. 'I just don't want to have this conversation in this place –'

'Don't mind me,' said Helen. 'I could always go and walk on the Heath.'

Sarah ignored this.

'If I can just collect my son,' she said. She went to the door and called upstairs. 'Daniel! . . . Daniel!'

Daniel's voice floated down, distant but determined.

'No! I'm not coming! I'm staying here!'

'Sarah,' said Paul, 'it's going to be like that time you took him to nursery school. He'll do the screaming-and-biting scene.'

'Only this time,' said Sarah, 'it'll be in front of Helen.'

'Is that really what you want?'

'Daniel!' shouted Sarah, 'if you don't come in here –'

'I shall not!' called Daniel, a little closer now.

'Listen, Sarah,' said Paul, 'let me just say something. I'm not going to spirit him away to the Seychelles or somewhere. Apart from anything else, I don't have the money.'

'Let him just stay the night,' suggested Helen.

'*Here*?' asked Sarah.

'Come on,' said Helen. 'You slept here. Last New Year's Eve. Before all this happened – It's not contaminated.'

'Let him stay, and tomorrow I'll persuade him,' said Paul. 'Bring him back to you.'

'You'll persuade him to come home?' asked Sarah. 'Oh, for this relief, much thanks. You'll persuade him to come back to the meals I make him. The clothes I buy him. The house I maintain for him. The computer I got him. The entire United States Navy in miniature I've had to find for him –'

She paused, then went to the door and called.

'Daniel, love, you seem to be staying the night with Aunty Helen, and your father is going to persuade you home tomorrow. Do you want to come down and kiss me goodbye?'

There was no response. Sarah picked up her coat, and said, more quietly: 'Daniel. I'm waiting.'

Silence.

Sarah went out the door, into the hall.

'Enjoy the evening,' she said to Helen. 'I'll go home and burn his bloody battleships.'

While Sarah was driving south from Helen Marriott's flat, her account director, Stephen Hallam, was in the Firenze Brasserie. Stephen was talking to journalists from AdMap. AdMap was the advertising industry's best-known trade journal and, over drinks, Stephen was giving its reporters a late and off-the-record briefing on his plans for a new creative agency. He did not notice two men in suits walking towards him, until one of them spoke.

'Mr Hallam?' he asked. 'Mr Stephen Hallam?'

Stephen was in the middle of an intimately humorous exchange with Rebecca Hind, AdMap's marketing writer.

'As ever,' he said. 'And you are –?'

'Detective Inspector Bell, sir,' said the newcomer. He introduced his companion. 'And this is Sergeant Clyde. We're looking into an alleged leak of Ministerial documents –'

Stephen glanced at the fascinated reporters.

'Inspector,' he said, 'I shall be delighted to help you. But, please: not now.'

The two men moved unobtrusively closer to Stephen.

'I'm sorry, sir,' said Inspector Bell, 'but we wondered if you could just come with us for a while? Perhaps help us with a few questions?'

'Excuse me,' said Rebecca Hind, backing away. 'Just need to find a phone.'

'Shouldn't take long, sir,' said Sergeant Clyde to Stephen.

Sarah reached home well after the polls had closed. She parked outside her house, and sat looking at it for a while. It was dark; Rose must have gone to bed. Sarah started the BMW and drove back to the agency.

The agency, too, was in semi-darkness. Only the restaurant

and bar were brightly lit. From inside, Sarah could hear the sound of the post-election party. It sounded as if it was on the way to being a riotous affair. At the moment, that was not what Sarah wanted. She went across the darkened first floor to David Postgate's office.

As Sarah was about to enter the office, Sally came out, looking back, and almost walked into her. Both women were momentarily at a loss. Then Sally said: 'Sarah – I was just speaking to David –'

She went down toward reception at a half-run, and Sarah heard her stumble on the stairs.

In the office, David was sitting in front of the television, watching election results come in. There was a bubble of blood on his lower lip.

The screen showed a huge election-night set and, in foreground, Sir Alun Corbyn commenting on the latest batch of results.

'The Prime Minister,' Sir Alun was saying, 'is now watching television from a comfortable hospital bed, where he is making a rapid recovery from the effects of the Birmingham riot. But these latest results are hardly calculated to help his recovery. Our present computer prediction indicates a very close finish indeed, as we return to our experts in the studio –'

Sarah looked from the screen to David.

'It's a bad habit,' she said. 'Biting your lip.'

David dabbed at his lip with a handkerchief. He said nothing, and did not take his eyes from the screen. Sarah remained standing.

'I saw Sally,' she said.

David nodded.

'She just dropped in to say she wasn't going to marry me. Couldn't contemplate breaking up my present union.' For the first time, he looked at Sarah. 'You knew she was pregnant?'

Sarah drew breath, then shook her head.

'She's going back to him,' said David.

'Going back to whom?'

'To that copywriter,' said David. He used a keypad to switch channels.

Sarah experienced an irrational sense of desolation. It was overtaken by an equally intense anger.

'She's going back to Nick?'

David nodded, and switched back to his first channel.

'Nick's leaving us,' said Sarah.

'Does he know that?' asked David.

'Not yet,' said Sarah. 'I'll go and leave him a note.'

When Sarah reached her office, the light was already on. Gordon Lochhead was sitting in her chair. Sarah stopped in the doorway and stared at him.

'Gordon,' she said finally. 'I didn't expect to see you back in the agency. Not after you –'

'Resigned,' said Gordon. 'I didn't expect to be back here either. But I need to copy some files, and I now have no keys to the cabinets.'

'Files?' said Sarah.

'The truth is,' said Gordon, 'I am becoming a consultant.'

'I don't believe it,' said Sarah.

Gordon nodded.

'You're going to say it's an admission of failure. To which I reply that I'm in advertising, I have no offers, and I have no job. Further, I am over forty. Apart from consultancy, what else can I do?'

'Over forty,' murmured Sarah. Then she said: 'Of course you can have the files.' She took a set of keys from her bag and handed them to Gordon. 'What does your wife say? About your change of role?'

Gordon took the keys and went across to the filing cabinet.

'Anne? She doesn't know I've resigned.'

'She doesn't *know* you've resigned? She doesn't know about the breakaway? . . . Anne still thinks you still work here?'

Gordon was searching through the cabinet.

'I go off at the same time every morning. Anne never calls the office. She's – she's in the garden.' He paused. 'She loves gardening. Grows tuber begonias.'

Sarah looked at him for a moment in silence. Then she said:

'Lock up when you finish. Leave the keys in my desk.' She pointed downstairs. 'There's a fancy dress party going on. You're unlikely to meet anyone sober enough to recognise you.'

'Of course,' said Gordon, 'I will have to tell her.'

Sarah paused on her way out of the office.

'Tell who? . . . What?'

'My wife.' said Gordon. 'Anne. I'll have to tell her we're selling the place. . . . It's the garden she'll miss. Not the house. Never liked the house. Too modern.'

Sarah stood looking at him.

'You'll have money again.'

Gordon said: 'Well. No country for old men.'

'Keep in touch,' said Sarah, and went back down to the first floor.

Outside David's office, Sarah met Alessandra, who was wearing a skin-tight sequinned dress, six-inch heels, and a gunbelt.

'What the hell is that?' asked Sarah.

'Imelda Marcos,' Alessandra explained. 'For the party.' She indicated David's office. 'I was trying to get him to come. Maybe you can do it.'

Sarah went in to the office. David was still watching the screen, on which a computer was rapidly generating more electoral information than any audience would ever wish to know. Sarah took David's arm and pulled him away from the television.

'You should get away from this thing. Come and have a drink.'

David was reluctant to leave the election results.

'It's very close,' he said, 'Next thing, the government's going to lose the election – and I'm going to lose the agency.' He followed Sarah out of the office. 'This may turn out not to be my night.'

'Our night,' said Sarah. 'For better or worse, we seem to be in this together.'

* * *

In the restaurant, the fancy-dress party was at its noisiest. Most of the Hamilton Forbes staff were crowded into the small area of the bar. Their political costumes gave a curious effect to the gathering: Nixon was drinking with Roosevelt and Christine Keeler; Genghis Khan with Mrs Pankhurst.

Nick, in the mask of Charles de Gaulle, was struggling to get a round of drinks which, he suspected, he would be better without. Next to him, President Reagan was shouting at the barman.

'Mineral water,' ordered the President. 'Make it a large one. Ice and lemon.'

Nick peered at the President.

'If you weren't ordering water,' he said, 'I'd swear that was Warren.'

Warren pushed his mask up into his hair.

'Later,' he said, 'I may have a serious drink.' He caught sight of Dee, unmasked, pushing her way through the crowd. 'Just don't tell Dee.'

'This is farewell to the agency?' Nick asked Warren.

Dee answered for him.

'This is a celebration,' she said. 'New career.'

Warren grabbed his drink, and ordered for Dee.

'You may not know,' he said. 'I have purchased an exotic pet shop.'

'You did say – exotic pet shop?' said Nick.

Revellers were beginning to move toward the television at the far end of the bar.

'Sells your toads – snakes – piranha fish –' said Dee.

'Uses all my past experience,' said Warren.

Sarah and David walked slowly across the darkened reception area.

'You have to make at least an appearance at the party,' she said.

'I doubt you'll believe this,' said David, 'but I would rather have had Sally than the agency.'

'If that were true, you'd still have her,' said Sarah. She looked at David. 'Any moment now, you'll know whether you still have the agency. You'll know whether we got the government back. Whether the advertising worked.'

'Oh, the *advertising* works –' said David. He stopped suddenly.

From inside the bar came Mike Sutherland's powerful voice, raised in a bellow of triumph. '*Majority*!' he was shouting. '*Majority*!'

Sarah took David's arm and led him into the celebrating crowd.

'What's the rest of that sentence?' she asked. 'Pity about the product?'

More compulsive fiction from Headline:

The explosive novel of abuse and betrayal

Silk & Satin

MARCIA WOLFSON

They are known as 'The Sisters' – five charismatic women who seem to enjoy every luxury and privilege money can buy. But beneath the glossy surface, each one hides a dark secret – a secret that Mark Saunders' murder threatens to reveal . . .

Darleen – is she really the grieving widow?

Joy – she chooses to celebrate Mark's death in a provocatively sensual way.

Deborah – the councillor whose public respectability conceals dark appetites.

Aida – actress and drug addict.

Samantha – her Oriental fragility masks her ruthless ambition.

Combining the sensuality of LACE with the hedonism of HOLLYWOOD WIVES, SILK AND SATIN is the pulsing novel of power and revenge.

FICTION 0-7472-3007-2 £2.95